What's everyone saying about
WAITING FOR CALLBACK?

'A witty, feel-good romp of a book. *Waiting for Callback* is my new favourite teen read!'

Emma Carroll author of
Letters from the Lighthouse

'So warm and funny with characters who feel like friends'

Karis Stainton author of
Starring Kitty

'A fabulously funny read with a very big heart'

Abi Elphinstone author of
Sky Song

'Fresh and funny and sweet'

Lisa Williamson author of
The Art of Being Normal

'This is a chocolate cake of a book, a good sugary and rich wedge of hyper-real characters doing screamingly funny things with straight faces...'

Harriet Reuter-Hapgood author of
The Square Root of Summer

'Funny, heartwarming and just properly brilliant'

Maximum Pop

TAKE TWO

PERDITA & HONOR CARGILL

SIMON & SCHUSTER

This new edition published 2018
First published in Great Britain in 2017 by Simon & Schuster UK Ltd
A CBS COMPANY

1 3 5 7 9 10 8 6 4 2

Simon & Schuster UK Ltd
1st Floor, 222 Gray's Inn Road
London WC1X 8HB

www.simonandschuster.co.uk

Simon & Schuster Australia, Sydney
Simon & Schuster India, New Delhi

A CIP catalogue record for this book
is available from the British Library.

PB ISBN 978-1-4711-7522-0
eBook ISBN 978-1-4711-4486-8

Typeset in the UK by M Rules
Printed and bound by CPI Group (UK) Ltd, Croydon, CR0 4YY

Simon & Schuster UK Ltd are committed to sourcing paper
that is made from wood grown in sustainable forests and support the
Forest Stewardship Council, the leading international forest
certification organisation. Our books displaying the
FSC logo are printed on FSC certified paper.

For Jonathan, with our love

TheBizz.com

27th June

Finally! The apocalypse is here!

That's not something even we at The Bizz, eternal pessimists that we are, saw coming. Remember *Straker? Sorry Straker (working title)*? No? We don't blame you. There's been a very loud silence on this project over the last few months. So here's what you need to know:

Straker is a post-apocalyptic drama that sees two tribes battle it out for survival and the power to shape a new civilisation. One wants to rely on tech (think 'gimme all the iPhones') and the other on nature (think 'back to mother-earth duuuude'). We'd been promised natural disasters, tons of violence, breathtaking CGI and 'love stories to rival *Romeo and Juliet*' (credit to the Panda Productions publicity department for that subtle and humble turn of phrase). So naturally we were pretty bummed when it dropped off our radar. BUT, drumroll please ... we finally have news!

Panda productions have nabbed master-money-maker, director Sergei Havelski fresh off the top grossing Terror Island franchise. Even more excitingly we have ourselves a male lead! A-Lister Sam Gross (aka our favourite bar-room brawl hottie) will play Raw, the leader of one of the tribes. We're expecting lots of action on and off screen. The actress who will play Winona, the leader of the other tribe is yet to be announced. Our informant is torturing us by hinting that the casting decision is proving controversial but wouldn't tell us any more. We're no longer speaking.

This production is also rocking a bit of a Hunger Games vibe with two juicy teenage roles for the children of the tribe leaders. Sam's adopted son and heir will be played by 17-year-old Carlo Winn. And – defibrillators at the ready – _here_ is his Instagram. He's a relative newcomer with only a few TV credits to his name.

Oh, and a completely unknown fifteen-year-old London girl will play female teenage lead Straker!

We think this is going to be one sweet, sweet apocalypse. Especially for one London school-girl...

★ CHAPTER 1

*'He's the director. He's the writer. I'm only the
actor, so what do I know?'*

Chloë Sevigny

I was under a tree in my garden with the guy of my
dreams and there was a Hollywood director on the
phone. For me.

'Hello?' I squeaked.

'So?' There was a long and worrying pause.
Mr Havelski was waiting for an answer. But what
exactly was the *question*? 'So?' Another scary pause.

My mum – she was there too and there was
literally no way to ignore her because she was doing
some sort of weird panicky dance in front of me –
mouthed, *'What? What?'* Our genetic link was at its
most obvious.

'So ... Is that my Straker I'm speaking to?'

'It's Elektra,' I squeaked, starting to stress that he'd got the wrong number.

'And ... is Elektra my Straker?'

'I ... I don't know ...' This suspense was killing me. I was better with statements from adults than questions. Ask any of my teachers. Was Havelski offering me the part? Was he just really confused? Was this an elaborate form of psychological torture? Maybe this was the final and defining test of my suitability for the role – what would Straker do?

'I mean ... I ... I think so ...' I stuttered. I'm pretty sure that this is not what Straker, world-saving action heroine, would have done.

'You *think* so?' Mr Havelski sounded confused.

My inner seven-year-old wanted to hand the phone to my mum. 'No. I mean ... yes. I mean, if you mean ...' If this went on any longer he was going to call one of the other girls on the shortlist and ask if *she* was his Straker. I pulled myself together. 'I'd *love* to be your Straker if you'll have me.'

'I would like that very much.' I could tell Mr Havelski was smiling all the way from LA. 'I'll see you soon.' He hung up before I could say goodbye; he was a very busy man.

I let the phone slip out of my very sweaty hand and threw myself into Archie's arms. He laughed and picked me up and spun me around. This had been my very favourite fantasy through months of near tragic crushing.

'Elektra, help!'

'How did you end up in the bush?' I asked my mum, as Archie and I each gave her a hand and hauled her upright. This hadn't featured in my fantasy. Obviously.

'I was sort of ... dancing and the path must be uneven.' She glared at the innocent little paving stones and untangled a hydrangea leaf from her hair.

'Sure,' I said. 'Are you happy?' It's fair to say that my mum had been conflicted about the idea of me taking a big film role.

'Of course I am. I'm beyond excited for you!'

A vision of Kris Jenner style momaging flashed before my eyes. 'Is Dad home?'

'He went to get another newspaper because Digby vomited on the sports section. He should be back any minute. Let's go inside and have celebratory tea and wait for him.'

'I should go,' said Archie, but he was still holding on to my hand.

I didn't want him to leave for obvious reasons but the thought of him sitting around the kitchen table with my mum and dad was too weird. Especially because Mum was now trying to persuade him to stay like he was her very favourite person in the world. I think he was scared she was going to hug him. As a) he'd never met her before, b) all he'd seen her do was 'dance' and fall in a bush and c) it was less than twenty-four hours since he'd got with me for the first time, this was possibly too much, too soon.

'No really, Mrs James, I should get home. I'll text you, Elektra. Er ... bye then.'

And we both just sort of stood there. Neither of us knew how to say goodbye. Mum was standing in between us, smiling amiably. Hopeless. There was a very real threat of awkward waves.

'Why don't you show Archie out, Elektra?' said Mum finally.

That took quite a long time in the end. There are some things that shouldn't be hurried.

'I'm just very proud of you,' said Dad later.

'Mum told you? I wanted to tell you!' I'd been dispatched to buy cake but she might have waited ten minutes for me to get home.

'Sorry, I couldn't keep it in.' Mum cut me a huge slice of the lemon cake by way of apology. 'And I told Digby.'

I was good with that. Digby might be an elderly Dalmatian but he was very much part of the family and it was right and proper that he should be one of the first to know. He came over and licked my hand. It might have been the crumbs but I was taking it as congratulations. 'Have you seen my phone? I need to call Eulalie.' Eulalie was my *fabulous* Coco Chanel/Dolly Parton mash-up of a step-grandmother.

'In the drawer, you left it in the garden. But, er ...' Mum looked shamefaced. 'I told Eulalie too. I know I shouldn't have, but you were taking ages and I was all excited and I just had to tell someone.'

Someone? It sounded like she'd told everyone. 'Was she pleased?'

Mum laughed. 'She said lots of things in very fast French that I didn't understand but yes, she was definitely pleased.'

MOSS! If I didn't text my best friend straight away there was a risk that Mum would do it for me. **MOSSSSSS!!**

What's up? Did Archie come over? ♥ ♥ ♥ ♥ ♥

Yes and SOMETHING JUST HAPPENED

With Archie? WHAT WHAT? I'm panicking here. Something good or something bad?

Something good. Very good. Like, THE DREAM

You had The Conversation?! You're exclusive with Archie? In LESS THAN 24 HOURS. 🐝🐝🐝🐝🐝 I am literally in awe. You guys are PERFECT together.

Are you mad?

Own it, Elektra. You're irresistible

That is true but we did not have The Conversation. Obviously.

I am so confused

It's nothing to do with Archie I considered getting into an in-depth analysis of what was wrong with the assumption that my every communication was about Archie – but only very briefly.

Then WHAT? JUST TELL ME

Havelski phoned me . . .

Oh. My. God. Yo

'Yo?' That was not the response I'd been hoping for. There was a long pause.

Sorry, I fell off my chair when I was typing. *You* are going to be a FILM STAR ★ ★ ★ ★

Hahahahaha

Dad stood right in front of me and waved until he got my attention. 'Talk to me, I want to know every last detail.' He sounded like Mum. 'What did Mr Havelski say? What did you say?'

'Mum's probably already told you everything. Although I bet she didn't tell you she fell in a bush.'

He didn't look surprised. 'But I want you to tell me.'

'I didn't tell him about . . . Archie,' said Mum. The pause was fake, she knew his name well enough. She probably also knew his date of birth and predicted GCSE grades. 'Don't miss out those bits.'

'Who's Archie?'

'*He's the boy from the party last night*,' Mum mouthed at Dad over my head.

Great. Not only had my mad mum stayed up to interrogate me on what had in fact been a very good night (thank you, Stephanie, random party-throwing girl who I barely knew) but she'd immediately briefed my dad. This was how things worked in my family. It was quite trying being an only child.

'I am right here,' I said.

'But what's he got to do with Mr Havelski?' asked Dad, looking confused.

'Absolutely nothing,' I replied firmly and rerouted the conversation back to business. And after an hour of me recounting (re-enacting) the two-minute phone call (and nothing else) I'd exhausted them both so much that I was left in peace to get down to the serious business of checking whether Archie had messaged me since he left.

'Elektra, is there any chance you could get off the phone for two minutes. I appreciate that you are now a very important person but I have asked you to get the door twice already.' Ah, Mum was beginning to sound more like herself.

I couldn't even see the person behind the petals when I opened the door.

'Miss Elektra Ophelia James?' he said, in a

tone that suggested he'd never had to deliver to somebody with a stupid name before.

I was living the dream. I nodded.

'Sign here.'

The delivery man thrust a little machine at me and I did a sort of squiggle that didn't look like it could be anyone's name, but he shoved the flowers at me anyway. I would need to work on my autograph now I was going to be a film star. I staggered giddily back into the kitchen. I'd never known that flowers could be this heavy.

'Oh, my!' sighed Mum happily. 'Who sent me flowers? Today is just getting better and better.'

Maybe I should have been worried that she didn't even look at Dad, just made a frankly undignified lunge for *my* flowers. 'Noooo, you don't. They're for me.' I pulled them back.

'Who's sending you flowers? Are they from your director? Is this what life is going to be like now? Film offers and flowers every five minutes?' Dad sounded a bit troubled.

'No,' I said, reading the note pinned to the cellophane. 'They're not from Mr Havelski.' That would have been amazing, but this was even better.

'Your *boyfriend* sent you those! That was quick,' said Mum.

'He's not my boyfriend,' I said, adding a silent, hopeful 'yet' in my head.

'He was certainly behaving like he was your boyfriend in the garden.' I cringed. 'And he must be keen,' she went on. 'Look at these roses. I'm jealous.' Now she did look at Dad (accusingly).

'They're not from Archie. *Obviously*,' I said.

'Then who sent them?' Mum looked at me suspiciously as if I might have a clutch of undisclosed millionaire boyfriends.

'Eulalie. How could you not guess that? Over-the-top? Super expensive? Pink? Beautiful? Got here quicker than the speed of sound?' I buried my nose in them; they smelled good. Once I stopped sneezing I read the note again and again.

Cherie, I am so very, very proud of you. Many people will give you flowers in all the exciting years to come but I wanted to be the first. I love you. xxxx

It made me want to cry. But in a good way.

To Do This Summer

I wrote this list last night in a fit of post-being-cast-in-a-Hollywood-blockbuster-excitement. I had to annotate it quite extensively this morning.

1. ~~Share an ice cream with Archie.~~ *I just put that one on so I had something to cross out.*
2. ~~Get cast in a film.~~ Also make a film. *I'm on fire.*
3. Get a tan. *Or at least a combination of sunburn and freckles that looks kind of like a tan.*
4. Avoid family holiday in Scotland. **Achievable**. Go on a girls' holiday with Moss, preferably at a time when Archie is also on holiday. (Possibly to a destination quite close to his??) *Would have to get rid of both mums for this to happen ... Definitely not achievable.*
5. Go to A Pool Party. *First I need to meet the kind of person who just happens to have an actual pool in their house/garden and make friends with them, which will probably involve convincing them that a) I am a perfectly seasoned pool party guest and b)*

not someone who just wants to use and abuse their prime real estate.

6. Learn Italian. **A noble intention but deeply unrealistic.**

7. Lie in a meadow with Archie picking wild flowers and having deep conversations about our relationship. **Must Google 'deserted wild meadows on the Circle line' asap. Also the deep conversations do sort of assume the relationship is a thing. Also our 'relationship' might go better if we avoid deep conversations?? Also it is less than forty-eight hours since we first got with each other – I might slightly be losing my mind.**

8. Write a poem. **???????????????????**

9. Roll down a grassy hill. **I'm so up for this. This is my kind of life goal.**

It was going to be a spectacular summer.

From: Stella at the Haden Agency
Date: 29 June 11:25
To: Elektra James; Julia James
Cc: Charlotte at the Haden Agency
Subject: GREAT NEWS!
Attachments: Performance Licence Application Form.doc;
Chaperone Security & Clearance Forms.doc

Dear Both,

Charlie and I wanted to be among the first to say
CONGRATULATIONS!! You'll be a perfect Straker, Elektra. We're
very proud of you – and it's lovely having a Haden Agency actor
landing such a big role, we've been doing little happy jigs in the
office all morning!

I'm sure that even though it's Monday morning you're all still busy
celebrating (or is Elektra at school?!) but can I just flag up some
important housekeeping that we need to get sorted out *as soon as
possible*. This is all going to happen really fast now.

I've made a list with everything that needs to be dealt with.

1. Elektra needs a performance licence. I'm attaching the
application form and you need to get this submitted to your local
authority *asap*.

2. The licence application needs an up-to-date medical certificate
too, so if Elektra could be seen by her doctor *asap* that would be
perfect!

3. We also need a letter from Elektra's headmistress authorizing
her to be absent from school for the production dates. As you
know, everyone is confident that everything is running *ahead of*

schedule and that Elektra's scenes will be completed during the summer holidays, but they have added on a fortnight just to be on the safe side. I'm sure that her school will share her excitement and be happy to help!

4. The production locations are now listed as **London and (unconfirmed) Hungary** so can you also let me have two passport photos and a copy of the 'magic page' of her passport.

5. Julia, if you are still keen to act as Elektra's chaperone then I'm afraid there are a lot of forms to fill in for you too (attached). I appreciate that this seems a little crazy but Panda Productions insists on every minor having an allocated, licenced chaperone.

6. Mr Havelski wants another meeting with Elektra and Carlo Winn (Jan) as soon as possible. His assistant is suggesting **Wednesday 1 July at 5 p.m. at Claridge's Hotel** where he will be staying (Charlie and I are very jealous). It's short notice but Mr Havelski is *a very busy man*. It's important, Julia, that you (and/or Elektra's father) also attend as this is a good opportunity to raise any questions you might have with Mr Havelski and his team.

I will be getting draft contracts out to you within the next few days and don't hesitate to call me to talk them through. I know that this probably seems rather daunting but do all try to enjoy it every step of the way!

With renewed felicitations to all!

Stella x

CHAPTER 2

'Why can't you understand that there's no such thing as privacy? That's just dumb.'

Lisa Kudrow

'You still haven't finished telling me what happened,' said Moss accusingly, as we walked to assembly. 'You were halfway through the whole celebrating-with-Archie-in-the-garden moment and you just went completely dead on me.'

'Sorry, I had a major emergency.'

'Really? What does a soon-to-be-movie-star count as a major emergency? Did your nail polish chip? Did your adoring fans give you the wrong colour of roses?'

'Don't mock me. I had a genuinely traumatic experience. I dropped my phone in the bath mid-text to you.'

'Did ... did it make it?' This was real concern; Moss knew how deep my phone dependency was.

'Only just,' I pulled it out of my pocket and gave it a little stroke. 'I got it into a massive bowl of rice. I've never run so fast in my life.'

'You've never run, full stop.'

'It was full-on like something out of *Grey's Anatomy*. I sat by its bedside for hours watching for signs of life. It only pulled through this morning.'

'Well now you have to tell me every single detail. Wait—' Moss tugged at me – 'who have they cast as your *lurve* interest?'

'Carlo Winn.'

'The American one?'

On the unlikely chance that I'd get this part I'd briefed Moss on the shortlist. 'The British one that lived in New York, yes.'

'Was he the one you fancied at the final audition?'

'No!' (A little bit, yes.)

'Should Archie be worried?'

'Moss, no!'

'Good, I really like Archie.'

'Not as much as I like Archie.' I gave a little swoony sigh and Moss laughed. I had to get that under control. 'I'm not going anywhere near Carlo. He *terrifies* me.'

'Interesting. Let's stalk him.' She grabbed my phone.

'We're not friends,' I said, trying unsuccessfully to wrestle it off her.

Talking of not friends, Flissy and Talia stalked past flicking their blow-dries and giving it the full Regina George.

'You will be,' said Moss. 'I've just sent Carlo a friend request.'

I loved Moss but she did struggle with boundaries. 'You're a nightmare. He'll think I'm into him.'

'Why? It's just a friend request and you're going to be co-stars.' She found that quite funny.

'Carlo's that kind of guy. He thinks everyone is into him.'

'Then the friend request won't make any difference ... Anyway, he's accepted already. You are his 1,735th friend, congrats.' She stood stock-still in the school corridor, oblivious to girls shoving past left and right, and scrolled. 'But I'm not sure I can be friends with you any more.' She zoomed in on a photo of Carlo in swimming trunks, caught the second after he'd jumped off some boat.

'That looks all right to me,' I said, dragging her along the corridor.

'It's like an advert for some stupidly expensive holiday or preppy lifestyle swimming brand. You—' insulting pause – '*you* are getting paid to get with *him*.'

'Not exactly,' I said. The bell went. We were going to be late for assembly.

'Does the script contain kissing scenes?'

'I think so.'

'Is there or is there not a beautiful romance between Straker and Jan?' Moss's mum's long-running campaign to turn Moss into a lawyer was paying off.

'Well … yes, there is. A romance so meaningful that dark turns to light and the world is saved. Probably. Or maybe everyone dies, but I think that's less likely.'

'I rest my case,' said Moss, as we were shooed into the hall. 'You're getting paid to kiss this almost-man-god and the only money I'm going to make in the next six months is going to come from babysitting. There is no justice in the world.'

'Good morning, girls!' exclaimed our head teacher, Mrs Haroun, from the stage. 'It's lovely to see you all here looking so fresh-faced and bright-eyed after the weekend.' Talia and Flissy slid down a little bit in their chairs. 'First things first, *uniform*.' There was a collective groan. 'One day of mild weather is no excuse for turning up at school practically wearing beachwear. *Dignity, girls, dignity.* And I'd just like to say to any of you who may be considering signing the anti-uniform petition that is currently circulating the corridors – yes, I know about it – that, whilst Berkeley Academy is a very democratic seat of learning, the petition WILL FAIL.' There was a murmur of misery. 'Anyway, you are in for a treat from the maths department this morning who will be giving you an account of their trip to the Xtreme Calculus Convention in Birmingham – in part, I hear, through the medium of an original song.' Mr Glenson brandished a ukulele ominously from the sidelines. 'But first we have some announcements. Feminism Society will be meeting in room A12 at four fifteen on Tuesday to discuss: *Should we hate men?* Boys from St John's are invited to attend.' There was a brave attempt at applause that Mrs Haroun quelled with one look. 'I would also like to clarify that after last year's fiasco at the *fiesta* we will *not* be offering the Spanish exchange this year. Which reminds me,' she went on, 'let's all give a warm Berkeley Academy "welcome back" to Señora Perez who has returned from her ... leave of absence, just in time for the end-of-term fun.' We all turned to stare at Señora Perez who was shuddering in the corner (probably PTSD).

Mrs Haroun looked over to where our year group usually sat. 'Elektra James?' I sank down in my chair. 'Where's Elektra James?' I was practically on the floor, but any number of 'helpful' girls pointed me out. Very, very slowly I got to my feet. 'Ah, there you are – could you join me onstage?' This was a first. I didn't *think* I'd done anything wrong but I wasn't entirely confident that I'd done anything right either. I climbed the steps to the stage, painfully aware of eight hundred and sixty pairs of eyes. There were good audiences and then there was school.

'Last night I received a very *interesting* email from Elektra's mother.' I had a bad feeling. 'Mrs James tells me that ...' Mrs Haroun paused for dramatic effect – 'Elektra has been offered the title role in a movie and will be filming over the summer holidays!' Flissy and Talia sat upright in perfect unison. I was starting to enjoy this. 'A movie called ...' Mrs Haroun squinted at the paper in her hand. 'STREAKER.' Scrap that. I was definitely *not* enjoying this. 'STREAKER,' she read, 'is a fast-paced run through a world that is post-apocalyptic and dystopian.' Flissy snorted. Mrs Haroun went on, 'STREAKER lays bare the bad and the good of the human condition.' Quite a few people snorted. Where was dignity now? 'I'm sure you'll all join me in congratulating Elektra – we look forward to seeing you *in all your glory* on the big screen in STREAKER!'

How could a woman who had worked with teenagers for so long be so utterly, utterly oblivious?

'Come on, girls, sit down and steady down,' said Mrs Lawal when we piled into the physics classroom. 'I know you're all very excited and happy for Elektra ...' Excited and happy wasn't the vibe Flissy and Talia were giving off. 'But in just two days' time, you'll be turning over your papers for the end-of-term exam. And – if you can come back down to earth and *concentrate* – I know you're all going to do *brilliantly*.'

It really wasn't going to matter which planet I was on. I was not going to do brilliantly.

'Think of the test as a chance to show off everything you've learned this year,' Mrs Lawal went on. 'You'll *enjoy* it.' Judging from the swell of groans, I wasn't the only one struggling with the concept of 'enjoying' a two-hour physics paper on the origins of the universe. 'I've set this session aside for quiet revision. If any of you experience a sudden blankness on the difference between the Oscillating Theory and the Steady State Theory then come and find me in the staffroom, otherwise I'll be back five minutes before the bell.' She was already halfway out of the door.

'Brilliant,' said Maia. 'The only lesson of the year when I'm extremely motivated and she decides to leave us to our own resources. She's probably off to FaceTime her new boyfriend.'

'Lawal has a boyfriend?' asked, well, all of us.

'She does, and he's younger than her and hot. My mum saw them together outside Tesco. We've basically been out-pulled by our physics teacher. And why didn't you tell me about *Streaker*, Elektra?'

'*Straker*,' I corrected for the umpteenth time that morning. 'It's only just happened,' I said, which was true but not the whole reason. I wasn't as close to Maia as I used to be, after she blew my reservations about Moss and Torr (Moss's sort-of boyfriend) massively out of proportion and nearly ruined our whole friendship.

'Such a pity you're not playing another talking *squirrel*,' said Flissy. '"Ooooh it's just so utterly nutterly!"'

My Squirrelina had sounded nothing like Flissy's Squirrelina but she got laughs (even Moss was struggling not to smile). This had been happening quite a lot since they'd released the Utterly Nutterly Nuts advert. I'm not sure the advert had shifted many nuts but it had definitely got a lot of air-time at Berkeley Academy.

'Can you just stop talking,' wailed Molly. 'Or at least stop shouting. *Nobody cares about Skillerina.*'

'Squirrelina,' I corrected her, very quietly.

'Yeah, but she's not just playing another squirrel this time, is she, Flissy?' said Moss, who was probably enjoying the attention more than I was.

Flissy shrugged. 'Or maybe it's just another part that she's boasting about that won't happen.' I flinched. One time I'd done that, *one time*, and I was never going to be allowed to forget it.

'What even is the Oscillating Theory?' said Jenny, her face scrumpled with worry, and everyone was dragged back to the misery at hand.

'Who cares?' said Flissy. 'Year Ten exams don't count.'

'They're the last ever exams that don't matter,' said

Moss darkly. The room got a lot quieter. I'd say that a chill fell over us, but the radiator was stuck on high (the radiator was always stuck on high – except for the months between November and February). Right, I'd spend five minutes checking Facebook and Insta and then I'd be filled with the sort of calm resolve that would bring mastery of the origin of the universe easily within my reach. Maybe.

Carlo had messaged me. My life really had changed a lot in the last forty-eight hours.

Psyched for the meeting with Havelski?

Bit nervous, I replied, which was a lie. I was *very* nervous.

Why? he sent back straight away. **Decision's made. We've done the hard part**

I'm no expert but I've got a feeling the 'hard part' might be making the movie, not getting cast

Bet you wouldn't have said that before you got cast

He was right about that. The biggest hurdle was always the one coming up (which was the only reason I was currently more worried about my physics test than maths).

They could still change their mind. Nothing's signed, I replied. And that was a really good reason to apply myself to the Big Bang Theory. I opened my book. *More matter means more gravity which could slow down expansion causing the so-called 'big crunch'.* A Crunchie right now would be a beautiful thing.

I was hungry. I couldn't concentrate so I checked my phone again.

My agent says we'll get contracts any day. Anyway, Havelski's too busy to change his mind

So do you know what this meeting's for?

Nope, but did you see where it's happening? What are the chances we'll run into Kate Moss?

Slim, I'd have thought, but I was really excited about going to Claridge's too so I didn't mock him.

The food will be awesome, Carlo added.

It's not like he's invited us to have tea and scones with him

Trust me, there'll be food. There's always food at these things and usually no one's eating it. I need your phone number, Elektra James . . .

'Aaaw, sweet, Elektra's texting her new boyfriend,' said Flissy.

I didn't say anything, just slid the phone back into my bag.

'Have you seen Archie since Stephanie's party?' asked Talia, coming over and perching on the edge of my desk.

I didn't want to answer her but clearly she wasn't going to move until I did. A voice in my head was going: 'Tell her EVERYTHING', but a louder (and saner) voice was saying: 'Are you mad? You don't like her. She *really* doesn't like you. Do NOT trust her. Also it is too early to tell anyone ANYTHING.' Finally I had common ground with Talia. We'd both got with Archie Mortimer. 'I saw him yesterday.'

'Seriously?' She couldn't have sounded more surprised if I'd said I'd met up with Chuck Bass. 'Did *you* ask *him* to meet up?'

'We're friends from acting,' I said, not quite answering the question.

'Close friends,' sniggered Flissy. 'You looked like very close friends on Saturday from where I was standing.' Flissy had been at the party too.

'So how was that for you, Elektra?'

Was Talia actually asking me what it was like to get with Archie? This was very uncomfortable. 'Er ... cool,' I said, which wasn't a very cool answer and certainly didn't do justice to the occasion, but I wasn't about to give her a moment-by-moment account.

'I don't think Elektra's got anything to compare it with,' said Flissy, which was fair (if you don't count a very creepy lunge-kiss in the traumatic final *Straker* callback) but annoying.

Mrs Lawal swept back into the room and saved me. She looked very pleased with herself. 'So, girls! I hope that was a productive revision session. We have—' she looked at her watch – 'precisely seven minutes left, so let's put it to the test with a quick test. See what I did there?'

It was going to be a long seven minutes.

★
CHAPTER 3

*'You rarely hear a man described as difficult, which
a woman is if she has an opinion that is not popular.'*
Kate Beckinsale

I messed up before I even made it into the ridiculously glamorous gilded foyer. I'm pretty sure I'm the only person ever to have visited Claridge's in a purple school uniform, and I'm absolutely certain that I'm the only person in purple school uniform to have got stuck in the revolving door. I had to be rescued by a doorman in a top hat, who was nice enough not to say anything to me and not even to raise his extremely bushy eyebrows at the very non-five-star-hotel state of me.

'Are you nervous, Elektra?' Mum asked in a too-loud whisper. 'Do you need to nip to the loo before the meeting?'

I despaired. I tried to catch my dad's eye but he was too busy gazing up at some architectural detail on the ceiling that only he could see. (To be fair, he is an architect.)

'I'm *fine*,' I said in a tone intended to close down both lines of enquiry. Although now, of course, I did want to go to the loo. My shoes were making too much noise on the polished black-and-white marble floor.

'Well, you shouldn't be nervous. You're entitled to be here,' said Mum.

This reassurance told me two things: she was also nervous and neither of us *really* believed that I was entitled to be here. Not at Claridge's and definitely not at a meeting with Mr Havelski.

I wouldn't feel entitled until I signed a contract.

No, I wouldn't feel entitled until I started filming.

Noooo. I wouldn't feel entitled until I'd *finished* filming. I'd read enough *The Bizz* posts to know that there were some brutal firings in this world.

Oh God. What if this meeting was because Mr Havelski wasn't sure about casting me at all? Now I definitely needed to go to the loo. My phone barked with a text. A miniature pug shot me a withering glance from a passing socialite's handbag. It wasn't a very Claridge's-y ring tone, so I switched it to silent.

Say bonjour to Michael for me. It was Eulalie.

Who's Michael?

The doorman. The large one with the bushy eye-brows. Were you not meeting him?

Sort of, but not to chat

But you must always chat to doormen! They are knowing everything

It wasn't the moment. Pretty sure I made an impression though

Of course you did. You are perfectly wonderful

No, it was how I looked that made the impression

Bien sûr, you are perfectly beautiful

Eulalie was loyal to the point of myopia but I was about to disappoint her.

I came straight from school

NON! Please do not be telling me that you are in Claridge's in that terrible uniform?! Like a prune. What is your mother thinking?

Yes I am ☹ And I never know what my mother is thinking. Never.

Is it being too late to rescue the situation? Le shopping?

It's way too late for le shopping. My fate is sealed. My humiliation is complete

'May I help you?' asked the man behind the desk.

'We have a meeting here with Mr Sergei Havelski,' said my mother. I couldn't speak because I'd just noticed that the lift opposite the desk came complete with a lift man, floor-to-ceiling gilded mirrors and a sofa. A *real* sofa in case you got so exhausted from standing in your fabulous heels between the ground and second floors that you needed to sit down.

'Ah, yes, Mr Havelski is receiving his guests in the French Salon,' said the desk man and, like magic, someone appeared to take his place so he could escort us to the room. We followed him nervously, just a little bit distracted by the fact that he was wearing what I think is called a tailcoat. He opened a door decorated with winged cherubs and showed us into a room that was all panelling and marble fireplaces, with a large chandelier hanging above a table. It smelled warm and expensive like salted caramel truffles. Eulalie would have been very much at home. Me? Less so.

There was a different cast this time: me, Carlo, my parents, his mum, Mr Havelski and his assistants Selim and Rhona, and a man in a black suit whose name I didn't catch but who was Production something or other. The relief that there were no other possible 'Strakers' in the room was enough to make me feel slightly faint.

'So you must all call me Sergei,' Mr Havelski said in his meerkat accent. I still wanted to call him 'Sir'. Actually, I was still a bit scared to call him anything. Really I wanted to say as little as possible to him, to delay the inevitable moment when he realized that he'd made a terrible mistake in casting me. A sort of director-y buyer's remorse. 'We're going to make a wonderful film together.' Mr Havelski – *Sergei* – was pacing around in front of us like a small stressy bear. He was doing a lot of smiling. The last time we'd met he'd been in full 'scary dictator' character and now he was trying to pull off 'everyone's favourite uncle' and I wasn't entirely convinced by the metamorphosis. 'First, we have the presentation and then we'll talk over tea.' Carlo, who was sitting next to me, nudged me at the mention of tea. 'We'll have a big tea and we'll talk. Selim, lights, screen; Rhona, doors.'

The year is 2077. The 'civilisations' that tyrannised Mother Nature have been obliterated by the Great Disaster *[flood/ rain/ wind/ fire/ comet/ nuclear: all encompassing eco-disaster to be decided]*. The few survivors who made it to higher ground *[this may rule out nuclear disaster? Talk to research team]* have watched the world as they know it destroyed and now the future of the human race lies in their hands. The survivors resolve to work together to save themselves, find other survivors and rebuild civilisation. But soon personal grudges and different views on how to build a new society cause them to revert to tribalism which quickly *[around 5 mins screentime]* becomes all out warfare.

The Hunger Games meets *Planet of the Apes* meets *Romeo & Juliet* meets the *Odyssey* meets *Avatar* meets *Mean Girls*; *STRAKER* tells the universally relatable story of forbidden teenage love against a post apocalyptic backdrop.

I'm not going to lie, I was almost hysterically excited. The rest of the slides were a bit quieter. Some of them were a bit weird.

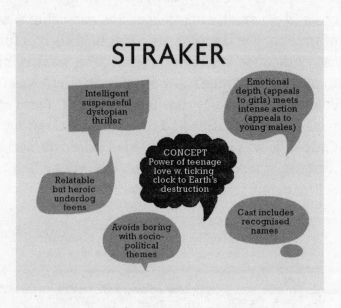

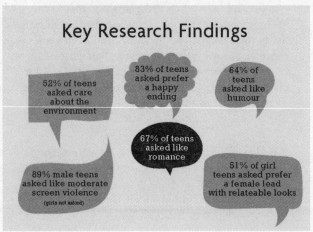

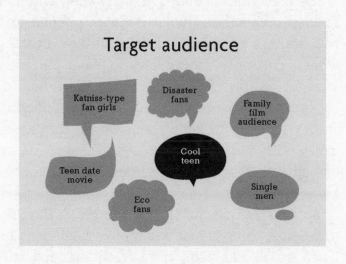

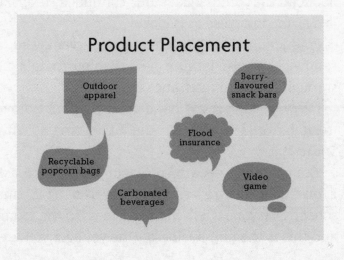

51% of girl teens asked prefer a female lead with relatable looks. I was grateful to them.

The presentation ended; nobody knew whether to clap or not but then the doors opened and two waiters wheeled in silver trolleys bearing what I can only describe as a feast: perfectly straight sandwiches upstanding in a feat of engineering, scones plain and fruit cocooned in snowy napkins to keep them warm, miniature cakes with twirls of chocolate, swirls of cream and icing so glossy I could see my own reflection. I was loving this.

'So, who has questions?' asked ~~Sergei~~ Mr Havelski (the Sergei thing is just wrong) five minutes later, when we all had stripy mint-green tea cups, stiff napkins and ten varieties of jam. 'And don't bother about all the commercial stuff,' continued Havelski, 'it's as meaningless as it looks.'

Production Suit glowered as he swallowed a sandwich whole. I think he'd wanted to talk us through the flood insurance tie-in.

I very slowly put my hand up, trying to be brave (relatable and brave). 'Is the title going to stay *Straker?*'

'So, you don't need to put your hand up to ask a question, Elektra,' said Mr Havelski. This isn't school. Everyone who's in the room is "in the room" and this is the film business – the younger you are, the more likely that we'll listen to you. To answer your question, for now we think the title will stay *Straker*.'

'But I'm not the lead character,' I blurted.

'True, but we want teens to identify with the film. Teenagers are where the money is so *Straker* it is … for now. Have more cake.'

I reached for the miniature Victoria sponge and struggled to get my head around the idea that teenagers were 'where the money was'. 'But I'm not even the lead *teenager*,' I continued. From the pages I'd seen, Carlo/Jan had more lines and way more of the action. I struggled to get the words out. The cake may have been miniature, but it was still four layers of fluffy sponge and buttercream and jam, so there was no way to eat it elegantly. Far less eat it elegantly and ask Havelski questions. What was I even doing?

Havelski looked at me over his glasses in a way that very much reminded me of my maths teacher. 'Tell me, Elektra.' He spoke very slowly. 'I give you a choice, yes? You can go and see a movie called *Jan* or you can go and see a movie called *Straker*, which do you choose?'

Fair point. '*Straker and Jan?*' I suggested, spraying out some crumbs. I seemed to be suffering from some weird brain/mouth disconnect that meant I couldn't stop asking questions.

He sighed. '*Straker and Jan* sounds like a family sitcom, not a dystopian movie.'

'They could maybe change my character's name?' suggested Carlo. 'I'm not bothered about the title thing, but Jan is kind of a lame name.'

'Interesting input Carlo,' said Havelski dryly. 'I'll put your suggestion to the writers.' I was one hundred per cent certain that he wasn't going to do that. So much for giving weight to the teen vote.

Production Suit began to speak. A deathly chill fell over the room like he was some film industry Dementor. 'Our extensive market research suggests that it's good marketing to have a girl's name in the title.'

Even a girl's name that sounds like a boy's name? Even a girl's name where the girl has fewer lines than every adult and the guy?

He was still talking. 'It's more on trend and it might earn us some coverage from *the feminist press.*'

'Parents?' Mr Havelski definitely didn't have a clue what their names were but he'd obviously had enough of Production Suit. 'Later we talk with your people about the details but for now you need to know we are going to take very good care of your children. So, you have no questions? So? Everything is good? Yes?' Maybe he'd had enough of all of us.

'Timing,' my mum said, and every adult in the room stiffened. Timing was clearly a big deal. 'I just need to be absolutely sure that there won't be any overlap with school term dates.' She had her little pocket calendar out and a highlighter all ready. It was a bit tragic. Mum nudged Dad (who'd closed his eyes to shut out the colour of my school uniform and/or the fact that there was a carved cupid in his eyeline) and he nodded as if, yes, timing had been exactly what he too had been worrying about.

'Casting the main child parts was one of the last things we did,' said Rhona, 'and the start date that we're working with as of today is the twentieth of July. Where we can, we'll bring the scenes featuring the children right up in the filming schedule. And although Straker and Jan are important, they're not in every scene so there's a high chance we'll be finished and able to release them *ahead of schedule*.'

'Yes,' said Production Suit and Mr Havelski as one. 'We are very much ahead of schedule.'

CHAPTER 4

'Actors have a childlike quality. You're relying on that make-believe game you used to play as a child but this time you're hopefully getting paid for it.'
Asa Butterfield

'Can I do my revision in here?' I asked, making myself a bit of space on the kitchen table. Normally I very much preferred to work in my own room away from my mum, but I was too hyped after the meeting. Also I'd run out of bedroom emergency provisions. I got up and rummaged through the cupboards. 'There are no biscuits in this house,' I declared, after a very thorough search.

'How can you possibly want biscuits after Mr Havelski fed us that enormous tea?' said Mum.

'That was hours ago and it was you that decided to cancel supper, not me. Seriously aren't there any?'

'Yes, but they're hidden behind the cookbooks on the top shelf.'

'Are they hidden from me?'

'No!'

'Then you've hidden them from yourself *but* you know where they are ... Please tell me you're not on a diet.'

'It's not exactly a diet.'

'If you've hidden the biscuits, it's a diet. How many times have you lectured me on the *stupidity* of dieting?' I hoped I sounded stern. 'OK, we have two options. One: you have to watch me eating them ...'

'Elektra,' she whispered. 'I'm not strong enough.'

'Then it will have be option two: I'm going to get these biscuits and we are both going to approach them in a rational free-from-fear sort of way. Agreed?' I stood on a chair to get to the top shelf and started pulling out cookbooks. Mum's avoidance tactic was impressively hardcore.

'They're behind Nigella,' she said, after I'd managed to knock both Jamie Oliver and Paul Hollywood to the ground. 'Can I help with your revision?'

'I don't think so. It's a practice maths test.' She was nearly as bad as me at maths.

'Then I'll just make you tea?'

I sat back at the table and nodded appreciatively. Mum turned into a sort of house elf whenever I was studying, pandering to my every whim and feeding me carbs at every opportunity. I liked it more than I admitted. Digby came over and laid his head on my knee. I tried not to mind that he was a bit slobbery.

> **Q. 1: Fred travels from a to b and at a speed of 90km per hour. It takes him time 't'. Krisha travels from a to b at a speed of 70km per hour. It takes her time 't+ 1 hour'. How long did it take for Fred to complete his journey?**

I was pretty sure Fred and Krisha were having a thing (they were certainly both in a rush to get to location 'b') but beyond that, nope, not a clue. I doodled a little heart in the answer box. I'd come back to that one.

> **Q. 2: CALCULATOR: A circular table top has a diameter of 140cm. Calculate the area of the table top in cm², giving your answer as a multiple of ϖ.**

The little pi symbol made me hungry. 'Can I have another biscuit?'

'Concentrate.'

So easy to say; so hard to do. I drew a little fruit

pie in the answer box. My mind wasn't on anything but pie and *Straker*. 'When will the contract come?'

'It already did. A courier delivered it when you were in the shower.'

'Whaaaat? Why didn't you tell me? Show me.'

'After you've finished your revision. Now *concentrate*.'

Even if every single question had been about calculating actors' fees and expenses I wasn't going to get any maths done. I faked for a bit. 'Done.' I wasn't.

She put a plate of biscuits and a slim plastic folder in front of me.

I reached for the folder even before the biscuits. *This Agreement is made between Panda Productions (hereinafter 'Producer') and Elektra Ophelia James (hereinafter 'Artist').* I'd never been called an 'Artist' before, mostly because I was very poor at art, but I liked it. Ten pages in and three (small) biscuits later I was a muddle of excitement and panic and mostly confusion. 'There's a lot in here I don't quite get,' I said. This was an understatement. It was like deciphering the Rosetta Stone.

'Nor me. Don't worry, I'm going to talk it all through with Stella tomorrow. I'm not sure I should even have shown it to you. We didn't mean for you to know how much you were going to be paid.'

I'd like to say that now I was 'an Artist', material

wealth meant nothing to me. But that would be a big fat lie. I flicked to the back page and my eyes nearly popped out. The total was in a little black box at the bottom and it was probably about a thousand times all the money I'd had in my life. Ever.

Of course I wasn't going to get out of bed for anything less now.

A couple of minutes later I was starting to stress out.

I was going to have to be *worth all this money* or, as it said in clause 3.1, *perform the part in a proper, diligent, competent and professional manner.* As I could barely make it through the school day without getting a detention for basically being a mess, this troubled me. I ate another biscuit and felt a bit better. I offered one to Digby but he shook his head. 'Diggers is dissing our biscuits, Mum.'

'I know. He's been off his food. I'm going to take him down to the vet and get him checked out.'

'Is he OK? He looks very . . . sad.'

'He's probably just worrying in case you're going to be the next child actor trainwreck.' It was Mum who looked worried. Her initial unbridled joy at me getting the *Straker* role had fast subsided into mild panic (which would have been more surprising were mild panic not her default state). I swear Digby rolled his eyes. But he'd definitely been a bit *flat* recently. He looked at me and coughed. Did he

40

have dog flu? I scratched him behind his ear. No question he still liked that.

'Do I actually get the money?' I asked, enjoying visions of shopping trips with Moss and Eulalie.

'Well, you won't be able to get your hands on most of it. Not for a few years yet. That wouldn't be good for you at all.'

My visions of shopping trips with Moss and Eulalie crashed and burned. I read on. 'I get a dressing room!' I wondered if it would be tacky to ask for one of those mirrors with lights. 'And *toilet facilities!*' I took a snap of that page and sent it to Eulalie, who was an enthusiastic user of any and all social media.

'Did you read the bits about the tutor?' Mum asked, ferreting through my schoolbag and coming up with one sock. She said 'tutor' in the same tone I'd have said 'Ryan Gosling'. 'Where's the other sock?'

'In my school locker.' It wasn't. It had just *gone*. 'Where are the tutor bits?' It wasn't easy to find anything in this document. She leaned over my shoulder and pointed to clause 7.3(i).

I steeled myself and read the clause. 'I think ...' I trailed off, then read it again. How clever did you need to be to write something that made this little sense? 'I think it's only during term time,' I said happily. 'And we probably won't run into term time.'

'You certainly won't run into term time,' said Mum, as though it were entirely within her control. 'It's a shame, though. It might be worth asking them if they can have someone on hand for holiday work.'

Making a movie wasn't achievement enough over a summer holiday?

My phone barked. **A dressing room! I will fill it with chocolates.** I loved Eulalie. **Do you have a robe?**

What??

For relaxing

I wasn't sure how much relaxing there'd be. Waiting? Yes – but I was an expert on waiting, and waiting wasn't relaxing. **I have a dressing gown. But it is woollen and has a sheep pattern on it**

Actors are not being relaxing in woollen sheep. Actors are being relaxing in silk

I wasn't sure I was going to be the sort of actor who would be relaxing in silk.

My phone barked again. **Want to do something this week?**

'Is that Archie texting you?' My mum had come up close behind me in a frankly stealthy way.

'No,' I lied.

'I think it was. Was he asking you out on a date?'

This conversation could not end well. 'No.'

'But he was asking if you wanted to do something.'

42

Oh, God. I put my phone in my bag, but the damage was done. 'If you saw the text was from Archie, why did you ask?'

She looked a bit sheepish, but not sheepish enough. 'So are you going to meet up with him?'

'Can I help you tidy up?' I tried distraction.

'Are you? And when? It's not the holidays yet.'

'Shall I load the dishwasher? Scrub the floors?'

'Stop trying to change the subject.'

I gave up. 'Maybe I'll meet up with him,' I said, because in my world such things were not to be counted on. 'And it's nearly the end of term. Even you have to let me go out a bit.'

'I don't *have* to let you do anything. What's he like?'

'He's nice.'

'Nice, like, would make a good *boyfriend* nice?' That word again. 'Or nice to pets and old people, nice? Or both? Nice doesn't tell me much.'

Well, yes, Sherlock, that was the point. I shrugged and pretended to be reading a newspaper article about a 'large humming object' spotted in the night sky above David Beckham's house.

'It's amazing how little I know about him, considering how long you've had a crush on him. Does Moss like him?'

I nodded distractedly. The article had turned out to be quite interesting so I was now real-reading it.

Mum had a lot of respect for Moss's judgment but then there were lots of things Moss did that my mother knew nothing about.

'Can we follow him?'

'What do you mean?' I had a troubling vision of my mum watching Archie from behind a bush. Now I came to think about it, that wasn't a vision, it was a memory.

'On Facebook or whatever that other one is with all the pictures.'

'Instagram?'

'Yes, that thing.'

'No, we can't *stalk* Archie online. Obviously.'

'Moss showed me *her* boyfriend.' That was true, and now my mum was over-invested in Moss and Torr's relationship (whatever that was). 'Come on, it'll be fun.' She looked at the laptop greedily.

'No.' But I knew I was weakening. I couldn't rule out the risk she'd do it on her own if I kept saying no. Also Archie was undeniably fit and a small bit of me did want to show her.

'And I'd be very worried about you going out to meet a near *stranger.*'

'Come on! Archie doesn't look like an axe murderer, does he?'

'It was hard to get a clear picture of him as he was so busy kissing you under our tree.'

This was painful.

'I *really* want to.' She was literally begging to be allowed to stalk a sixteen-year-old boy.

'No.' I held firm.

'That's a shame. Well, I suppose I'll see him the next time he wants to come over and *enjoy* our garden. I'll make an effort to get to know him properly. Maybe tell him that story about the time you and Moss hid—'

'Are you *blackmailing* me?'

'No. I would be blackmailing you if, to take a random example, I were to send him that photo of you from Halloween last year. Yes, the spider costume one ... the *dancing* spider costume one.'

It was official: my mother was blackmailing me. No wonder the production company wanted to run *extensive* checks before accepting her as a chaperone. I know that you're not meant to give into blackmail and that it always ends badly with bankruptcy or murder or something, but that photo was *really* bad.

I gave in. I negotiated with terrorists.

Facebook or Instagram? I had a sudden blank about what was on either. I'd probably spent more time stalking Archie than I had on all of my coursework combined but I couldn't remember anything. I opened up the laptop very nervously.

Archie's Facebook profile picture was Mum-friendly; his hair looked like it had been polished by a keen butler and he had a healthy glow (possibly because he was at a party rather than doing a wholesome outdoor activity, but she didn't have to know that).

'Ooooh, I like his jumper.' Of course Mum liked his jumper – it was a cricket jumper. The dream. 'Next.'

His only other profile picture was safe too, not least because it had been taken when he was about ten. What is it with boys failing to keep up with their public relations? I made to close the laptop lid.

'Let's look at his tagged photos?'

There was no good explanation for how Mum could have become this Facebook-savvy. I blamed Moss. But I hadn't given Archie's perfection enough credit. The first twenty-odd photos were of him winning football matches. There was one of him filming in period costume, which was basically what my mum thought boys should wear twenty-four seven anyway. One of him smiling slightly manically for a school prospectus – which his friend had posted with a caption so ironic that my mum commented on how nice it was that Archie had such supportive friends. I was mildly surprised that there weren't any pictures of Archie saving starving children or single-handedly diffusing political tensions in the Middle East. I was beginning to worry that instead of being banned from ever seeing

Archie-the-delinquent again, I was going to end up pressured into an early marriage so I could produce a stable of perfectly behaved grandchildren.

Oh, God. My relief was premature. I tried to flick over one of Archie buried under about seven girls. Next.

'Wait, what was that?'

'Nothing, nothing,' I squeaked, flicking as fast as I could. Why were there suddenly no safe football photos for me to stop on? Oh no, this one was Archie and Talia. How could I have forgotten this was here?

'Is that Talia?' Mum gasped, as if I'd shown her a picture of the Dalai Lama kicking a kitten to death. And how could she identify Talia? Literally all you could see was a blow-dry and a YSL shoulder bag. 'Archie *snogged* Talia?'

'Can you *please* never say snog again?'

'But I thought *you* were snogging Archie?'

'Oh my God, can you please never say *any* part of that sentence again?'

'Has Archie *cheated* on you?'

'Firstly, me and Archie are not officially going out.'

'*Clearly.*'

'Secondly, this happened months ago.'

She looked sceptical. 'Well, I hope you're going to ask him about it.'

I was not going to ask him about it.

'Do you still want to see him?'

'Yes, I do.' *Obviously.*

She gave me the full your-judgment-is-poor stare and asked, 'So what are your plans for the weekend?'

'We don't have *plans.*'

'But he was texting you about meeting up.'

'Yes, but we don't need to decide what to do now.'

'Then how can you *plan?*'

I shrugged like I was way too cool to need more than an hour or two to plan a meet-up, but inside I was agreeing with her.

'Why don't you ask him to come round here?'

So she could ask him all about his 'relationship' with Talia? No, thanks.

'I think that might be a tiny bit awkward.'

'Oh, you mean Dad might embarrass you?'

That wasn't *exactly* what I'd meant. 'I think we'll just go for a drink or something.'

'A drink?'

'Coffee?'

'You hate coffee.'

'Coffee doesn't mean coffee.'

'What does coffee mean?'

'Tea. I meant tea. That's all I meant. Can we just not talk any more?'

From: Stella at the Haden Agency
Date: 6 July 11:03
To: Elektra James; Julia James
Cc: Charlotte at the Haden Agency
Subject: *Straker* (working title): Trainer Dick Murphy joins the team!
Attachments: Richard Murphy (RT Screen Combat Training) contact details.doc

Dear Both,

I've just had Rhona on the phone chasing about the licence. I've assured her that it's all in hand but she's reminded me to ask if Elektra is up to date with her tetanus shots? Maybe something to check when she's having her medical tomorrow. Good luck with that, Elektra!

And as you know, Straker has some brilliant fight and action scenes, so the production has engaged a really experienced combat trainer (Dick Murphy) to work with Elektra and Carlo on their general fitness levels, knife skills and swordsmanship. Free personal training is one of the perks of the job! Can I just check that Elektra is confident with basic skills like climbing and diving? I see that these are now checked off on her online Spotlight but if she needs any practice, now really is the time to shout!

Stella x

P.S. I got your message about your background checks, Julia, and I will chase that up again today. *Of course* we know that you're not the Julia James guilty of masterminding large-scale financial fraud in Oregon! We might have to think about making *interim* chaperone arrangements though because these things do tend to run at their own pace. Leave it with me.

★ CHAPTER 5

'*You have to have a certain amount of self-delusion
to get anywhere in the arts.*'

Mia Wasikowska

'Just slip your shoes off, Elektra, and we'll get you weighed. Your friend can take a seat over there.'

Dr Chukwu obviously thought it was a bit weird that I'd brought Moss with me but a) I'm quite scared of doctors, b) I was very scared of this doctor (who had that whole 'sweetie-nicey on the outside, psychotic on the inside' thing going on – like a medical Dolores Umbridge) and c) I'm very, very terrified of injections and I was pretty sure she was going to make me have one. Also – and this may or may not have been the main reason – we were meeting up with Archie and Torr afterwards.

'So explain to me exactly what you have to be fit *for* in this *movie*.' Dr Chukwu looked at me searchingly for signs of germs or possibly stupidity.

'Well ... acting,' I said.

'Is it an *action movie?*' She had a form in front of her with little boxes to tick and cross. I didn't usually do well on forms like that.

'There is some action in it, yes,' I said. Hopefully not too much.

'She's playing a girl who saves the world,' said Moss proudly.

I was getting stressy about the 'girl saving the world' thing. Not with the concept that a girl could save the world, although that's ridiculous for a billion reasons, none of which have anything to do with gender. I was more immediately worried about being low on world-saving *skills*. I famously have no combat skills. I can't climb trees or mountains or towers (even towers that aren't on fire, as they so often seem to be). There are stairs I struggle with. I can't build a shelter – any sort of shelter. I struggle to get the duvet cover on. I'd literally woken up at 3 a.m. this morning, panicking because I didn't know how to start a fire with matches and firelighters, far less twigs or flints or whatever people who can save the world use. It's my parents' fault for not calling me something like Bear.

'Well, if there's *action*,' said the doctor, after she'd

listened to my now-racing heart, 'we need to check your fitness levels and record your history of sports injuries.'

The second bit was easy. 'I haven't had any.'

'That's because she doesn't do any sport,' added Moss helpfully.

'I need the patient to answer, thank you, if I'm to assess her fitness for purpose,' said Dr Chukwu, checking my blood pressure. Moss shrank back, nearly tipping over a hideously over-scaled anatomical model of an eye. I was pretty sure I wasn't technically a patient, although I was beginning to feel a bit feverish. 'So you wouldn't say you were particularly used to doing strenuous exercise?'

'Not on a *daily* basis,' I said, sort of truthfully.

She made a little cross on her pad.

'But I'm getting a personal trainer so I'll probably be really fit soon.'

Moss snorted and the doctor didn't look much more convinced. 'We have a record of one fractured digit from a rounders' incident and ...' she flicked through the file in front of her, 'one broken arm from a fall. How did that happen?'

'I tripped.' There was no need to tell her that I'd tripped over a paving stone because I'd been staring at a six-metre high poster of Alex Pettyfer. No need at all.

'Making movies can be dangerous,' she said. 'A patient of mine nearly broke his back when a stunt went wrong.' This is the point where my mum would have gathered me up like an umbrella and left. 'I think his harness snapped during some aerial work. Nasty spinal compression fracture. But if it's what you *want* to do ...' She tutted. 'Well, I'm sure you're very excited.'

'I *am* very excited. I can't wait.' Embarrassingly I made a little *squee* sound and Dr Chukwu made a note. Possibly about my mental state. 'But I'm sure I won't be doing any aerial thingies,' I said. I very much hoped not, now more than ever before.

'Will you be in extreme heat or cold?' I shook my head nervously. Another reluctant tick. 'Underwater to depths of two metres or more?' The pen was back in the air.

'I ... I really don't think so.'

'Well, this certificate won't cover your fitness for diving, so if you're wrong on that you'll need to come back.'

That would be the least of my worries in that eventuality. Diving (sky or water) was another missing skill. I could only swim if I put my feet down between lengths. That tiny exaggeration on my Spotlight form was haunting me.

'When was your last tetanus injection?'

'I'm not sure.' Quite a long time ago.

'Let me see, the last one noted down in our records was … eight years previously, so you're overdue one.'

'I could maybe pop back and have that another day?' I asked hopefully (desperately).

'No. If you want this certificate signed today then you'll have to have the injection today. I just need to run through some quick questions. Any history of pregnancy?'

'No.' Seriously?

'Any chance that you could be pregnant?'

'No!'

Moss sniggered.

'Would you like your friend to go out of the room while you answer these questions?'

'No. It's fine. The answer's no.' *Obviously.*

'I've filmed that bit for your mum,' said Moss.

'I hope that's a joke,' said Dr Chukwu giving Moss's phone a death stare.

'Of course,' said Moss so innocently that I knew it wasn't.

'I need to get to your upper arm, dear.'

I inched my sleeve up as far as it would go, which wasn't far enough.

'No, not like that. Just slip down your jumper.' And then she left me sitting there panicking *and freezing* while she broke out the syringe. 'Right, here we go … No, don't jerk away, I need you to stay still for this … just a tiny prick … There we go, all done.' She put a little plaster over the hole she'd made in me and I resisted the urge to ask for one of the *I've been a Brave Bear Today* stickers.

'Well, at least I got the certificate,' I said, rubbing my wounded arm. It felt like we'd been in the surgery for hours, but we'd still got to the cafe before the boys. 'There was a nasty moment when I thought she was going to refuse to sign it because I'd had chickenpox in Year Five or something. She was so revoltingly thorough. If I'd had Dr Ness, he'd just have asked where to sign.'

'That's because Dr Ness is about a hundred and five and can't remember any medicine any more,' said Moss.

'He'd have given me a sticker, though,' I said.

'I *knew* you wanted one,' she said, taking three out of her bag and decorating my face with them. 'There, all better now?'

Yes, actually. 'How long do you guess before they get here? Do I need to put on mascara?' Now that I had a romantic … *thing* and a film deal, I was going to become one of those women who could whip out emergency make-up supplies because they never knew where their spontaneous and glamorous lives would take them.

'Nope, you don't want to set the bar too high

early on.' Moss brutally slayed my fantasy. 'Anyway, it's too late, Archie's just walked in.' She waved at him energetically.

Archie came over and there was a long moment when he just stared at me. 'I'm early, right? I'm always early. It's a curse,' he said.

'It's good to be early,' said Moss, her eyes on the door. 'Torr is always late.'

'To be fair,' I said, 'you're pretty famous for your own lateness.'

'Do you want another drink? Something to eat?' said Archie.

'More hot chocolate, please,' I said, because I'd spilled most of mine over a 'highbrow' essay on the Kardashians in *Heat* magazine. 'That was weirdly awkward,' I said to Moss, when Archie had gone to the back of the very long queue.

'I'm not sure,' said Moss, sniggering. 'But I think it might have something to do with the brave bear stickers all over your face.'

Great.

'Or maybe it's just seeing you in all the glory of this uniform,' she added.

I pulled off the stickers. I pulled off the purple cardigan. There wasn't anything more I could decently remove. Also it was the coldest July ever and the air conditioning was on way too high. 'Have I got red marks all over my face now?'

'No,' she said, though I wasn't sure that I believed her. This wasn't the impression I'd been hoping to make.

Moss kept looking at the door.

'Torr will be here soon,' I said.

She shrugged. 'He's flaked on me a couple of times recently.'

'You looked pretty happy together at Stephanie's party.'

'It was a *party* and he was my plus one. It doesn't count.'

'Remind me, Moss, when was Torr's last GCSE exam?'

'Er ... a couple of weeks ago?'

'So it's possible he's been a tiny bit distracted? Also just how late is he?'

She checked. 'Eleven minutes.'

'This might be the worst thing I have ever said to you, but you are currently reminding me of my mother.'

'I've met Elektra's mum,' said Archie, setting down the mugs and pulling up a chair between us. He reached his arm across the back of mine and I leaned back a little nervously.

'God, Elektra, you're always cold. You don't wear enough clothes,' he said.

I went red. Archie took off his hoodie and gave it to me and I pulled it over my head very slowly, so I had time to return to a normal colour. It was warm from his body but I didn't dwell on that.

'So how did that whole "meet the mother" thing go?' asked Moss.

'It wasn't like that,' I said. 'Trust me, it was one hundred per cent an accident that Archie met my mother.'

'She seemed nice; she fell in a bush,' said Archie.

'That doesn't sound very like your mum,' said Moss.

'I think she was just really surprised to see me with a boy,' I said, and immediately regretted it. I had to stop being so honest. It was undermining my whole 'I'm cool' vibe that I'd spent literally hours practising in my head this morning. 'By the way, Moss, Torr's just walked in and he's making gooey love eyes at you so you've been panicking about nothing.'

'Moss told me about the *Straker* thing,' said Torr, arriving at our table. 'Congratulations.'

'It still doesn't feel real,' I said. 'I haven't had to do anything yet.' This was the easy bit.

'It's definitely real now it's been announced in assembly,' said Moss, and I gave a little shiver of nervousness. 'Oh, no, sorry, that was *Streaker*.'

Torr looked confused. 'So you guys met through acting?' he asked Archie.

'Yeah, we go to the same after-school class.'

'Do you act professionally as well?' Torr asked him.

Archie shrugged. 'I was in a TV thing ages ago, but not so much. It can be months when I don't hear from my agent.'

'You did that biscuit commercial too.' I jumped back into the conversation.

'Oooh, yes, the blueberry and oat thing,' said Moss.

Archie looked puzzled. He wasn't to know that Moss was *very* familiar with his voice-over promoting the B-Oat Bic ('row, row, row your way to slow release carbs' being one of the more memorable lines). We've watched it so many times on YouTube that it comes up as a suggested page.

'Are you going to keep doing it?' asked Torr.

'I'm up for something at the moment,' said Archie, 'but I've only had one audition and it probably won't come off.'

'What is it?'

'Er ... it's quite hard to explain. A vampire thing.' Archie looked a bit embarrassed.

'A vampire? What, like the sparkly guy in *Twilight?*' asked Moss, impressed.

'I've never seen that movie,' said Torr, not even trying to hide how tragically mainstream he thought we were.

'No. I'm up for the vampire hunter. Or like a bear

hunter turned vampire hunter ...' Archie trailed off. 'They're going to film it in Transylvania. Some of it anyway.'

'Is Transylvania a real place?' I asked.

'Well, yes,' said Archie. 'It's in Romania.'

I'd thought it was just a figment of Bram Stoker's pervy imagination, full of vampires and blood-soaked myths playing out in crumbling castles and forests filled with nameless things. Who knew?

'It's just *weird*,' said Torr suddenly.

'I *know*. Who even lives there?' I said.

'Not Transylvania,' said Torr. 'You guys.' He gestured at me and Archie with his mug.

'Er ... what exactly is weird about us?' asked Archie.

'Well, you talk about doing this drama stuff like it's normal and *it's not normal*.'

'Harsh,' I said, and Moss gave him a look.

'Not weird in a bad way just ... outside the usual. Like you both have *agents* and Archie's just casually done an *advert* and you've just casually been cast in a *film*.'

I wasn't even a tiny bit casual about being cast in a film. 'Well, I think it's weird when people in your year talk about life after GCSEs,' I said. 'To me that's too far away to seem real.'

'When do you guys turn sixteen?' asked Torr.

'You know when my birthday is,' said Moss. There

was an awkward pause. She looked deflated. 'It's in March.'

'Mine's in October,' I chipped in quickly.

'That reminds me.' Moss turned to me. 'We need to arrange a time ...' She waggled her eyebrows at me. 'You know.' She waggled them more. I had no idea what she was on about, but she looked deranged. 'To *plan* ...' Nope, still too cryptic for me. 'The PARTY,' she mouthed.

'Why are you mouthing the word party?' Torr looked utterly perplexed.

Moss went red. I went red. How to explain that we needed urgently to start planning my birthday party that might or might not be happening some time in *October*?

Archie shrugged. 'I'm guessing it's a party we're not invited to.' He sounded disappointingly cool about that.

'Or maybe it's an imaginary party,' said Torr brutally.

'Even an imaginary party is more exciting than talking about GCSEs,' said Archie.

'GCSEs aren't that bad,' said Torr. 'They're basically just a test of stamina.'

'You weren't saying they were easy two weeks ago,' said Moss.

'We probably won't be saying it the week before results either,' said Archie.

'CAN EVERYONE JUST STOP TALKING ABOUT EXAMS?' I said. 'Seriously, please stop.'

'Nobody is going to stop talking about exams for at least two years and probably not even then,' said Archie, pulling me in to him to lessen the blow. I yelped and jerked away and then had to explain that my injection really hurt. 'Sorry, sorry, sorry,' he said, trying again more carefully. 'Would you rather talk about holidays? What's everyone doing? Everyone, that is, who isn't filming the title role in an action movie.'

'Are you going to go and sit in Elektra's *trailer* all summer?' Moss asked Archie.

'No he isn't,' I answered for him.

'What? Do you not want me there? Waiting for you to come off-set, ready to make you tea and read lines with you and massage your shoulders ... ?'

It was awkward because Archie was joking but that was literally my dream.

CHAPTER 6

'It is probably a goal for me to remain entirely in a state of behaviour that in the real world would be totally inappropriate and infantilizing.'

Jesse Eisenberg

'I knew you were going to get the Straker role,' said Daisy tipping everything off the only chair in my bedroom and making herself at home.

'No you didn't,' I said. Daisy might have spent at least ten of her sixteen years acting, but she didn't have that sort of insider knowledge. 'Casting is a complete mystery, a dark art intelligible only to the Illuminati.'

'Maybe I am one of the Illuminati,' she said. It would have sounded more sinister if she hadn't been halfway through a custard cream. 'I knew you'd get Archie Mortimer too.'

'That's a lie,' I said.

'OK, I didn't think you'd achieve both these feats within a twenty-four hour period, but I did guess that they were very much on the cards.'

'I haven't "got" Archie anyway.' I had to keep reminding myself of that tiny, inconvenient fact.

'Yeah, but you've got *with* him and that is an excellent start.' She looked at me closely. 'You really want to go out with him, don't you?'

'Is it very obvious?'

Judging from Daisy's expression, it was. 'It'll happen. Archie's a really nice guy.' Daisy was the only one of my friends who knew Archie, because we all used to go to the same acting class. 'And you've been friends for a bit – he wasn't going to make a move if he wasn't into it.'

'We were sort of friends. I mean, I didn't talk to him that much.' Because it's really hard to talk to someone when you have a massive crush on them.

My phone barked. **TABLE READ on Saturday**

'Who is it?' asked Daisy.

'It's Carlo Winn, the guy playing Jan.'

'Ah, fit Carlo from the casting?'

'I don't think he's that . . .'

She gave me a 'don't even try' look. The Illuminati claim was becoming more believable.

'What's a table read?' I asked.

'It's when everyone sits around a table and reads the script,' explained Daisy.

Ah, quite literal then. My phone barked again.

Pumped for meeting Sam Gross

There was a zero per cent chance of me pulling this off. Maybe Carlo had hung out with famous people, but I'd never met one in the wild. What did you even say to them? I'd stalked enough of them on Insta to know that they were definitely not 'just like us'. I'd be too scared to look Sam Gross in the eye – also, he's shorter than me and I wasn't sure how I was going to pull off the metaphorical 'looking up to' with the physical 'looking down at'.

My extensive research on Sam Gross wasn't making me feel any more chill.

1. He's been in rehab seven and a half times (I'm counting the time he arrived, stayed for two hours, punched a male nurse and left as a half).
2. He turned down the lead role in two blockbuster action movies in favour of a Harley Davidson road trip to Mongolia.
3. He owns forty pairs of red leather loafers with concealed heels which were handmade in Italy.
4. He threw a tantrum on a talk show because they asked him for his views on male plastic

surgery (OK, it was a stupid question, but he possibly took it too far when he punched the interviewer).

5. He owns one hundred white shirts handmade in Italy.

6. He has been married to three beautiful women. He has also been divorced by three beautiful women.

7. He owns sixty identical black suits handmade in Italy.

8. He has his own brand of whisky, and a cocktail named after him (whisky, chilli and lemon – allegedly it's lethal).

9. He has a pet goat called Demon and if *The Enquirer* is to be believed (is *The Enquirer* ever to be believed?), it has play dates with George Clooney's pig.

10. He is handsome. Normal-people-can't-look-him-in-the-eye-and-tend-to-forgive-him-everything-including-the-anger-issues handsome. *That* handsome.

'Sam Gross will probably fall in love with you and there will be a SCANDAL,' said Daisy.

I looked at her. 'Sam Gross is *forty-three* years old. He will be *forty-four* in three weeks. That wouldn't be scandal, that would be CRIME.' Digby stirred, shifted creakily over to me and absent-mindedly licked my leg, as if to establish that he was my one and only elderly love interest.

'When you put it like that . . .' Daisy looked a bit shamefaced. 'He is so ridiculously hot though. I would totally go back to acting if I could star with Sam Gross.'

'Would you actually?' She'd given it up because she didn't want to do it any more, which was a good reason even if I didn't really understand it.

'Well, no, definitely not. But I do still fancy him.'

I *almost* raised an eyebrow. My intensive practice was beginning to pay off.

'You're judging me,' said Daisy.

'A little bit,' I said. 'Maybe it's OK when it's on the screen.' I wasn't at all sure it was OK even then, but given my crush on Prince Harry I was in no position to judge. Also Gross looked a lot taller on-screen.

'Can I come and visit you on set?'

'Only if you promise not to drool all over Sam Gross.'

'I can't make that promise. Can I visit anyway?'

'I will lock you in my dressing room, but yes.'

'You're getting your own dressing room? With a star on the door, right?'

'Obviously. I literally can no longer go into rooms without stars on the doors.'

'You're going to get tired of looking at the walls of that dressing room. It gets so, so boring.'

'I'll take lots of books and box sets,' I said.

'You won't be able to concentrate. And you won't be allowed outside in case you get a suntan or mess up continuity in some other random way and they won't let you go on Facebook and they definitely won't let you use Snapchat or send any pics because of confidentiality and you'll end up spending hours playing *Cut the Rope* and scrolling through BuzzFeed.' Daisy had had more acting jobs than anyone else I knew.

'Do you miss it?' I asked. 'The acting.'

'Not even a little bit. Real life is way less stressful.'

Seriously? At our age real life was pretty stressful.

'But that reminds me,' she went on, 'I've got some gossip on *Fortuneswell*.' *Fortuneswell* is a classy British rip-off of *Little Women* that we both auditioned for and neither of us got. 'They've cast Georgie Dunn as Mary.'

'Eeeeeugh, that is disgusting!' I said.

'She's actually quite a good actress,' said Daisy.

'Not that, Digby's just cough-sicked up half a custard cream and I've put my hand in it.' I flapped hopelessly for a bit.

'I'm not sure how you're going to cope with a post-apocalyptic world, Elektra James, or a diet of grubs and berries.' Daisy cleaned my hand with a wet wipe, like I was a toddler. She was the only person my age I knew who would have wet wipes conveniently to hand. 'And what about wild animals?' she asked, after we'd cleared up as best we could. 'You can't even manage your dog.'

'There won't be real wild animals on-set ... will there?' I asked, cuddling Digby to make us both feel better. If there were real wild animals, I was in trouble. If there was a snake, I was going to fire myself. It was my red line.

'Probably not,' she said, but she didn't sound sure. She pulled the conversation back to *Fortuneswell*. 'So, Georgie Dunn, brand new beloved of the sidebar of shame. What do you think?' Georgie Dunn had played a wild child in a TV thing and hadn't exactly snapped out of character when they'd wrapped.

'It's a ... brave choice.' Mary was the feistiest of the four daughters and the part I'd gone up for so I was invested. 'How did you find out?'

'My friend Lucy's been cast as the eldest sister so she's giving me all the gossip.'

'Ask her if it's true that Georgie got with Harry Styles.'

'I *really* doubt it. But I'll ask.'

'Isn't Georgie Dunn a bit old to play Mary? She must be at least eighteen.'

'She can play down. She's got that whole wide-eyed, freckly, innocent thing going on. She's a good actress,' said Daisy.

I nodded. 'As long as she gets to set in one piece, she'll be fine.'

My phone barked. Daisy checked the screen. 'It's Carlo *again*. Is he into you?'

'No. He really isn't.' I read his message. 'It's just a big news day.'

Female lead confirmed

'I thought you were the female lead?' said Daisy.

'Hahaha, no, they're just bigging up the Straker role to tap into the teen market.'

Daisy nodded like this made perfect sense.

Who is it?

You'll never guess

I don't need to guess because you are going to tell me. How did Carlo always find out everything before me?

No. GUESS

You're so annoying. I suddenly couldn't think of a single actress.

'Oh my God,' said Daisy. 'Is it Jennifer Lawrence?'

'Of course it isn't Jennifer Lawrence.' **Is it Jennifer Lawrence?**

Are you mad? No

Is it Emma Watson?

In my dreams

In my dreams too. **Just tell me**

It's Amber Leigh

TheBizz.com

11th July

Excitement was high when Sergei Havelski, award-winning director of some of our favourite movies here at The Bizz (*Terror Island*, *Straight Down* and, of course, *Forgotten*), was hired to kick the *Straker* project into life. But if early rumours are to be believed, this one might be *Straight Down*-hill to better *Forgotten* ...

We've heard from more than one reliable source that the decision to cast Amber Leigh in the role of Winona was taken at producer level and that Havelski is NOT HAPPY. Everyone on the planet knows that Sam Gross and his leading lady had a brief but turbulent relationship and it's going to be 'interesting' to see how the 'Samber' reunion plays out. But that's not all, because Havelski is himself rumoured to have had an under-the-radar 'dalliance' with Amber ... She isn't exactly renowned for her resilience and sense of perspective (watch her epic rant at an LA barista *here*). We sense there could be trouble ahead ...

Pass the popcorn.

CHAPTER 7

'I know you know who I am, but let's cut through this fame crap.'

Daniel Radcliffe

'It's weird being back in this room,' said Carlo, coming to sit next to me at the big conference table. This wasn't by choice, every place had a name card. Mine read 'STRAKER' and, underneath that, in smaller letters, 'Elektra James'. On one side of me was 'JAN' ('Carlo Winn') and next to him was 'WINONA' ('Amber Leigh'). Her chair was empty. This was surreal.

'It looks completely different,' Carlo said. 'But it's still got the same vibe.'

'Which is fear,' I said. The last time we'd been here had been for the final *Straker* callback. Carlo didn't contradict me about the fear thing. I strongly suspected that I wasn't the only one who'd googled,

'Can actors get fired after a table read?' last night. (They can.)

More people were filing in and taking their seats. I recognized Rhona and Selim and Production Suit from the Claridge's meeting. Mr Havelski (I still couldn't bring myself to call him Sergei) was wandering around, clapping the guys on the back and double-cheek-kissing the women. It had a sort of first-day-of-term feel to it. But with more place cards. Oh, and Hollywood stars – more of them, too.

Rhona kept bringing people over to meet us and I kept bobbing up and down and smiling nervously and agreeing that, yes, it was all very exciting and immediately forgetting the name and role of whoever I was introduced to.

There was a bottle of water and a neat stack of printed pages in front of every place.

<u>STRAKER</u>
Written by
Mitch Ivor
Hal Denton
Amy Prudhorn

That was two more writers than the last time I'd seen the title page. Then came an address and then, in little letters: 'Straker is a working title.' I turned to page one.

Sc. 1. EXTERIOR. FOREST: EVENING

Dark, dank, threatening. It could be any time, past or future.

Closer ...

Shapes, dark shapes, start to detach from the trees. They are human and yet there is something animal about them, something feral.

Closer ...

A woman and a girl hold hands. It is a connection of fear as well as love. The girl is about fifteen, but her face is the face of someone who has seen many dark things. The woman speaks to comfort the girl ...

WINONA

This is the safe place. We don't need to go any further. Here we stop. All of us. Here we rebuild.

STRAKER

I don't feel safe here. I don't think I'll ever feel safe anywhere. Not ever again ...

Except ... it wasn't the same as the first line I'd practised. Oh, God, I felt a bit sick. I skipped a couple of pages.

STRAKER

I can't remember how to sleep ...

That was the same. I scrolled down a couple of lines.

STRAKER

You want me to rest beside the dead people.

That was different (also, very intense). I picked up the pen that had been helpfully provided. A bit of underlining always helped. But then I got distracted because the pen was decorated with little coloured pandas – *Because Panda Productions are not just black and white.*

There was some commotion by the door and Sam Gross came in.

Let me say that again.

Sam Gross, Hollywood star/heart-throb/nurse-puncher, came into a room that I was in. I stood up, like when the headmistress came into the classroom, and then (because I was scared of being noticed) I sat down again.

'Sergei!' Sam roared, with a strange attempt at Havelski's accent. 'It's good to see you. It's been a while ... Cannes, right? What a night!' There was lots of man-hugging. 'I brought you a present, mate.'

Sam slammed a bottle of his own-brand whisky on the table. 'We can share, right?' He looked around the table. 'Except maybe for the kids. Who's going to introduce me to the kids?'

Carlo bristled at being called a kid. I didn't care. Sam Gross had just referred to me directly – I would take patronising. We were now very much the centre of attention (which is odd when you're in a room with Sam Gross). Rhona brought him over to us and I stood up again.

'She's tall, this one,' he said, like I couldn't hear. 'Good to meet you, sweetheart.' He kissed me on the cheek. He smelled very expensive and also a tiny bit of whisky. 'Ha, she's blushing, cute.' I blushed more. He turned to Carlo and there was a dodgy moment when I thought he might say, 'He's black, this one,' but then he just went for the man hug. Carlo blushed too, but some sort of bro code must have stopped Sam from pointing it out.

'Where's Amber?' Sam asked.

'Running late,' said Rhona nervously.

'Typical,' said Sam. (Well, actually, he swore and then said, 'Typical'.)

'For the first and last time on my production,' said Mr Havelski darkly. 'OK, everyone,' he said, raising his voice just a fraction. We all fell silent immediately. 'As you've just heard, Ms Leigh is running late, but we're going to get started. Time is money and I'm not waiting for anyone. Also we've got a lot to get through; the script appears to be even longer than the last time I saw it.' He didn't sound delighted by that. The two young guys and the middle-aged woman sitting together at the end of the table looked tense. 'I'll read Amber's lines as well as the stage directions. Elektra and Carlo, have you ever done one of these?'

I muttered, 'No.' This was definitely my first, and quite possibly my last, table read.

'I have,' said Carlo, but he didn't sound as cocky as usual.

'So, for Elektra's benefit, a couple of pointers before we go. It's not a big dramatic performance, but try to bring us a little something of your Straker. Everyone bring something, but not so much that you scare us.' He laughed. Rhona and Selim laughed. The writers laughed. The producers laughed. None of the actors laughed. 'Let's get started.'

He read out the directions in his normal voice (well, in the voice that was normal for him), but when he got to the opening line, Winona's line, he definitely went up an octave.

WINONA
This is the safe place. We don't need to
go any further.

It wasn't a funny line, it's just that when I'm nervous I sometimes get this really inappropriate urge to laugh, like a laugh-vomit. I bit down hard on my lip. I could sense Carlo sitting tensely beside me and I was pretty sure that he was having the same problem. I wasn't going to risk looking at him. I focused on Mr Havelski instead. That was a mistake. He was channelling his inner Winona.

WINONA
Here we stop. All of us. Here we rebuild.

I suppressed a snort (which is always an uncomfortable thing to do). Focus. My line was next and I didn't want to laugh any more. None of the actors I'd googled last night had been fired after just one line at a table read. Setting a new record wasn't the professional impression I was aiming for.

STRAKER
I don't feel safe here. I don't think
I'll ever feel safe anywhere. Not ever
again . . .

I was pretty sure that I was pulling off the insecure part of the characterisation anyway.

Mr Havelski/Winona was frowning in con-centration.

WINONA

We're together, Straker, and that is what
matters. We are each other's place of
safety.

Mr Havelski looked at me as a mother looks at her frightened child (obviously) and then read, in his normal voice, 'Straker runs into her mother's arms and the two of them stand united against the dark times ahead.' Octave change.

WINONA

We are the lucky ones, Straker, because we
have each other. So many have lost loved
ones—

He broke off and turned to the writers. 'Strike that line. It's just bad.'

There was a noise at the door, and all of a sudden Amber Leigh was in the room and one hundred per cent the centre of attention.

If Sam Gross had glowed, Amber Leigh was in a different category. I don't know what it was – make-up? Green juice? Money? It wasn't that she looked different to what I'd expected, it was that she looked *exactly* like she did on magazine covers. She was a genuine air-brushed human being.

'Sergei!' She rushed at Mr Havelski and

hugged him like they were in the final scene of a particularly frothy romcom. I can only assume he enjoyed it; his face was unreadable. She gave a sort of twirl and then scanned all the faces turned to her. 'Sam.' She nodded at him.

'Amber.' Sam didn't get up and she didn't move towards him.

There was what felt like a very long pause before Havelski said, 'Meet your daughter,' and pointed me out.

Amber Leigh looked at me and looked again, and then looked around the room as if there might be another fifteen-year-old hanging around somewhere. 'Oh!' she said. There was no way to interpret it other than as surprise.

'Hello,' I said awkwardly.

'Hair and make-up, darling,' Amber muttered to the table at large. 'Hair and make-up.' She seemed to find that quite comforting. 'I'll wait to say hello to everyone properly until teatime,' she announced, and turned to Rhona who she'd obviously identified as the person (i.e. woman) in charge of such important detail. 'There will be *green* tea, darling, won't there?' Rhona nodded and Amber sat down at the one empty seat at the table, between Carlo – who looked smug – and a silent man in a denim suit. Amber picked up her name card and laid it face down in front of her. Then she moved the bottle of water and the pages of script aside and placed her very large handbag on the table. 'You stay there, darling, where Mummy can see you,' she said. It looked like she was literally talking to the handbag, but then if I'd owned that handbag I'd probably have married it. She turned to Rhona, 'Sweetie, would it be too much trouble to have some mineral water in a little bowl?' Odd.

'It's not still alive, is it?' asked Sam in a tone of disgust.

'Sorry?'

'The,' he swore, '... dog.'

'No.' Amber sniffed. 'Coco has passed.' She gave us all a moment to grieve and, as a dog person, I did my very best. 'But Mummy has a new little baby, doesn't she?' she cooed at the bag which was now rocking gently from side to side.

'I love dogs,' said (simpered) Carlo, who I suspected would have said he loved cobras if a cobra had been residing in Amber Leigh's handbag.

Amber looked at Carlo appraisingly. She obviously liked what she saw, because she drew the bag closer and pulled down the side. A very small, very determined, possibly deranged ball of fluff and attitude exploded on to the table. It lifted its leg against a snowy white stack of pages and peed, looking around at everybody as if daring them to ask him to stop. We were literally playing mind games with a miniature Pomeranian. And it was winning. Carlo put out his hand and the pom-pom snarled.

'Come on, Kale, come back to Mummy,' said Amber, ignoring the whole weeing incident.

'Kill?' said Sam. 'You named him Kill?' He laughed and the dog growled. 'OK, fair play,' said Sam, inching his chair away from the puddle of wee.

'Right, everyone,' said Mr Havelski, accepting the inevitable, 'we're going to take a break, ten minutes tops, and then we'll get stuck back into it.'

'Rhona,' I whispered, because she was the least frightening person in the room, 'where are the loos again?'

'Where are what?' she asked loudly.

'The loos,' I mouthed. I'm not quite sure why I was embarrassed but I was.

'Oh, the loos,' she repeated in an even louder voice. Everybody turned round. 'Down the corridor, turn left and on your right. You'll need the code for the hall door. It's four-seven-five-six.'

'Four-five-seven-six?'

'No, four-seven-five-six,' she repeated. 'Look, if you forget it, just bang. Someone will eventually hear you.'

All the people who'd stopped their own conversations to listen to this one made murmuring noises which I think were meant to be reassuring.

It was cooler in the hall and it was nice to be on my own. I dawdled down the corridor checking out all the posters on the walls. One featured a scantily clad Sam Gross in *The Lock Down*, something that wasn't going to make me more cool, calm and collected around him when I went back in the room. Turns out the imagine-famous-people-naked-to-make-yourself-less-nervous thing is a myth.

I got out my phone the minute I sat down on the loo; it's perfectly natural multi-tasking whatever my mum may say. I had lots of messages from Moss saying not very much other than she was bored and wanted stalker pics of Sam. I had two messages from Archie, one wishing me luck for the table read and the other saying that he wanted stalker pics of Amber. And one message from Eulalie asking me whether Sam Gross was as hot in the flesh as on the screen (highly inappropriate, but I put her mind at rest anyway).

Four-five-seven-six. Back out in the corridor I tapped out the door code and twisted the latch. I did it again. And again. Five-four-seven-six. Five-four-six-seven. There was plainly something wrong with this door.

Just bang. That's what Rhona had said, so I banged.

Quite quietly, obviously, because I didn't really want to draw attention to myself.

Then a bit more loudly, because, after all, I probably did want to draw attention to myself.

Then very loudly, so that my fists hurt. It was probably a bit like being an extra in *The Lock Down*.

And then I just sat down for a bit. At least I had topless Sam for company.

I am stuck in the loo, I texted Moss. **Well, not in the loo, in the corridor**

How did you get stuck in a corridor?

Forgot a door code

Ah ☹ 😩 Phone your mum

She's at home. Also she doesn't know the code. Met my film mum, though

What's she like?

Very shiny. Possibly made in a lab in Beverly Hills. Scary handbag dog named after a vegetable. Don't think they will persuade viewers of genetic link. And then, **I'm freaking out. I need to get back in there before they recast me**

Shout? Someone will come eventually. Do you have provisions? Emergency chocolate?

The door is really thick and there is no one on this side of it. It's like being in space, no one can hear me scream. I am slightly panicking. And, no, I don't have any chocolate. It's not like I was planning a long excursion . . .

Is Carlo there?

Not in the corridor, no. In the room where I should be, yes

Text him

He'll laugh at me

Possibly, but what choice do you have?

True. I texted: **Hey Carlo, can you ask Rhona for the code to the corridor door, please?**

Long pause. **Hahahahahahaha** and then, **We all thought you'd fallen down the loo or were being sick or something**

Their concern was touching. Glad I'd helped with the whole team-bonding thing. Within seconds, Rhona was opening the door and apologizing and being nice and I was scanning the room to check there wasn't a new Straker at the table.

I could have done without the round of applause. But I was pretty sure they all knew what my name was now.

Amber Leigh
(in her own words)

1.

On why she thinks all actors should be in therapy:

'To really "be" another person you have to know yourself.'

2.

On being asked if she struggled with her weight:

'I'm naturally very skinny. If anything I'd like to be a bit bigger, but I just find it really difficult to put on weight. My absolutely favourite thing is french fries!'

3.

On being asked about her contributions to charity:

'All good actresses give of themselves. Of course I give off-screen too. I just don't talk about it as much as some other people.'

4.

On the perils of being a child star:

'Sure, it was tough. Sure, there were dark days. It made me grow up fast, but it made me the creative person I am today. I'm just so grateful.'

5.

On being asked about starting a family:

'Of course I want to adopt a baby. Who wouldn't? Kids are cute. But right now I'm focusing on my doggy baby!'

6.
On wearing couture at the Oscars:
'I feel so blessed and lucky but to be honest I'm happier in yoga pants. I'm very down to earth .'

7.
On Sam Gross:
'Our values were just very different. I respect this beautiful planet,
I respect animals, I respect the nursing profession.'

8.
On Sam Gross:
'Look, I've made mistakes too, but at least I've made them sober.'

9.
On Sam Gross:
'I don't want to judge the guy, but seriously he has more pairs of shoes than I do!'

10.
On Sam Gross:
'I wouldn't go so far as to call it a relationship.'

From: Charlotte at the Haden Agency
Date: 13 July 12:01
To: Elektra James; Julia James
Cc: Stella at the Haden Agency
Subject: *Straker* (working title): Costumes!!
Attachments: Maud Granger, Costume Designer contact details. doc

Dear Both,

Sorry about this, because I know Elektra was all psyched up for her first day on the *Straker* set on 20 July, but the start date has now been shifted to **Monday 27 July**. There's some complex set-building going on so the *very slight* delay is understandable.

The people from Panda have been in touch to arrange an appointment for Elektra to go in for a costume meeting (details attached). There will be a costume department on set but one of the lead designers would like to meet with Elektra *as soon as possible* for a preliminary fitting. Now that it's the summer holidays, we've arranged this for **Thursday 16 July at 2 p.m.** We can't wait to hear what they've got planned! So much fun, I'm jealous ... Send pics, Elektra!

Charlie x

★
CHAPTER 8

'I ain't Thor without the costume and the hammer.'
Chris Hemsworth

'Sorry to keep you waiting.' The woman coming towards us was very tall with wild, curly hair and she was wearing one of those dresses that looks like it's only held together by a safety pin. She was struggling with three mugs of tea and a large scrapbook. I reached for the tea; Moss reached for the scrapbook. 'I'm Maud. You're Elektra?' I nodded. 'And—' she turned to Moss – 'you must be the fashiony friend? Great skirt.'

'She made it herself,' I said, because I could tell from her face that Moss had temporarily lost the power of speech.

'It's awesome. Want a job?'

'I'd leave school and start tomorrow,' said Moss,

who probably would (but over her mother's dead body). Then they started complimenting each other on every detail of what they were wearing. It turned out Maud's dress *was* only held together by a safety pin.

'Follow me and we'll get going.' Maud took us through to a huge room stuffed with rails of clothes – one bearing white Victorian lace blouses and another, twenties flapper dresses winking with tiny jewels and glittery thread. There were stands bursting with hats like dysfunctional fruit trees and three headless dummies sporting corsets and crinolines. There were boxes of shoes and old-fashioned boots with little buttons up the side and a crate of ruffs. One small table was covered only in coils of (presumably fake) pearls. This wasn't fashion; this was dressing up. Maud led us into a smaller room. One whole wall was mirrored and there were mirrored screens too.

'Measuring bit first. Are you OK with stripping down to your undies, Elektra? It's just that tape-measuring doesn't quite do it. I need to get a real feel for your body.'

Great. If I'd known that this morning, I'd have selected something more fetching than the originally-white, now grey sports bra I was wearing. (There was no point keeping it for sport because I didn't do sport.)

Maud read my face. 'Nobody likes this bit. You wouldn't believe the number of gorgeous actors I've had standing in this room apologizing for their thighs or their odd-shaped boobs or their mismatched undies.'

I was torn between wanting to know which actors she was talking about, and really wanting to stop talking about 'undies'.

'I'm not wearing a bra,' said Moss in a brave but probably untrue intervention. I loved Moss.

'I never do, so freeing,' said Maud. 'Use the screen if you want, Elektra.'

I had on the wrong clothes for easy disrobing. I should have worn a dress held together with a safety pin. Instead I nearly knocked over the screen trying to take off my jeans and, once I was out of them, I had a red line up each leg from the seams. But despite all that, when Maud set to measuring me, she was so matter-of-fact that even I couldn't manage to make it awkward.

'I'm excited for my costumes,' I said, when I was back in my clothes. This was an understatement, but I thought even Maud would have judged us if I'd told her how often Moss and I had talked about this.

'I can show you some sketches now, if you want?'

Er, yes, we did want. Obviously.

Maud opened up the huge scrapbook onto the coffee table and we crowded round it. She turned each page slowly. Drawings, little pinned bits of material, photos of costumes from other films. I was making little gasps of excitement. Moss was making *really loud* gasps of excitement. This was heaven.

'Oh, *this one.*' I pointed at a short, silky sliver of a dress, all silvery, the pinned piece of fabric changing in the light like fish scales. I would look good in that dress. (Obviously I didn't say that out loud.) 'Can I take a photo?'

'Sorry, no photos,' said Maud. 'Production like to control the release of any images.'

Production wouldn't have much to fear from my one hundred and thirty-seven Instagram followers but I put my phone away.

Maud turned over another page: more silver slips of deliciousness.

'They're gorgeous ... they glow,' Moss said, and I just nodded in mute admiration. This was so much better than I'd expected.

'These are the Warri Tribe costumes. I'm glad you like them.'

I did, but Straker wasn't in the Warri Tribe. I was even more excited to see my own costume now. 'We're coming to the Terra Tribe.' Maud sounded excited too. She turned more pages. 'There's a Winona robe ... and these are Straker's.'

I looked, and I looked again. 'They're all very ... *brown,*' I said.

'Yes, we're working with the classic dystopian colour palette for the Terra Tribe,' said Maud proudly.

Moss nodded as if she understood.

'There's a good range of tones.' Maud ran her finger over the tiny swatches. 'Look, not too much taupe, more russet and sienna and lots of chocolate and mocha shades, even a hint of caramel.'

If she worked in Starbucks, everything she was saying would be a good thing. But in brown clothes with my brown hair and probably some brown mud I was basically going to look like a twig – no, I remembered the measurements – a log. I was going to be a log fighting for survival in a ruined world.

'You've gone quiet, Elektra,' said Maud. Moss was still *ooh*-ing over every sketch. I think she was a bit in love with Maud.

'No, I LOVE them! They're AMAZING!' I lied.

'No, you don't,' said Maud mildly.

I'm a hopeless liar. I need to work on that, it's a huge life skill to be lacking (especially for an actor).

'But it's fine,' went on Maud, 'sometimes it just takes a bit of time to come round to costumes. You're going to look gorgeous and, even more important, you're going to look like Straker.'

Ah, yes, that was the important bit. I'd forgotten. My narcissism had got the better of my professionalism.

'And the blood helps,' said Maud.

'Sorry?'

'Blood. It will be super-flattering for your colouring. There's the *fresh* blood, which is really vibrant, and on the version of the script I've seen, you're covered in *dried* blood from about scene seven right through to the end, and that's more of a wine/mahogany/currant-y kind of shade.'

Moss was looking at Maud with pure adoration.

'Those are the shades we're picking up. So the cloak lining is a deep dark red and we've asked for the detailing in the sword hilt to be picked out with garnets – not real garnets, but still.'

'But it's some time in the future and there's just been a world-threatening eco-catastrophe.' I was still a bit hazy on the details. 'Would they really have been decorating sword hilts?'

'You haven't watched a lot of dystopian films, have you, Elektra?'

'Not *very* many.' None. Well, none all the way to the end. I had a tiny problem because I couldn't watch violence. Not even not-very-violent violence. It was the blood. The sort of blood that Maud was going to douse me in for the whole of filming.

'You need costumes you can move easily in.' Maud was really trying to sell it to me. 'You need to be able to run, jump, climb and fight. Outfits you can save the world in.'

Moss laughed. I laughed too, but nervously. It was going to take more than brown costumes to make me an action hero.

'That's totally what I'm going to do when I leave school,' said Moss, as we walked back out into the sunshine. (It was like leaving the cinema in the afternoon; it took a bit of adjusting to.)

'Save the world?'

'No. Design costumes.'

'Sure. After you've done that degree in international law your mum has picked out for you.'

'I seriously am. I had a lightbulb moment in there. Finally! I've always wanted to have a lightbulb moment. I'll go to art college and get a degree in costume design then I'll go back in there and work with Maud.'

'Making brown tunics?' The silver costumes were still glistening and blinking at the back of my mind, just out of reach. I had costume envy before I even had any actual costumes. They should reverse the tribes. Carlo didn't need silver slips of deliciousness. Carlo could pull off brown sludge with blood accents.

'They were amazing. All those rips and frayed edges and *cuff detail*.'

Cuff detail?

'The *topstitching* . . .'

Topstitching?

'The *primitive pleating* technique ...'

Sometimes our friendship baffled me.

'I am finally one of these sorted women with a life plan.' Moss paused and then added fiercely, 'I'll be happy every single day. I'm going to forget guys and become a strong and independent creative woman.'

'Has Torr still not texted you back?' I asked, reading between the feminist lines.

'No. He has not.'

'How long now?'

'Two and a half days.'

This had to be seen in perspective – a drop from an average two and a half minutes' reply time. 'When did you see him last?'

'I went over to his house on Sunday.'

'And?'

'He was ... nice.'

'That's good, isn't it?'

'He was nice in a really polite way. Like I was the daughter of a friend of his mum's or something. In the end I just made up a really lame excuse and went home because it was too awkward.'

'What did you say?'

'I said I had to wash my hair.'

'Oh, Mossy!'

'I *know*.'

'Did he laugh?'

'No, he just behaved like that was a perfectly legitimate reason to blow him off. I swear he was *grateful*.'

'Come home with me. Mum's out and Eulalie should be there. She can advise you on your love life and you can tell her about your life plan and I can tell her about that silver dress that I'm NOT going to be wearing on-screen.'

If Eulalie couldn't help Moss, I was out of suggestions.

★ CHAPTER 9

'If I felt I was being employed just for my looks, I'd stop acting.'

Kit Harrington

It seemed weird (in a good way, but still *weird*) that Archie was sprawled over my sofa. Dad was away at a conference on Retaining Walls – *thrilling* – and Mum had gone to bed early, after lots of deeply embarrassing and pointed *and unnecessary* comments about 'trusting' us. Only marginally less embarrassing than the thirty minutes when she'd hung around and asked Archie a) what his parents did (baker dad and accountant mum), b) whether he had any siblings (just a tribe of mini half-siblings who lived in Canada with his dad) and c) what subjects he was taking for A levels (French, Spanish and English).

It was like some strange parental version of speed dating.

We'd been going to watch a film. That was totally the plan. We'd managed ten minutes of the sort of deep indie flick that Torr would have very much enjoyed (chosen because we wanted to impress each other) and then ten minutes of a film so deeply shallow (chosen because we wanted to show that we were too cool to care about impressing each other) that even we couldn't cope and now we'd given up the pretence.

'The callback for *The Corpse of Peter Plogojowitz* is tomorrow and I'm not ready,' said Archie.

'Is that your vampire thing?'

He nodded.

'Catchy title. Are you meant to be off-book?'

'They haven't said so, but everyone will be. Not knowing the lines is not really how I want to stand out. I've had six auditions and two callbacks this year and I haven't got one part.'

'Is it getting to you?'

'Not really, it's just beginning to seem a bit pointless. When you google yourself and "Is Archie Mortimer dead?" comes up, it's probably time to get a part or move on.'

I ignored the fact that he'd googled himself because it wasn't like I hadn't done the same thing. 'What was the answer?'

'About one thousand, three hundred people voted I was dead.'

'And the count for alive?'

'Twenty-three.'

Oh. 'It's impressive that so many people voted.'

'That is the best that can be said, yes.'

'Do you want me to read your lines with you? Have you got them with you?'

'They're on my phone. You don't mind? Really?'

'Sure.' At this stage I'd do pretty much anything for Archie, but I wasn't going to say that. He was a nice guy, but he was still a guy, so chances were his ego was already pretty healthy.

SC.4: EXTERIOR. COUNTRY INN: DARK, COLD NIGHT.
The only light comes from a single candle held aloft by a beautiful young maiden (Ana). She is waiting — waiting for Tibor Snoloky. As he rides up she steps forward to greet him.

ANA
Tibor, you're safe! We've been worried.
(beat) I've been worried.

TIBOR
I saw nothing. There's nothing there.

There's nothing to fear. The castle is
empty. Everyone has left.

ANA
Then you are the only one who is not
afraid.

TIBOR
Afraid of shadows and cobwebs? Afraid of
rumours and women's whispers? Afraid of
bats? No, Ana, I'm not afraid.
(A wolf howls.)

'I think you should be the wolf too,' said Archie.

I wasn't yet confident enough in our relationship
(whatever our 'relationship' was) to risk humiliating
myself by making wolf noises.

'Digby can be the wolf,' I suggested. Digby heard
his name and raised his head from Archie's leg. He
didn't look like he could be bothered to be a wolf.
He hadn't bothered to do anything for days. Just
sleep and look sorry for himself. Now he rearranged
himself more comfortably. He'd basically fallen in
love with Archie. He had no dignity. 'OK, not Digby.
You'll have to be the wolf.'

'I can't be the wolf. I'm the wolf *hunter*.'

'I thought you were a bear hunter? Tibor Snoloky,
teenage bear hunter extraordinaire.'

'I think I'm a bear hunter turned wolf hunter ...
turned vampire hunter. It's not one hundred per
cent clear.'

'Who's going up for Ana? Anyone we know?'

'Doubt it. And I don't think we'll be reading with
the possible Anas, not at first callback.'

Good. The description of Ana on the casting
brief I'd read upside down on Charlotte's desk was
simply '*Caucasian maiden of staggering beauty*'. Even
if I hadn't been blocked out for *Straker* I don't think
I'd have been put up for that one. Or even for one of
the sidekick maidens who were merely described as
'*outstandingly beautiful*'.

'And I doubt I'll get past this stage,' continued
Archie.

'You will. I know it.' He just looked at me like
I was a bit of an idiot, which was fair. 'Sorry,' I
clarified, 'what I meant was you *should* get past the
first audition. You *should* get past all the auditions.
You'd make an awesome Tibor.'

'Except for the fact that I can't sword-fight or
ride.' He looked very worried and pretended to be
fussing over Digby who was sneezing.

'Did you by any chance tell them you *could* sword-
fight and ride?' I asked.

'It's just possible that I may have implied a degree
more confidence in those skills than I possess.'

'How hard can it be?' Occasionally I can be

optimistic. (Also, I'd lied on my Spotlight form too.)

'That's what I thought. I'm just a little bit less sure now than when I ticked the form … and I've got a feeling I'd be even less sure if I was about to sign a health and safety waiver.'

'Maybe have a couple of lessons? To be on the safe side. At least on the riding.' Horses scared me. They are bigger in real life than you think they're going to be.

'Yeah. Once round Hyde Park and I should be ready for the "galloping through Hoia-Baciu forest" scene.'

'Hoia-Baciu sounds like it should be in Hawaii, not Transylvania.'

'I looked it up,' he said. 'It's the world's most haunted forest.'

'Seriously?'

'If you believe everything Wikipedia says, then yes.' I did believe everything Wikipedia said. It had got me through many an essay crisis. Digby sensed that Archie needed a bit of reassurance and licked him enthusiastically. 'My friend's got a house full of Dalmatians.' Archie didn't seem to mind about the slobber. 'His mum breeds them and there are always, like, thirty puppies to try not to step on. She keeps trying to give me one, like other mums give you cake to take away.'

'You should take her up on the offer.'

'I can't. My mum's allergic.' He didn't look happy about that.

'I'd love to live in a house with thirty Dalmatian puppies.'

'To be honest, it smells a bit,' he said. 'They are cute, though.'

'It sounds like 101 *Dalmatians*,' I said, forgetting I was trying to be cool.

'Love that film,' he said with a grin.

It took us a bit of time to get back to the lines.

(Without losing eye contact, Ana unclasps the small crucifix that hangs around her neck and reaches up to fix it around his.)

ANA
This was my grandmother's. If you're going to go after them, you must promise to wear it . . .

TIBOR
(pressing the precious talisman back into her hands) Something so precious belongs around your neck, Ana, not mine.

We both went a bit 'method' on that bit.

'Elektra,' my mother yelled from upstairs. 'Is Archie *still* here?'

Her timing was scarily on point.

'He's just going,' I yelled back. I hoped that wasn't true. I also hoped she'd go to sleep soon.

'It's late.' Why did her voice suddenly sound closer?

She wouldn't, would she?

Archie and I looked at each other.

Yes, she would.

We sprang to opposite ends of the sofa.

My mother *would* come downstairs in her dressing gown (which *clung*) and hover by the door.

'Um, sorry if we woke you, Mrs James.' Archie was an unnaturally polite teenage boy. 'We'd kind of lost track of time.' I don't think even I would have said something so unsubtle.

'Does your mother know you're still here?' Mum replied. She didn't sound cross exactly, but there was a tinge of something a tiny bit threatening in her voice.

'Yes, she's cool as long as I keep my phone on.' And she probably was. Archie's mother sounded insanely chilled. 'But I should … probably go now.'

'How are you getting home?' asked Mum.

Any minute now she was going to tell him it was dark outside.

'It's dark outside.'

I was losing the will to live.

'I'll get the bus.' Archie was literally backing out

of the room (shadowed by Digby) and I didn't blame either of them.

'At this time of night!' You'd have thought he'd suggested walking naked through the snow. 'I'll drive you.'

'No, no, really, please don't go to the trouble.' He looked terrified.

'Just let me find my keys. I'm awake now anyway.'

Archie looked at me in desperation. It was too late for him. There was absolutely nothing I could do to protect him from a twenty-minute car ride with my dressing-gown-clad mother.

If I ever heard from him again, he was seriously into me.

I heard from him again even before my mum got home.

I had a good time tonight x

Me too x

I'd have stayed longer if your mum hadn't come in

Sorry about that

It was sweet getting a lift home

Did she talk all the way?

Yep

?????!

Well, there was the time when you were four and took off all your clothes on the teacup ride

That never happened. That did happen.

And the time when you were five and took off all your clothes on the school trip to the British Museum. That was a good one

I will kill her. Also that never happened. Obviously. That did happen. Obviously.

And she told me that your middle name was Ophelia and then she asked me in a mildly awkward way if I liked you . . .

After I've killed her, I will kill myself

And then there was a pause. A long pause. A pause so long it implied serious texting doubt.

Soz my mum just came in

Or maybe it just implied that his mum had come in. This was stressful.

I watched the typing dots appear and disappear. Was he deleting? I couldn't deal with this level of suspense.

You want to hang out again soon?

Where and when? I had literally turned into my mum. **Sure. Whenever**

I'll text you tomorrow x

And the weird thing was that I was one hundred per cent sure that he would.

From: Charlotte at the Haden Agency
Date: 23 July 10:56
To: Julia James; Elektra James
Cc: Stella at the Haden Agency; Rhona Muir at Panda
Productions
Subject: *Straker* (working title) – Naomi Pritt joins the team!
Attachments: Chaperone contact details.doc; CV.doc

Dear Both,

First of all we've just had notice that the start date has been put
back again, but only by a week – to **Monday 3 August**. I hope
Elektra is relaxing and enjoying some chilled holiday time. *But no
suntan, please!* Also no haircuts. No *anything* that might impact
on how Elektra looks on-screen.

I'm so sorry, Julia, that the chaperone background checks are
still ongoing. They are VERY thorough, aren't they?! Of course
we know that you're not the Julia James accused of animal
cruelty in 2003! The good news is that Naomi Pritt (who is
engaged as Elektra's tutor *just in case* filming runs into term
time) is also a qualified on-set chaperone. Naomi will be able
to act *in loco parentis* until all the approvals are through. As
the regulations put it – she'll be *'exercising the same care as
a good parent might reasonably be expected to give'*. In other
words she'll be a safe and reliable stand-in for you, Julia. It's a
perfect solution!

Kind regards,

Charlotte

P.S. Of course you'd be very *welcome* on set too, Julia, but frankly with Naomi doing the chaperoning, there wouldn't be anything for you to do. It's totally up to you, but we'd advise against.

P.P.S. We know you'll be thrilled that Naomi's special subject is French (you'll get a bit of sneaky holiday tuition in as a bonus, Elektra!!).

From: Charlotte at the Haden Agency
Date: 23 July 10:58
To: Julia James
Cc: Stella at the Haden Agency; Elektra James
Subject: *Straker* (working title) – Scheduling [2]

Dear Julia,

I've just read your message. <u>Please do not worry</u>! *The production company do not anticipate running into term time with Elektra.* As I said, Naomi's engagement was on a 'just in case' basis. And in the circumstances it's lucky for us that they put the arrangements in place. She will make an excellent chaperone!

Kind regards,

Charlotte

From: Stella at The Haden Agency
Date: 23 July 11:25
To: Julia James; Elektra James
Cc: Charlotte at The Haden Agency
Subject: *Straker* (working title) – Scheduling *again* [3]

Dear Julia and Elektra,

Please ignore Charlotte's last email!

Elektra's first day now looks set to be **Monday 10 August**. The decision to film some of the forest scenes in the Fairmount studio instead of on location has meant adjustments to the built set. They're going to prioritize all the Straker and Jan scenes in the schedule but unfortunately, realistically **Elektra's scenes won't be finished before the end of the holidays**. I know that you won't be happy about this, Julia, but the overrun should be manageable. Elektra can still be at school every day she isn't needed on set! ☺

Panda are keen to *make the very best use* of the *minor delays* and want to step up Elektra's training sessions with her trainer. Don't panic, Elektra. We're sure that lots of actors find these sorts of physical skills TRICKY! We believe in you!!

Stella x

P.S. I hope Digby's feeling better!

CHAPTER 10

'*When I fall, I fall pretty hard. The first love feeling is the best in the world.*'

Lily James

'*Exercise the care which a good parent might reasonably be expected to give.* I'm sorry but I'm still not comfortable with the idea that we outsource that. Elektra has a perfectly good parent already.' My mother was ironing.

'I'd like to think she has *two* good parents,' said Dad mildly.

'And only one of them is being investigated by the chaperone checkers for large-scale financial fraud *and* animal cruelty,' I added helpfully.

'Where are you meant to have committed animal cruelty?' asked Dad. 'Was it part of your Oregon crime spree?'

'No,' said Mum shortly. 'It was in Dakota.'

'Allegedly,' I added. Dad laughed, Mum didn't. Another aggressively pressed school shirt was added to the pile.

'Charlotte says you'd hate doing it anyway,' I said. 'Apparently it's super boring. Remember how much you hated hanging around with me when I was doing that student film project? And that was just one day.'

'It was one day in a freezing warehouse with no proper toilets. This will be different.' *Slam, press, fold.*

'Well, they said you could come too,' I pointed out.

'They *plainly* don't think that's a good idea and if I'm going to have to sit in your dressing room all day it's probably not worth it. Anyway, someone's got to stay at home to look after Digby and make sure he takes all his pills.' Digby was on so many doggy vitamins that he was rattling. 'It will be this Naomi woman who'll be with you at every second whether I'm there or not.'

I wasn't entirely comfortable with the 'with me at every second' thing either. I'd googled chaperones and theoretically Naomi was even meant to accompany me to the toilet (well, to the door). Basically I was getting a nanny.

'And what if she's still in charge when you go and film in Hungary?'

Well, presumably I wouldn't have to suffer the sightseeing and river cruise planned by my mum, but I didn't say that because she was plainly suffering some serious maternal redundancy stress. 'Carlo says that his agent says that location filming is "uncertain" now, whatever that means.'

'Nobody gives us any clear information,' said Mum, and I nodded sadly. She moved on to ironing my underwear – she only did that when she was really angry. I felt sorry for my knickers, they were now 2D. 'And nothing ever happens when it's meant to.'

'I'm sure Naomi is highly competent if she does this for a living,' said Dad, bravely but stupidly. I think he was on edge because there was a pink jumper in the ironing pile. (He struggles with colour, it's an architect thing.) 'Anyway, Elektra's nearly sixteen, I doubt she'll need much chaperoning.'

'Which reminds me,' said Mum – *slam, press, fold* – 'Elektra wants to have a sixteenth birthday party.'

'Maybe,' I said. The more I thought about it, the less sure I was. Moss might think we couldn't avoid throwing parties for ever but I wasn't convinced I wanted to be the first one to go over the top. 'Would you be OK with that, Dad?'

'I might be missing something here, but isn't your birthday in *October*?' That was a question? 'So unless you're planning something with marquees and elephants, isn't it a bit early to be thinking about a party?' He looked worried. 'You're not planning on elephants, are you?'

'No, there will be no animals at my party. *If* there's a party.'

'But you want us to say you can have a party?' asked Mum.

'Well, yes.'

'I'm not at all sure,' she said. *Slam, press, fold.*

'Maybe we can talk about it later?' I offered. Like next month. Or the month after. It was too intense in this kitchen. 'Or you can talk about it when I've gone out?'

'Gone out where?' Oh, God, now Mum had the spray starch out. Hardcore.

'Out. I already asked you.'

'But that was before your training session. You must be shattered.'

I was, but I was still going out. 'You said it was OK.'

'I said it was OK before you fell through the door looking like you'd had a heart attack. What on earth did that trainer make you *do*?'

'Climb a rope,' I said, shuddering at the memory. Dad snorted, Mum looked worried. I fished the offending pink jumper out of the pile and pulled it on (slowly, so as not to tax my poor little brand-new arm muscles). 'I'm fine now.' I really wasn't.

'Are you meeting Moss?' asked Mum. 'And I haven't ironed that yet.'

I was tempted to say yes, but I didn't dare. Despite diligent practice, I was still a terrible liar. 'No.'

'*Archie?*'

I sighed. 'Yes.'

'Where?'

'A cafe.'

'You're suddenly spending a lot of time in *cafes*, what's wrong with people's houses?'

Where to start?

'You must be spending all your allowance on overpriced tea and biscuits when you could be getting those for free right here.'

It was a fair price to pay to get out of here right now.

'Which cafe are you going to?'

'I'm not sure yet.'

'Then how do you know where to go?'

'We're meeting at the tube station.'

'I don't know if that's OK.' *Slam, press, fold.*

'Come on, Mum, it's the holidays.'

'Stop trying to exercise the care a good parent might reasonably be expected to give, Julia – it's unhelpful,' said Dad, volunteering as tribute. I left him to be slaughtered by Mum and went out.

The good thing about being a bit late was that there was a higher chance that I'd get there after Archie and so wouldn't have to stand around tapping at my phone to assure random passers-by that I did actually have friends. The bad thing about being a bit late was that I was worried he wouldn't still be there and I couldn't text and check because then I'd look all insecure. Also I seemed to have left my phone at home in my haste to escape. Well, hopefully it was at home. It was definitely somewhere.

When I arrived, Archie was there and I wasn't even awkward about kissing him hello. I was getting the hang of this mature, sophisticated, meeting-up thing.

'Where do you want to go?' he asked.

'I don't mind,' I said, because a) I didn't and b) I'm a really indecisive person.

'Cafe or park?'

'Cake?' Maybe I was some way off the mature and sophisticated thing.

'So did you hear anything on *The Curse of Peter Plogojowitz?*' I asked Archie, when we were sitting down with cake and huge mugs of tea. He looked surprised by my perfect pronunciation, but there was absolutely no need for him to know that it was down to pressing the Google Translate button at least sixty times.

'Yeah, actually.'

'And?' He was unreadable. I was never unreadable. I needed to work on that.

'I haven't got another callback.'

'You might still hear,' I said. 'Daisy once heard she had a part two months after her audition.'

'No, I definitely won't get one, they've cast it.' He fiddled with his teaspoon and didn't look at me.

'Ah, I'm sorry.' I shouldn't have asked.

'I haven't got another callback because I've got the part.' He grinned.

I whacked him because that had been unforgiveable. It was unfortunate that I sent his mug of tea flying but the situation was still very much his fault.

'Is there any chance, Elektra, that you could restrict significant physical gestures to times when I'm not holding a mug of hot water?' But he didn't look annoyed. He just looked happy. Of course he looked happy.

I was happy for him.

It was just ... *Transylvania*.

'We are having a weirdly successful summer,' he

said, mopping himself down with somebody's left behind newspaper.

'We're like one of those acting power couples,' I agreed.

'Like Brad and Angelina,' he said enthusiastically. 'Well ... except for the nasty break-up,' he added quickly.

'We are *nothing* like Brad and Angelina.' I managed to stop myself adding 'all those children' in case he thought I subconsciously wanted to have his babies. 'We're more like ... No, sorry, I can't think of a single stable celebrity relationship.'

He sadly shook his head. 'I can't either.'

This was going downhill, so I changed the subject. 'Tell me everything. Who's playing Ana?'

'I'm still at the "don't know anything" stage.'

'Have they told you when you're filming though?'

'It looks like they're going to start pretty much now. I've just been told to sort out the licence and my passport and wait to hear.'

Passport. Of course. He'd need that to travel the two thousand three hundred kilometres to *Transylvania*. (It's possible that I'd googled that too.) 'So, literally at a moment's notice?'

'Weird, right. By the way, some girl is waving at you.'

119

I turned to see where Archie was looking. Oh, brilliant. The only reason that this particular girl would be waving at me was because I was sitting with Archie.

'I know her from somewhere,' he said. 'Flossy McNaughtie?'

'Flissy McNaughton. She goes to my school. We're not really friends.' Understatement.

'Is she the girl you slapped?'

Brilliant. He'd obviously just remembered where he knew Flissy from: a certain Facebook video.

'I didn't slap her.'

'No. You tried and failed to slap her.' He laughed. 'Over me, I think?' He was *loving* this.

'Elektra! Hi!' Flissy kissed me on both cheeks like one of those fake-accidental meet-ups on *Made in Chelsea*. She'd never kissed me before. Actually, she'd never said 'hi' to me before. 'It's Archie, isn't it? We met at Stephanie's party. I'm a friend of *Talia's*.'

Archie mumbled hello and looked extremely awkward at the mention of Talia.

'You've got some tea on your shirt,' Flissy said, and started dabbing at him with a tissue. It wasn't helping him relax. 'You met Elektra through drama, right?'

'Yes,' I said, answering for him. I really wanted

her to go away or at least stop pawing at Archie.

'I think Talia's thinking about auditioning for something soon,' she said, very much just to Archie.

I didn't think Talia had ever acted in her life, but as long as it wasn't for Ana or any of the other maidens of outstanding beauty, she could audition for whatever she wanted.

'Don't you think she'd be good?' Flissy asked, still only looking at Archie. I was surprised she didn't just ask me to move so she could continue the conversation more comfortably. 'I mean Talia would be amazing on film, she's just so gorgeous.'

'There's a bit more to it than that,' said Archie.

Sometimes only a little bit.

'Oh, she's *talented* too,' said Flissy, 'but then you already know that, don't you, Archie?' She giggled and then there was one of those really loud pauses. It went on so long and became so intense that I think even Flissy started to get mildly uncomfortable.

It's surprisingly hard to find the words to tell someone, even someone you really don't like, just to go away. Archie was going for the classic male 'no words' approach so he was no use.

She stood there for a couple more minutes. 'Right ...' she said eventually. 'I'm just going to leave you guys to it. I'll be sitting over there.' She gestured at a table in the corner that was not quite far enough away. A table in the original branch of Starbucks, which I believe is in Seattle, would have been not quite far enough away. She bent down to air-kiss Archie goodbye. 'I'll tell Talia you said hi.'

Tragically I didn't get a kiss.

'Um ... the Talia thing,' said Archie, when Flissy had gone up to the counter. He looked very uncomfortable. 'I mean, you know ...'

I didn't help him out.

'I got with her a couple of times.'

I stayed quiet. I was going to let him suffer through this one.

'It was never, like, a thing,' he said. 'Also it was ages ago.'

Any minute now he was going to apologize, and that wouldn't be fair. He had nothing to apologize about. (I hoped.)

'It's cool,' I said, and then I leaned over and kissed him, even though Flissy was in the same room. OK, maybe especially because Flissy was in the same room.

'Park?' he asked, carefully replacing the mug he'd swerved out of my way just in time.

'I'm going to miss you when I'm away,' he said, when we'd got a safe distance from the cafe.

'You'll be too busy killing vampires to miss me,' I said, and stopped myself from adding 'and hanging out with maidens of outstanding beauty'.

'Well, you'll be busy with *Straker* . . . and working out with Dick.' He tried not to laugh. We were walking really slowly because my leg muscles had started to seize up in a worrying way. 'Any news on the locations yet? Is Hungary definitely happening? Hungary's pretty much next door to Romania.'

That had occurred to me too. 'No, nothing's been confirmed.'

'Well, wherever you are, you're going to be hanging out on-set with Carlo.'

Wait a minute, was Archie *jealous*? I really hoped he was. I willed him to be a bit more explicit because that's pretty much always how The Conversation starts in romcoms.

Nothing. Archie stuck his hands in his pockets and stared intently at the ground. I gave it a bit longer. Still nothing. I changed the subject. 'Flissy was a bit intense,' I said.

'Terrifying, I thought,' said Archie. We stopped on one of those little islands in the middle of the road and he pulled me round so I was facing him. 'I'd "un-get" with Talia in a minute if I could,' he said.

'It really doesn't matter,' I said.

'Yeah, but I don't want you to think I'm that kind of guy because, well … because … you know how much I like you, right?'

'Well …' I sounded more doubtful than I was because I really, really wanted him to tell me how much he liked me.

'I'm pretty sure I've made it embarrassingly obvious how much I like you,' he said.

'Not quite embarrassingly obvious enough …' I said in a small voice.

'OK, you want me to be more embarrassing.' He laughed and looked round, maybe to check for paps, now that he was going to be a teenage vampire-hunting celebrity. 'How about this? I, Archie Mortimer, am incredibly into you, Elektra James. And, um … I was thinking … well, I was wondering …' He paused. 'And … anyway … I really want to make this official. What do you think?'

What I thought was that I should probably kiss him, even if the businessman loudly clearing his throat as he edged past us obviously thought that our tiny PDA was a shocking testament to the depravity of modern youth.

Traffic islands had definitely gone up in my estimation. I'd walked past so many without realizing their potential. This one was right up there with the all-time classic romantic destinations: Pemberley; the brooding, windswept, Yorkshire Moors; and the small expanse of concrete in the middle of the road between Starbucks and the park.

I officially had a boyfriend.

My boyfriend was flying to Transylvania.

I had to hope that was correlation not causation.

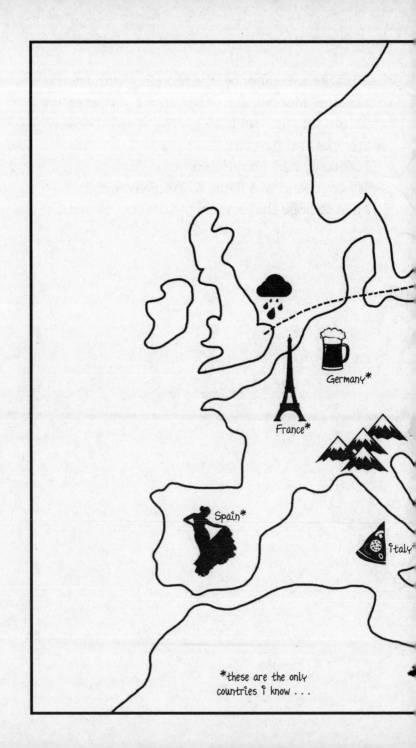

Germany*

France*

Spain*

Italy*

*these are the only
countries I know . . .

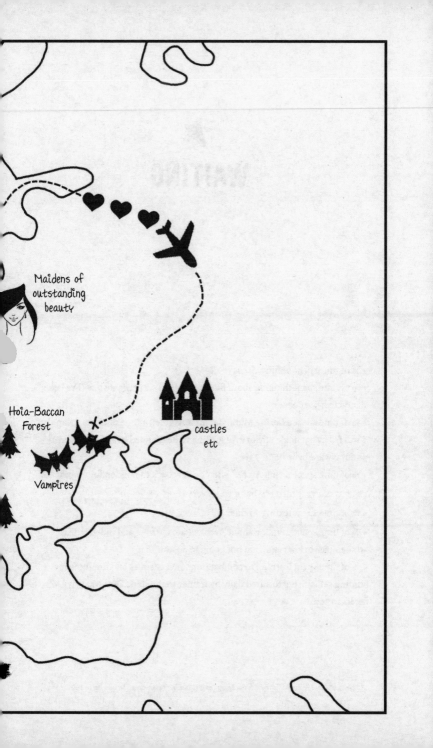

WAITING

- % of time spent filming *Straker*: 0%
- % of time spent thinking about filming *Straker*: surprisingly low (I've been distracted, see below)
- % of time spent assuring Mum that filming in term time does not mean that I will fail every single one of my GCSEs and be doomed to a life of illiteracy and wayward behaviour: 73%[1]
- % of time spent seeing Archie when he flew back to London for a weekend: 1%. It was a very nice 1%, but it was a very short 1%
- % of time spent texting Archie: 27%
- % of time spent thinking about Archie: I am a strong and independent woman (see below) and I am not going to answer that
- % of time spent learning to combat unknown enemies and fine-tune my hunting skills/being tortured daily by trainer to the stars, Dick Murphy: 36%, felt like 136%

---

[1] All percentages are approximate i.e. made up (and shouldn't be assumed to add up to 100).

CHAPTER 11

'When you go to [a movie set] and it's your job
and you go everyday, you do get a little immune to
how magical it is.'

Natalie Portman

'I can't drive *and* navigate,' said Mum, as if I'd suggested she simultaneously dance a rhumba and skin a chicken. 'I was relying on you.'

'But there was an *enormous* sign,' I said.

'Well, if you saw an enormous sign, why didn't you tell me about it?'

'Because you literally couldn't have missed it unless you were driving with your eyes closed. Please tell me you weren't driving with your eyes closed?' I looked at her.

'Just for a second at that big junction. It was terrifying.' For a woman who until recently had been obsessed with making me wear a vest on chilly days, my mum could be remarkably cavalier with my life. She was a bit sweaty and possibly regretting her decision to turn down the offer of a *limo* ride to the studio. It was raining heavily, more November than August. The buildings all looked grey and stained with damp. Half the billboards were covered in graffiti. 'It is a bit dystopian,' I said, as we finally turned off the motorway.

'That's an unkind way to describe Slough,' said Mum.

'I bet it's sunny in Hungary,' I said. (I knew that it was sunny in Transylvania because I had regular updates from Archie and, no, we didn't only talk about the weather.)

'Well, I'm happy it's Slough, at least for now,' said Mum for the hundredth time. 'While you're filming here you'll be coming home every night and eating properly. And I can be confident that the holiday homework is getting done. You're shivering. Are you cold?' I shrugged. 'Nervous?'

It was a stupid question. Of course I was nervous. There was a lot to be nervous about. Havelski always made me nervous because he was just a very scary person. Carlo made me nervous because he was too confident and hot and possibly didn't understand boundaries. Obviously I was scared of Sam Gross and was even more scared of Amber

Leigh now that I knew she was inseparable from a small deranged dog. I was scared of meeting anyone else from the table read, because to the brutally literal ones I would probably be known as 'toilet girl' and to the brutally ironic, 'Houdini'. And now I came to think about it, I was scared about all the people I hadn't met yet, because meeting new people always scared me.

'It's just first day nerves,' said Mum. 'I remember your first day at primary school. You were so scared you did a tiny wee in your knickers.'

Was that meant to be comforting?

'I'm sure there's nothing to worry about,' she went on, in her most anxious voice.

There was plenty to worry about. I wouldn't know where I was supposed to go. And then there was the whole action thing. I still couldn't run or jump or climb or *dive* like a normal human being, far less someone that might save the world with her survival skills.

I wasn't just worried; I was PANICKING.

The only thing scarier than it being Day One of actual filming was the thought that they'd postpone again and that Day One would never ever happen.

Mum fumbled to find her driving licence to show security at the entrance gate. Well, more border crossing than gate – Slough was feeling more exotic by the second. She narrowly missed driving into the little hut that homed the security guard.

He checked her licence, smirked at my passport photo and ticked us both off on a list. 'So, leave the car in Visitor Parking, take a seat in reception and there'll be someone along to collect you in five minutes. You'll need these.' He handed us passes to hang around our necks. Mum's was a standard paper guest pass in a little see-through envelope, but mine was sturdy plastic with *Straker* printed across the top and then my photo (unfortunately my passport one again) and then *CAST*. Five square centimetres of plastic, a photo that looked like the mug shot of a repeat criminal offender and irrational levels of excitement. The security guard smiled at me. 'Welcome to Fairmount.'

And suddenly Fairmount felt like Hollywood.

'Hello! You must be Elektra. I'm Naomi Pritt, your chaperone.' Naomi was taller than me, with a golden afro and the kind of winged eyeliner I have attempted many times but never achieved. I shook her hand. Her jeans might have been ripped but her nail polish was unchipped. I was officially in awe of her.

'And you must be Elektra's mother.' She smiled at my mum.

'Yes ... indeed I am. I am Elektra's mother.' Mum sounded a bit weird and manic. I think she was nervous.

'Sorry,' said Naomi. 'It must be annoying being referred to as "Elektra's mum". It's Julia, isn't it?'

Mum pulled herself together and smiled properly.

'Follow me,' said Naomi, and we did – into one of these golf buggy things, except because of the rain Naomi had to pin down the plastic covers so we were like three very large toddlers in an enormous weather-proofed pushchair. I was the one facing backwards. So, not *that* like Hollywood. It was a weird place: on the one hand we were passing lots of white ordinary-looking one-storey office blocks, on the other we were driving down a street called Godzilla Avenue. 'I'm just cutting round the back to the A Stage production offices. That'll be home for a while,' explained Naomi, who drove the buggy like it was a Ferrari. 'Most people are already here.'

Great, so my mother's inability to turn off the M25 at a junction even close to the right one meant that we were late.

'We'll need to get cracking, so let's skip coffee and so on and I'll just take you straight in.' Naomi rounded the corner in a way which made me think she'd already had a number of strong coffees that morning. 'It's the health and safety talk.' She looked at Mum. 'I'm guessing you want to stay for that?'

'OK,' shouted a tall, skinny man with a baseball cap pulled down low over his head. 'Find a seat, everyone. I'm Ahmed, I'm the first assistant director – AD – on this film and this is the most important talk you're going to have, so pay attention.'

Ahmed had the sort of vibe that made people do what he said. Within minutes, the room had stilled. It was packed, and I was glad Carlo had held spaces for us, even if it meant I was practically sitting on his lap.

'Health and safety on-set – the *basics*.'

Carlo groaned. A few other people groaned. I restrained myself from joining in. Given my own personal health and safety record, it was probably a good idea to pay attention.

Ahmed stared everyone into silence. 'Right, good, EVERYBODY listening? Why does health and safety matter?' Was that a rhetorical question? No. '*Because you could get hurt or die.* We don't want to dedicate this film to any one of you.' Nervous laughter, although it wasn't that funny. 'Also, we really don't want to get sued.' Nobody laughed at that.

Carlo silently offered me a Fruit Pastille.

Unfortunately it was an orange one, but better than nothing.

'Film sets are inherently dangerous places,' went on Ahmed. 'Massive amounts of electricity, hot lights, ladders, suspended equipment, power tools, cabling, stingers. TRIP HAZARDS – that's a big one, people.'

Mum scrabbled in her bag for a notebook and started making a list. A little something to look at in the unlikely event that she felt calm at any moment during the next few weeks.

'That's before you add in EXTRAS like weapons, explosives, chemicals. You're lucky there are no helicopters in this script.'

I could hear Mum deep-breathing.

'Except for the one that Sam Gross will turn up in every morning,' whispered Carlo, and went back to eyeing up a very pretty twenty-something sitting a couple of rows in front of us.

'Hey, the kids over there eating the Fruit Pastilles, pay attention.' Clearly Ahmed missed nothing, this was like being in the army. 'Fight scenes, falls, pyrotechnic incidents, malfunctioning fog machines. Flying objects can be an issue, boulders, heavy weaponry, winged creatures, elves.'

'There are elves in *Straker*?' Sam broke in. I hadn't thought he was listening – he'd seemed pretty glued to his phone – but then he'd probably heard it all before, like a frequent flyer and the safety drill. Anyway, Sam was a genuine action hero so he could probably outrun danger.

'There may or may not be elves in *Straker*. There are certainly flying boulders and multiple fight scenes.'

I mentally added 'elves' to the long list of unknowns.

'Cold, heatstroke, insect bites ...'

Mum had now reached the hyperventilating stage. Carlo was trying not to laugh. I was just confused. Slough was a more threatening place than I'd realized.

'Allergic reactions to make-up – that's a big one.'

I got that. Talia had once had a reaction to eyelash primer (a product I hadn't known existed) that had made her eyelid swell up to the size of a tennis ball. I think she just has extensions now, presumably because *gluing* bits of baby mink on to the ends of your eyelashes is safer.

Ahmed moved on to advise us on what we should do to avoid dying, and I listened very hard. Carlo, on the other hand, now had his phone propped up under his knee and was subtly checking his texts.

'If someone shouts "HOT SPOT", think *hazard* and *get out of the way*. If we run into you with a camera we could drop it and that could cost us tens of thousands of pounds.' Ahmed paused, then added as an afterthought, 'And you could get hurt. Do what you're told and if you're not sure then shout. Don't be scared of looking silly.'

Obviously I *would* be scared of looking silly, but maybe just a bit less scared than of the whole death or serious injury thing. I thought he'd finished, but no.

'Mobiles. I don't like them.' He glared at Sam. 'NEVER talk and walk. NEVER text and walk. Offset I can't ban them but, as I said, I don't like them. But never, NEVER have your mobile on-set.' He looked at Sam again. He looked at Carlo. 'There will be consequences.'

I believed him. So I was going to suffer social suicide, as well as risk actual death. Always good to finish a talk on an upbeat note.

Havelski wandered up to the front looking more relaxed than I'd ever seen him. Plainly pyrotechnic and other assorted risks were all in a day's work. 'Thanks, Ahmed,' he said. 'I just want to add one thing – thank you all for being here. Now we're going to make a great film.'

So Havelski, as well as having great taste in teen leads, was the master of the short speech. There was the muddle of noise that people make when they're being released from assembly, all scraping chairs and a sort of exhalation of relief.

'People!' Amber had made her way to the front of the room. 'People!' She made a shushing noise and motioned for everyone to sit back down. Everyone did (but then Amber had been on the Top Hundred International Beauties list for the past seven years, so I suppose even if you needed to go to the loo you'd just hold it in for a bit). 'I don't think we can wind this up without a little special moment. First, let's have a big round of applause for our lovely director ... OK.' She cut us off before anyone had a chance to make much noise, then took a deep breath. 'Now we need to get this film going with a blessing. Let's hold hands because we're stronger when we hold on to each other.' Had she forgotten we were in London, not LA? No one moved. A short guy in very long pressed shorts tried to back slowly out of the door. 'You!' She pointed at him. Short Guy looked terrified. 'You can start us off.' She was like a vindictive teacher. Short Guy moved forward very slowly and offered his hand to Rhona, who was looking extremely confused. I gave in and extended both hands, one to my mum (who was still hyperventilating) and one to Carlo. I was not in my comfort zone.

'Much better. I can feel the love in this room,' said Amber.

Carlo squeezed my hand, which would have

been creepy, except he was shaking with held-in laughter.

'I'm calling on every single one of you.' Amber raised her arms like some sort of High Priestess. 'Every single one.' She stared down a couple of fidgeters. 'To take a moment, close your eyes if you haven't already done so and just send waves of *love* to everyone else in the room, because we're *family* now. Come on, guys!' She sounded a bit testy, like we weren't trying hard enough. I had a bad feeling that my palms were sweaty. '*Project that love*,' she admonished, so we did.

Maybe.

Naomi was at the door waiting when we filed out. She looked at Mum. 'Are you all right, Julia?'

Mum just shuddered. 'I suppose I should leave now,' she said, but she obviously didn't want to go. To be fair, after that speech she was probably worried about abandoning me to the flying elves, random pyrotechnic risks and, worst of all, love gurus.

'Why don't you come and see Elektra's dressing room before you leave?' suggested Naomi gently. 'It's over on King Kong Place.'

'Can I come and see your dressing room?' Carlo asked me.

'Maybe wait to be invited?' suggested Naomi mildly.

'I'll give you the last Fruit Pastille, Elektra,' he offered.

I took it because I'm easily bribable. 'Maybe later,' I said. I could see Mum itching to add Carlo to her list of possible risks.

'Let's walk together anyway. My dressing room's next to yours.'

My mum looked at Naomi desperately. I think she was coming round to the idea of a professional chaperone.

'It's the third door on the left,' said Naomi, stopping to check a message on her phone and motioning us ahead of her. One, two— I stopped so abruptly that Mum and Carlo ran into me while I just stood and stared at the door. OK, there wasn't a gold star, but someone had sellotaped a square of paper with ELEKTRA JAMES/STRAKER on it to the door. This was officially MY dressing room, with MY NAME on it. It was a beautiful moment.

Naomi caught up with us and let us into a little room with a tiny sofa and coffee table nearly hidden under a bunch of pink flowers and – *the dream* – above the titchy dressing table was one of those mirrors with lights around it. I gave a little squeal and ran over to stroke it. I wasn't dignified. Carlo (who despite our earlier conversation had decided to invite himself along) sniggered.

'Is it the same as yours?' I asked him.

He paced the length and breadth of the room, which didn't take long, and reached his arm up and touched the ceiling. 'It's the same size,' he said, satisfied. 'But I didn't get flowers, which is sexist.'

'Did you get the fruit basket?'

'Yep. In fact ...' he looked at it closely, 'I think I probably got more fruit than you.' He seemed pleased about that. He sat down on my miniature sofa and put his feet up on my miniature coffee table.

'Make yourself at home,' I said. He stretched out a bit; plainly Carlo wasn't very good at picking up on sarcasm.

'Chuck me a plum will you, E?' he asked.

'No way. Not if you got more fruit than me.' I eyed the fruit basket and wondered if it was one of those fruit baskets that magically replenished itself every day.

'You go, girl,' said Naomi, abruptly kicking Carlo's feet off the table. I already loved Naomi. 'Anyway, there's no time.'

'Do we get to see the set?' I asked.

'Not today. It's closed to everyone except the set-builders. Tomorrow for sure. But you do get fittings.' She looked at her watch. 'We need to get over to the costume department in about half an hour.'

'I should probably go,' said Mum, and then stood there for a bit, waiting for someone to tell her not to. This time nobody did and I gave her a quick hug goodbye.

'I'll show you how to get out,' said Naomi, and Carlo and I were left behind in what oddly seemed like an even smaller space.

'So tell me all about the fit boyfriend,' said Carlo.

'What fit boyfriend?' Strangely enough, I hadn't been sharing confidences with Carlo.

'There obviously is one.'

'Why do you say that?'

'Because every time I flirt with you, you just get weird and pretend you haven't noticed.'

Why was he saying this out loud? I was too awkward to ask where the loo was, let alone demand why a near stranger wasn't flirting with me. I tried to laugh it off, attempting the sort of aloof amusement that comes easily to heroines in romcoms. 'You flirt with everyone, Carlo. You spent half that safety talk checking everyone out. Maybe I just don't take you very seriously.'

'You've gone really red.'

Not even close.

'Look, E, everyone takes me seriously ... unless there's a fit other in the picture.'

'He's in Transylvania,' I said, because Carlo wasn't going to drop it.

'Transylvania? Is that a real place?'

'Of course it is,' I said dismissively. I was now an expert on that particular corner of Romania.

'How did you manage to hook up with someone who lives in Transylvania? Typical.'

'I didn't – he lives in London.' I felt a bit defensive. Carlo didn't know me nearly well enough to make 'typical' comments. If he did he wouldn't have thought it was 'typical' for me to hook up with anyone, regardless of location.

'So what's your boyfriend doing in Transylvania? Vampire hunting?'

I waited for Carlo to stop laughing at his own wit and then said, 'Yes.'

'Oh, God, is he one of those Dracula weirdos? Does he, like, dress up and go on vampire tours?'

'No, he does not. Obviously. He's playing a vampire hunter in a TV thing.'

'Another drama boy. Damn. Competition. I hate coming up against other actors, we're like a super-race.'

'That's beyond untrue,' I said, thinking of Brian and Christian from ACT, and Damian from the auditions and so, so many others. 'Anyway, you and your ego could do with a bit more competition, Carlo.'

'Ha, that means you *do* fancy me.'

I just looked at him. I was going for condescending this time.

'Well, Dracula Boy is out of the picture so you should be looking around.'

'He gets back to London often enough.'

'Sure, how often have you seen him since he went?'

'Once.' Only once in two long weeks.

'How long for?'

'A couple of hours.' It turned out that although Archie's mum was cool, she was also quite demanding of his time now he'd basically moved to Romania.

'Exactly. Because he's *filming*. Out of sight, out of mind.'

'That's just not true. Archie and I are texting.'

He snorted. 'Maybe texting is enough for you, Elektra, but for guys ...' He trailed off like he couldn't disclose the secrets of the male cult.

I tried to stop thinking about Ana and the maidens.

'We two, for example, we are filming.' Carlo had read my mind. 'We are being *thrown together*.'

'What, us and a hundred-strong crew?'

Carlo didn't look impressed. 'If you get bored texting and waiting just let me know,' he said.

It was a relief when Naomi got back. She got rid of Carlo and we half-ran the two blocks to another long, low white building that was the costume department. Inside was strip-lighting and there were tall mirrors propped everywhere at weird angles. There were endless rows of costumes and, at the end of each row, a grid filled with polaroids of the outfits and details of their wearers. Shelves ran along the walls, filled to the brim with labelled boxes.

I slowed down to watch a woman being pinned into her costume. It was one of the silvery Warri slips I'd seen in Maud's scrapbook, but now it had layer upon layer of 'dystopian' embellishment. Tiny polished silver cogs and miniature bolts sparkled like gems, marking out a circuit pattern that crept up from the hem. I wanted that dress – the bitter rivalry between the tribes wasn't going to be hard to fake.

I was out of breath by the time we reached the far end of the huge room, partly because of costume awe, and partly because, despite Dick's best efforts, I was still cardio challenged. Amber was standing on a shallow pedestal in front of one of the mirrors and Maud was tending to her costume. As I arrived, they both gave me distracted air-kisses, Maud because she had pins in her mouth and Amber because she was far too interested in looking at her own reflection. I didn't blame her – she looked amazing. There had plainly been a bit of an *intervention* on the costume front. There was no brown-gritty-realism cloak for Amber. Instead she wore a deep wine-red Grecian-style gown. I wasn't sure where the ancient Greeks were going to come into the plot, but it was beautiful. Made of crimped silk – *crushed* was obviously as far as Amber was prepared to go on the post-apocalyptic front – and held together with an intricate criss-cross of twisted silk cords. Maud was sewing clusters of dark leaf shapes between the layers of semi-translucent silk. I began to feel more optimistic about my costumes.

I was bustled behind a screen by Maud's assistant and efficiently stripped down to my 'undies' and into a robe.

'Elektra!' Amber turned from the glow of her own reflection as I emerged and was motioned on to another little pedestal. 'Aren't the costumes *divine?*' she asked.

'Divine,' I repeated hopefully.

'We didn't have enough time to talk at the table read,' Amber went on. 'But we can really get to know each other now. *Bond*. Share lots of mother-daughter secrets.' She giggled. I wasn't sure what she meant. My actual mother-daughter relationship had not prepared me for Amber. 'I find it's always good to be open to sharing the love with your co-stars. Talking of which,' she continued, 'Carlo Winn is rather beautiful. You two will make for such a cute little subplot.'

I caught Maud's eye. Half the globe knew how fond Amber was of 'sharing the love' with her co-stars. I had no idea how to reply, but I was saved by Maud's assistant coming back with my costume over her arm.

Two minutes later, she swivelled my pedestal so that I, too, was facing the mirror.

Ah. Amber's costume revolution had clearly been more of an elite military coup than a democratic rising. My costume was still a sack.

The three of them turned to look at me. Amber cocked her head. 'It's so *real*,' she said.

'Ah!' Maud clasped her hands. 'It's *exactly* as I envisaged. You can really sense the trauma Straker has gone through.' What she was sensing was probably the trauma I was *going* through.

'It's ...' Everyone was waiting for me to say something. 'It's ... *wow*.'

Actually, it was a brown hessian sack gathered in with drawstrings at the neck and wrists, so kind of the opposite of wow. And, to make it worse, I was going to be wearing it while trying to maintain a long-distance relationship with a boyfriend who was playing a vampire-slaying heart-throb in a flattering range of breeches and tuxedos surrounded by fit maidens (who would not be wearing sacks).

*

How was long-awaited Day One? I'd fallen into bed within an hour of getting home, but I wasn't too tired to text with Archie.

😊 😁 💃 ❤️ 👍 😍

That good?

Better Costume trauma aside.

Did you see the set?

No, tomorrow. I literally cannot wait

Today's highlights?

I have my own DRESSING ROOM with MY NAME ON THE DOOR. And flowers in MY DRESSING ROOM. And there's a TV on MY DRESSING ROOM wall

I'm sensing a theme here. I'm not going to mention the twenty dressing room selfies you sent me

SORRY

Ha ha, I forgive you x By the way who were the flowers from?

'Elektra?' My mum put her head around the door and I shoved the phone under the covers. 'Are you on the phone?'

'No,' I said innocently.

'Yes, you are, your bed is glowing.' Ah. 'I'm not going to ask you who you're talking to at this time of night because I'm pretty sure I know. You should be asleep. He'll wait till the morning.'

'Sorry. OK, I'm going to sleep now,' I said, turning my face angelically on the pillow.

'Night night, both of you,' she said, and I thought

148

for one horrible minute that she was talking to me and *the phone,* but then I realized she meant Digby. She'd given up the pretence that she was ever going to make him go and sleep in his basket and he was curled at my feet like an unseasonal hot water bottle. I waited till she'd properly gone then fished out my phone.

Havelski

Cute. What else happened?

There were some low points

Such as?

I sent Archie a photo of me in my costume because under the circumstances there wasn't much point trying to keep it a secret.

Ha ha ha ha ha ha ha

You'd better think of something nice to say

Your legs look good

I'd take that.

Did they give you the 'you will almost certainly die in the making of this movie' lecture?

Yes. Also the studios are enormous and everything looks the same and I will never ever find my way around. And I may die in a golf buggy racing accident. Plus my fruit bowl was smaller than Carlo's

OK, this is getting quite hard to follow, but you can tell me everything in person as soon as I get a break and can fly back – I miss you xxx

I missed him too.

STRAKER (working title)
PANDA PRODUCTIONS
Scene 12
Ext: Cliff-face. Daytime.

_____
_____

_____
_____

_____
_____

_____
_____

_____
_____

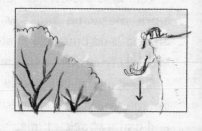
_____
_____

CHAPTER 12

'I suffer from a persistent fear. It manifests itself in nerves, and on film the camera sees even the tiniest evidence of this.'

Eddie Redmayne

'Hello, hello!' A very blond guy wearing chinos and carrying a clipboard knocked on the open door of my dressing room and came straight in, followed by the short shorts' wearer that Amber had tortured at the health and safety talk. 'So, the plan for today!' announced the blond guy. 'Mr Havelski is running ahead of time, so we're bringing forward Straker's call time.

Naomi looked horrified. 'But Elektra needs to eat breakfast, Eddie!'

I'd already eaten two croissants in the back of *my limo* – breakfast wasn't my problem.

'There's time for breakfast if she multitasks,' he said firmly. 'The new schedule is as follows: we'll convene at meeting point 1C at seven thirteen a.m.' I looked at the clock on my wall. It was now 7.08 a.m. 'From there you—' Eddie pointed his pen at Naomi – 'can marshall our Straker—' he paused and waggled the pen at me – 'over to Hair and Make-up at eight twenty a.m., where she can have a little something to eat and drink while she's having a blow-dry.' He made it sound like he'd planned me a spa day. '*Then* get her to Costume at nine twenty-five and *then* swiftly on to meeting point 3A on Sound Stage A, where we'll—'

'Eddie, where is meeting point 1C?' Naomi interrupted him wearily.

'Well, *Naomi*. Meeting point 1C was clearly marked on the second set map I handed out yesterday morning.'

'Could we not just meet *at* the set?'

He looked at her like it was the year eighteen hundred and she'd just suggested women should have the vote. He consulted his clipboard with such aggression that a lock of extremely blond hair actually fell *out of place*.

'He's hungover,' mouthed Short Guy to Naomi.

'Actually, Andy, I think you will find I am *not* hungover. It was indeed a bit of a mad one last night and it may be true that I found a lobster costume

152

among six other inexplicable ... items in my bed this morning. But I got up at six a.m. and did my abs to Abba. And I am feeling much better.'

'You did your what?' snorted Naomi.

'I did my abs to Abba.'

I was beginning to respect Eddie. He was a male in his early twenties who didn't feel the need to justify his love of Abba.

'I usually do legs to The Mikado, but I wasn't feeling up to singing along to opera this morning,' he said, as if that completely cleared up our confusion.

Naomi (who I'm confident had never listened to, far less exercised to, Abba) checked her watch and consulted her own clipboard. It was a stand-off. 'Can we just leave it that I'll get Elektra to set no later than ten a.m.? I have no idea where meeting point 3A is, so we'll meet just inside the main door.'

'Meeting point 3A is just inside the main door,' said Andy, who was trying and failing to be helpful.

Eddie glared at Naomi.

Naomi glared back. 'It's my job,' she said fiercely. 'Why don't you go check on Carlo Winn? He's unchaperoned. Also I'm pretty sure I heard him doing abs to One Direction earlier on.'

It was a lie, but an effective one.

*

It was rush hour in hair and make-up. I was waved into the one empty chair – between Sam and Amber.

Carlo was on the other side of Amber, bravely trying to bond with Kale who was having his own little blow-dry and set. 'Such a cute dog,' he said.

Sam rolled his eyes. 'That's not what I'd call a dog,' he said.

Amber ignored him and turned to Carlo. 'I have so much respect for men who care about animals.' Carlo visibly *melted* at the attention. 'Or the planet.' She turned back to Sam pointedly. 'Or, you know, other people.'

'Sorry, Mr Gross,' whispered Sam's make-up artist. 'Could you just relax your jaw a little?'

'Do you know your lines, kids?' asked Sam attempting a smile. Carlo nodded. I nodded. 'Do you want to run lines then, Amber? Check we've got that fight scene down?'

Amber glared at him. 'Trust me, Sam, I'm ready for the fight scene.'

A grandmotherly lady called Ruby took me off to get my hair washed. We returned to deathly silence. There was a plate with not one but two bacon rolls sitting at my station. My phone barked. I turned off the sound but checked the screen.

You missed so much beef

I looked over at Carlo. I think he'd have winked

except one of the make-up girls was sticking weirdly flattering plastic scars all over his forehead.

You started it. What did I miss?

Carlo smirked.

Breaking news. Sam hates small dogs just a bit less than he hates Amber. She hasn't forgiven him for the time he left Coco-the-predecessor-Pomeranian on a plane. It was a private plane. There were some VERY heated exchanges about the poor judgement of a man who keeps a pet goat in his Hollywood garden. That man being Sam. Obviously. Can I have one of your bacon rolls?

I passed over the plate.

'What are you two texting about?' Amber missed nothing.

'Er ... my dog,' I improvised.

'I just *love* dogs,' said Carlo (not for the first time). Sam snorted. Kale preened.

Ruby grabbed a pot of 'dirt' and started going full dreadlock on me. I wasn't sure why she'd bothered washing my hair, since she was now covering it in *lumps* of mud. I suppose it was volumizing. She grabbed a can of lacquer, forced me to hang my head upside down and went all out until I had a halo. I touched it nervously. A muddy halo so rock hard that it was no wonder I'd survived the apocalypse.

I looked over at Amber. Somehow she had

survived the apocalypse with a blow-dry, a fabulous set of extensions and some artful mud-contouring.

'That is some ... hair. Is it hair?' Carlo laughed at me.

'It's called commitment to the role, wise guy,' shot back Sam. If there were teams – and I was really beginning to think that there were – I was totally Team Sam.

'Come on, Elektra.' Naomi did her weird materializing-at-my-side thing just as Ruby was finished with me. 'You're due on set. You too, Carlo. I'll take you both. We don't want Eddie to get his knickers in a twist. Ready?'

Not exactly. I wasn't ready. I suddenly, absolutely did not know my lines, and there was a strong possibility that I would open my mouth and all that would come out would be semi-digested croissants and bacon.

Naomi looked at me closely. 'Maybe remember to breathe?' was all that she said. Then she summoned up a buggy like someone hailing a taxi. 'Can you drop us at Sound Stage A, please?'

A big guy in a black T-shirt and baggy shorts was having a cigarette by the enormous doors when we arrived. 'Hey, Naomi, you've brought us our Straker and Jan, right?' He had a growly warm voice. Costumes were essentially like wearing a name tag, so he had a huge advantage over me because I had no idea who he was. 'I'm Sound Dan,' he said, as if reading my mind. Then he hugged me and Carlo. 'I'm your friend with the boom,' he said. 'If you've got questions, ask me. They're setting up for your scene right now.' He ground out his half-finished cigarette. 'I'll come in with you.'

I thought that my extensive googling had prepared me for the five thousand metres-square hangar that was our set, but it turned out I wasn't prepared at all. It was like that bit in the *Harry Potter* film where Harry steps into Diagon Alley for the first time. THAT. Well, except for the wizards and owls and Hagrid. But one minute I was in reality and then I walked through double doors as high as three buses and I was in a *something* that wasn't like anything else. A world milling with people who looked like they knew what they were doing/ building/fixing; equipment in black boxes and on wheels and up ladders and on scaffolding and fixed to tracks; rigging everywhere. There were bright green walls and patches of what might or might not be grass and, in amongst the metal and plastic, there were hills and a sort of cliff and lots of rocks and any number of strange statues. There was *a river* – OK, maybe a *stream*, but still … There might as well have been wizards. And there, in the middle of it all, dressed entirely in black, was Havelski.

'Excited to go, yes?' he asked when we reached him. He seemed quite excited himself.

'Yes!' Carlo and I said together.

'So? You've had the lines, you've had the story boards. You know what you're doing?'

We both nodded, but maybe not as emphatically as he'd have liked. 'Quick recap, we're doing one of the early scenes. Jan and Straker have met but only a couple of times. You're wary of each other, but you want to keep each other alive.'

We both nodded.

'Jan has climbed some way to safety.' Havelski gestured at the 'cliff' which suddenly looked even higher and scarier. 'Straker is just behind him, but she needs his help.' Yes, she would, she really would. I felt a little bit sick. 'We're going to block it now, ignore the cameras.' That was easier said than done. They were huge and one of them was mounted on a sort of crane high above us. Havelski started pointing out to us exactly where we needed to be and Carlo was all of a sudden perching on a high outcrop and we were ready to run it through.

JAN
Get up here, Straker! Higher!

You couldn't say Carlo looked *chill* because he was a good actor and he was meant to be sheltering from rapacious wolfy things, but I also didn't think he was scared. He could have been on flat ground, for all the concern he was showing as he neared the edge.

JAN
Straker! Come on!

Carlo shifted even closer to the edge. He was wearing a wire harness, but it didn't look nearly sturdy enough to me. I suppressed the urge to shout at him to be careful because I was pretty sure that Havelski would take a dim view of that kind of improvisation.

'OK, that's looking great, Carlo, we've got that,' said Ahmed. There was a bit of huddling around the monitors and some nodding. 'Elektra, whenever you're ready ...'

STRAKER
I can't!

I'm scared of heights! I didn't actually say that last bit because, although true, it wasn't in the script. In my head I was screaming it.

'Try and move a little bit more to the left, the light's better ...' said Ahmed, and there was some more huddling. 'Let's do it again.'

JAN

(*Leans out as far as he dares and reaches out his hand to her.*)
Take my hand, Straker. I'll pull you up!

STRAKER
You can't, I'm too heavy.

This *was* in the script. It was also true. Even if it hadn't been, it wasn't entirely clear how I was supposed to get much help from a hand held out at least two metres above me. Was I meant to jump up to it? I did a bit of futile bouncing which was a) undignified and b) not very in character, so I wasn't surprised to hear various voices shouting at me to stop.

'Elektra,' said Havelski, coming over to me. 'You can't forget that in this scene you are being chased by seven wolf-like creatures, closely followed by seventeen armed members of the Warri Tribe and something nameless which the scriptwriters can't agree on.' He looked around darkly, and a woman that I recognized as one of the writers from the table read shifted further into the shadows. 'For now, let's call them The Dread.'

The Dread. I was feeling that. I nodded. 'Sorry, did I not look scared enough?'

'No, don't apologize. Never apologize on-set,'

said Havelski. 'You did look scared ... but you looked scared like "Elektra-James-English-schoolgirl-can't-climb-can't-jump scared". I need "Straker-feisty-heroine-from-who-knows-where scared".' He glanced at the scriptwriter again. Clearly they'd been having as much trouble writing this scene as I was acting it.

'Maybe she needs a quick break and some Haribo,' suggested Naomi from the sidelines.

'No, I'm fine.' I lied. If Carlo didn't need a break I definitely didn't need a break.

'So, I want more of *this*,' Havelski reached up in a dramatic fashion, all mingled terror and hope, 'and less of *this*.' He pulled an expression that made him look like he was scared he was going to wet himself. 'Let's go again.' And hordes of people all did whatever they had to do so we were good to go again.

(Straker falls back and screams.)

Take two.

Take three.

Take four.

I fall over ALL the time (it's my legs, they get tangled easily), so why is it so difficult to fall over when the script tells me. Oh, God, I was being *paid* for this. I hoped they couldn't ask for a refund.

161

STRAKER

It's my ankle. (*Straker clutches ankle and grimaces.*)

I was giving it the full damsel in distress now.

JAN

I'm coming down.

STRAKER

No, it's not safe.

JAN

That's *why* I'm coming down.

Carlo swung to the ground at the same time as I stumbled backwards and fell. Unfortunately, and yet somehow predictably, falling wasn't in the script this time.

'Stop, everyone!' yelled Havelski, sounding both very loud and a bit bored.

Naomi was over to me in seconds. 'Did you hurt yourself?'

'I'm *fine*,' I said, rearranging my costume and trying to reassemble my dignity.

'No, she's not, she's *crying*,' said Carlo, through his laughter. He was plainly no longer in character – Jan would have rescued me.

162

'I'm not!' I said. 'My eyes are just watering.' I really wasn't crying. It was embarrassment. I stood up and gave an awkward little wave to everyone who had gathered around, to show how fine I was. Yes, in the balance between embarrassment and pain, embarrassment was definitely coming out on top.

'What's the damage?' Havelski asked Naomi.

'I'm *fine*,' I said. I could answer for myself.

'Good,' said Havelski, checking his watch. 'It's always a win to get to the end of a day without an A and E crisis.' He patted me on the shoulder, which was less comforting than I think it was meant to be. I felt like Digby. 'Reset!' Havelski called, and a horde of people scurried around to make that happen. 'So the thing is, Elektra, you can do this scene. It's not *that* high, you're really securely rigged up and we're not going to let anything happen to you. I promise.' I nodded. 'Right, everyone, let's film this.'

CHAPTER 13

*'I don't have a period look because I cut off all
my hair.'*

James Norton

'You can't go out tonight, you're too tired,' said
Mum.

'I'm fine,' I said for the seven hundredth time.
OK, I was creaking *slightly* whenever I sat down, a
bit like Digby, but that was because of the twenty
minutes kickboxing training Dick had added to the
schedule as a sort of 'treat'. It was a no-filming day,
but that didn't mean rest. 'I'm fine to go out.'

'Where will you even go at this time of night?'
said Mum. She was whipping up a gourmet meal of
chicken and rice to tempt Digby, who still seemed
to have no appetite. I'd had a pasta ready meal,
because, well, priorities.

'It's seven thirty! *Everywhere* will be open.'

'Archie can come over here.'

'Yes, but you and Dad are here. Unless you want to go out?' I added hopefully.

'No, Elektra, I don't think we do really want to be chased out of our own home so you can be here alone with a boy.'

She made it sound so dodgy. How to explain that it wasn't the need to be alone so much as the need not to have them there? It was better to spend every single penny that I could get hold of (thank you, Eulalie) in cafes and avoid the awkward.

'And seven thirty is late when you've had a week of being up at dawn. Besides, I wanted us all to have dinner together tonight because you still haven't told me everything that's been going on.'

'I have!' I protested. 'I've told you everything.'

'All I got last night was two and a half minutes informing me that you'd remembered all your lines and that everything was *fine.*'

'Well, that's exactly what happened. That, and lots of sitting around waiting and eating.'

'But I want to know all the *details.* Has Mr Havelksi been nice to you? What have you been eating?' She literally wanted me to tell her in real time. 'And has Naomi been looking after you properly?'

'The food's the best food I've ever eaten and Naomi looks after me brilliantly,' I said. Mum looked a bit put out. 'If I promise to tell you *every single tiny thing* I can remember tomorrow, please can I go out now? I haven't seen Archie in ages! He's had nearly eight hours of travelling and crossed multiple bits of Europe and his mum is letting him go out.'

'I am not Archie's mum.' Obviously. 'Stella said that it was important that off-set time was calm and restful.'

'Well, I really feel quite lively.' She narrowed her eyes at me; that had been a bad choice of words. 'Pleeease, Mum. I'm not on-set tomorrow either so I don't even need to get up early. I won't be long. I'll make you a cup of tea before I go. Pleeease. I love you.'

'You are manipulating me, Elektra Ophelia,' she said. I was, and it was working. 'You win, but you need to be home by ten at the latest. *Latest.*'

As that was a full hour later than I had been hoping for I gave her a hug to seal the deal. 'You can have a lovely quiet romantic evening with Dad,' I said because he'd just come into the kitchen. 'And Digby,' I added, because nobody put Digby in the corner.

'Why are you arranging for me to have a quiet romantic evening with your mother? Delightful though that sounds, I suspect an agenda.'

'Archie is back in London,' said Mum, tucking

a tartan blanket round Digby who was shivering a bit.

'Ah, the eagle has landed,' said Dad inexplicably. 'What. Is. That?' He clutched his chest and pointed theatrically to the table.

'What?' I asked, looking in the direction he was pointing. 'It's a *Post-it Note*, Dad. It's really not that scary.'

'It's ... *pink*, very pink. And it's heart-shaped. It is an *abomination*.'

He looked like he was too scared to sit at the table, so I cleared the Post-it away to the drawer of shame, the one with the metallic gel pens and the novelty erasers and a purple pug-shaped phone charger. I loved that drawer. My phone barked and I checked my texts. Excellent. The eagle had not only landed but was walking from the tube to Starbucks.

'Any chance of a lift, Dad?'

Archie was waiting for me at what I very much wanted to call 'our table'.

'Hey.' I gave an embarrassed little wave.

'Elektra!'

This was the point at which I was meant to run into his arms, but I suddenly felt shy so I just stood there until he got up and came over to me. He leaned in to kiss me. We bumped noses and tried again. For a welcome-back kiss that had been *much imagined* it was … awkward. We ended up hugging and I was pretty sure Archie was nervous too – it's the only explanation for the weird back-patting that was going on.

'I'll get you a tea,' he said. 'You want a tea, right? You haven't got all sophisticated and finally started drinking coffee?'

No, I definitely hadn't got all sophisticated, as I think the previous five minutes had clearly demonstrated. Archie was probably glad that there was a long queue. I took the opportunity to text Moss.

In Starbucks with my elusive boyfriend and I'm suddenly so nervous that I have literally nothing to say

Tell him about Straker

Idk I don't want to go on about it. It's all our texts are about

Talk about Carlo. Make him really jealous

Are you mad?

Weather? GCSE results?

You give terrible advice

Still better than asking him if he met any fit girls in Transylvania

Now of course the only question I could think of when Archie came back to the table was: 'Did you meet any fit girls in Transylvania?' so instead I just looked at him for a bit. That wasn't so bad.

Elektra??? Don't ask how he's getting on with Ana and all the spare maidens.

Ah, yes, it would be stupid to ask if he'd met any fit girls in Transylvania, given he was in fact essentially *living* with fit girls in Transylvania. *Thanks for reminding me, Moss.* I put my phone on silent.

'You're staring at me,' said Archie. 'Have I gone all weirdly vampire hunter or something?'

'No,' I said, then hesitated because he *did* look a bit different.

'It's the hair, isn't it? I should have warned you.' He tugged at what was left of it. 'It looks like I'm about to join the army.'

In fact it looked like he had already joined the army and the severe haircut was some sort of unfortunate corporal punishment. I *mourned* his floppy hair.

'I like it,' I said (lied).

'You should hear my mum on the subject. It's like she's in *mourning*.'

'Bit of an extreme reaction ... Anyway, it'll grow.'

He looked at me. 'You hate it too.'

'NO!' I was way too emphatic. 'Nooo ...' There was a slightly uncomfortable pause.

'I brought you a present,' he said eventually, putting an enormous bar of Toblerone on the table. 'I got it at the airport, but it was that or a vampire souvenir mug so count yourself lucky.'

I did. 'Do you want some now?' I asked him.

'Yes, please,' he said, which was good because so did I.

'So tell me everything that's going on in *Straker*. How's life as an action hero?' He felt my arm muscles. 'Your biceps are getting bigger than mine.'

Sure. 'My inner action hero remains quite shy. I can't climb up the fake cliff, keep falling over at the wrong times and still run like a nervous chicken.'

Archie laughed.

'Seriously. The trainer says I do a weird hand-flapping thing when I run.'

'I've never noticed that,' he said.

'I don't think you've ever seen me run,' I said, but then not many people had.

'It's all camera tricks, anyway. They'll make you look good even if you're not the most natural runner in the world.'

I hoped that was true. 'Did you meet your horse yet?' Archie's equine co-star seemed like the safest one to ask him about.

'I did! I haven't had to ride her yet – I'm getting some lessons next week – but we've been bonding with Polo mints.'

'What's she called?'

'Angelina.'

'Is her surname "Jolie"?'

'I'm afraid it is, she's a very beautiful horse but ...'

'Highly strung?'

'I really hope not because I'm still seriously ... worried about those scenes.' I think he meant scared. 'Talking about hot co-stars, has Carlo tried to get with you yet?'

'No,' I said, which was sort of true. 'He's fallen in love with Amber Leigh.'

'Seriously?'

'Well, Amber Leigh, the pretty sound girl, two hot make-up girls, the tall lighting guy and probably Sam Gross. What can I say, Carlo's a friendly guy.'

'Sounds like an idiot.'

'He's OK. He's funny. You'd probably like him. And I have to get on with him because there isn't really anyone else our age on set. Our stand-ins are both about thirty.'

'What about the other tribe members?'

'The whole set-up is that we're the sole remaining teenagers. There's a baby, but it's being played by a doll so there hasn't been a lot of interaction there.'

'No one will see the Jan and Straker romance coming, then. No one.'

I laughed. 'The script changes every day, so maybe by the end Straker will decide she'd rather die alone in a cave than get with Jan.'

'I've just got to bribe the scriptwriters, then.'

He laughed awkwardly and started to stir his tea unnecessarily. 'Well, I am one hundred per cent available to read the "get with" scenes with you. We can practise them a lot.'

Now I was bright red and unnecessarily stirring *my* tea.

'The fewer takes you need on these scenes, the happier I will be,' he said.

I met his eye. 'You *are* jealous, Archie Mortimer.' *Please, please, please let him be jealous.*

TheBizz.com

17th August

Drop everything! We have a new obsession. Introducing Archie Mortimer: Very fit, apparently very talented and soon to be hitting our screens as a Transylvanian vampire hunter in teatime Gothic thriller, *The Curse of Peter Plogojowitz.* Check out Archie's headshots *here* if you think you can handle it.

See what we mean?

Voice of Reason: But he's only 16!

Our Base Instincts: We don't care, he looks older and he's insanely hot!

We don't know if he's single, but if he is we don't think he'll stay that way (sadly). The rest of the cast members are equally beautiful and ALL FEMALE. There are blooming Transylvanian peasant maidens, mysterious vampire hunters and the drop-dead gorgeous wives of Dracula. We don't know if the BBC is singlehandedly trying to close the gulf in employment opportunities between the genders, but we haven't seen a cast list with this kind of ratio since *Sister Act.*

We have a feeling this will be the summer of their lives…

CHAPTER 14

'When I was on the set of Mad Max I
learned how to knit and threw myself into
it wholeheartedly. I knitted 24/7 pretty
much. It got to the point when I wasn't fun
anymore.'

Nicholas Hoult

'So the *other* hot drama boy in your life is back
in the country, is he?' Carlo was doing press-ups
before our scene, not because Dick was making
him, but so that his arm muscles would look
pumped. Half of me thought that was tragic and
half of me remembered that this film was going
to be in 3D on a three-metre-high screen. I would
have judged Carlo more harshly, but given I'd just
spent twenty extra minutes in Make-up having
the spot on my forehead *blended* away it wasn't

really fair. Make-up artist Bo (part woman, part white witch) was one of my new favourite people.

'He was, but now he's back in Transylvania.'

'Still weird,' said Carlo, who annoyingly wasn't even out of breath.

'What?'

'Transylvania. I'm not convinced he didn't make it up to escape you.'

'Hilarious. Besides, how do you always know what's going on in my life?' I asked him, wondering for the hundredth time why people said girls gossiped more than guys.

'It's one of the perks of being on a film set, you get to know everything about everyone.'

'Did Naomi tell you Archie was visiting?' I said, getting out of the way of a breathless electrician carrying a light bigger than himself.

'No. Naomi doesn't tell me anything.' That was good to hear because I'd shared things with Naomi that I didn't want to share with Carlo. 'Sound Dan overheard you talking to Naomi yesterday and warned me about my competition so I would have time to hide my broken heart.'

'Yeah, right.'

'You just don't have faith in me, E,' he said, getting up and clutching the space where his heart should have been. 'How was the romantic reunion, then?'

A pretty girl from the costume department walked past and smiled at Carlo while ignoring me. He smouldered back. I waited patiently till their little moment had passed.

'It was nice, thank you,' I said primly.

'Distance hadn't dampened the passion?'

'Talking of passion,' I said, although Carlo was the last person I'd have that conversation with, 'the rewrite on today's scene is—' I broke off, unsure of the right description.

'I know,' said Carlo. He dropped his voice. 'It's getting worse, right? And not just because our parts are getting smaller and the adults' parts are getting bigger.' Ah, he'd noticed that too. 'Did you read the bit about Winona and Raw's "moment of love epiphany in the midst of human hatred"?'

'Or the "flowering of a single bough in the midst of natural bareness",' I added gloomily. They'd hired another two new scriptwriters and, judging from the rewrites we'd seen, at least one of them wanted to be the Next Great Novelist. Every scene now had an introduction so saturated with metaphors and similes it was like a fungal infection (it was catching).

'I'm not at all sure that you two are standing in the right place.' Eddie and his clipboard were upon us. He sounded so stressed it couldn't be healthy. 'And I think this phone is yours, Elektra?'

I reached out for it but he dodged me. 'I'll give it back to you later. I wouldn't make a habit of leaving it in Costume, Sam nearly stood on it when he was getting into his warrior boots.' Eddie looked at his schedule again. 'No, you two are *definitely* in the wrong place.'

'We're moving in five,' said Carlo.

'You must have left point 2D at least ten minutes before schedule,' said Eddie. 'That really doesn't make my job any easier.'

'Sorry,' I said.

'*Dancing Queen! Feel the beat from the tambourine …*' blasted out without warning from some hidden on-set speakers, making me jump way higher than I could when directed. '*Having the time of your liiiffffe!*' sang ten electricians in perfect harmony.

Eddie stopped, pen in mid-air, and smiled a wide and slightly vacant smile. Then a little sway and I'd swear a sneaky bit of core work.

'See,' whispered Sound Dan, who'd come up behind me. 'Works every time. He's like that three-headed dog in *The Philosopher's Stone*.'

We all swayed for a bit. Two of the electricians lay down and gave it the full crunch. The music died and Eddie blinked. 'So, guys.' He smiled benignly and stretched. 'Maybe move to behind that thing.' He waved his pen at some random construction covered in tarpaulin. 'Lie low and listen out for the "Quiet on-set", yeah?' And he strolled off, looking like he'd just left a yoga class.

They were resetting at the end of a big Winona/Raw scene that was filming immediately before the one that Carlo and I were in. We stood together, leaning against something that closely resembled an Easter Island statue and watched.

Amber was draped artfully over a large boulder, a remarkably neat trickle of blood from her 'possibly fatal wound' perfectly highlighting her cheekbone.

Sam rushed in across the 'mossy ledge', braving the half-a-metre 'unfathomable cavern' below to where Amber lay, and pulled her into his arms. The boulder squeaked.

'Cut!' shouted Havelski, turning on Ahmed. 'The boulder's squeaking again.'

'We can clean that up in post-production,' said Sound Dan.

'I want it sorted now,' said Havelski. 'It's distracting. So?'

Amber and Sam nodded gloomily. It was indeed distracting. They'd been filming this scene for some time.

Ahmed gave the production designer's assistant a look and he grabbed his walkie-talkie sheepishly. 'Hi? Yah, is that Mina from polystyrene construction?' From where I was sitting I could only hear one side of the conversation. 'Yah, yah, it is Milo! Ha ha, you recognized my voice ... yah ...' He caught himself and refocused. 'Well, yes, there is a tiny bit of a problem.' He looked around. 'Actually, there is definitely a problem with the set. Yes ... hmmm ... no, I know ... the thing is, the boulders are squeaking. No ... no, not *speaking*, *squeaking*.'

Everyone was completely silent. Sam shifted, the polystyrene squeaked again. It sounded even louder this time.

'Oh, right ... OK, yes.' Milo replaced the walkie-talkie very slowly and carefully, as if with one false move he'd be attacked by a wild animal.

'Well?' barked Havelski. (Milo hadn't underestimated the risk.)

'So ... Well, I'm just repeating Mina here ... but, yah, *Mina* says that that just sort of ... *happens* with polystyrene.'

'There is no way to stop the boulder from squeaking?' asked Havelski very slowly.

'No, I'm not saying that,' said Milo.

'Good. I'm glad you're not saying that.' This was painful to witness. 'So, how do we stop the boulder from squeaking?'

'*Mina* suggested maybe if ... if *Sam* sort of props himself up on his elbows a bit more?'

Havelski raised an eyebrow. Just one but it was enough to make Milo visibly crumble.

'Um ... *Sir*, I could ...' He looked around, as if for divine inspiration, and miraculously seemed to find it. 'What about if I put something underneath the boulder to make it more stable? Does anyone have some paper I could fold up?' As divine inspiration went, it was pretty poor. Havelski's other eyebrow slowly began to rise. 'Or ... may-maybe not.'

Havelski didn't even dignify the suggestion with a response. He sighed. 'So, we are going to go from "I won't leave you, Winona" and we are going to "prop ourselves up on our elbows a bit more".'

'Lights.'

'Set.'

'Roll sound.'

'Rolling.'

'Roll camera.'

'Camera rolling.'

'Mark.'

'Scene thirty-two, roll A, twenty-three, take seven.'

'Action!'

RAW
I won't leave you, Winona.

WINONA
I know you won't, Raw.

RAW
Everything's changed since I met you.

WINONA
Really? I thought it was just me who was
seeing the world differently.

Amber paused dramatically and whispered,
'Winona looks lovingly.'

'Stop, Amber! Stop! Keep the camera rolling.
Amber, that's a *stage direction* not your line.'

'What was?'

'Winona doesn't *say* "Winona looks lovingly" she
just *does* it.' Havelski rubbed his eyes and sounded
very tired.

'Oh!' Amber giggled. 'I always tell guys when I'm
being loving.'

Somehow I didn't doubt that was true.

Sam and Havelski looked at each other. It was a
look of deep understanding and misery, like they'd
just been reminded of a dark chapter in their lives.

'I think you mean *warn* them,' Sam muttered.
The boulder squeaked again. 'Also *we* are now
finding it quite hard to *prop* on our elbows.'

'OK, *OK*,' soothed Havelski, assuming the
air of a man trying to retain control over a
sensitive international incident. 'We'll take it from
"everything's changed since I met you."'

RAW

Everything's changed since I met you.

WINONA

Really, Raw? I thought it was just me who
was seeing the world differently.

RAW

How could I not see the world differently?
You are so beautiful, Winona.

WINONA

What does beauty matter any more, Raw?

Amber looked into the presumably desolate post-
apocalyptic distance.

RAW

You are the only true thing keeping
me going, Winona, through this barren
wilderness.

WINONA

Raw, no, there is still beauty everywhere
if you know where to look.

Winona was kind of contradicting herself there but
in the scheme of things that could probably slide.

I know to look into your eyes, Winona.

Sam held it together for (a noble) three or four seconds. 'Sorry,' he said, sitting up. The boulder squeaked emphatically. 'Why do we have to say each other's names in every line? Surely they know who they're addressing? They're stuck on a cliff ledge and most of the human race is dead – there isn't much ambiguity.'

'It's romantic, Sam,' cooed Amber with (as the screenwriters would say) just a *hint* of underlying steel.

'Who wrote this scene? It's new, right?' Sam demanded. He was on the 'Warri' path now.

'Deepak,' sighed the script supervisor. 'He's just got engaged.' She rolled her eyes.

'Look, Havelski,' said Sam. 'I was told this film was going to be a cutting-edge exploration of humankind pushed to its extremities, or at least – if not better – a commercially successful action movie. I didn't imagine that I was going to be playing out a screenwriter's screwed up fantasies of marital bliss.'

Havelski sighed deeply. 'Can you just say the line, Sam? For me? For old times' sake? Please.'

So Sam said it, maybe a bit for 'old times' sake' (whatever Havelski was referring to), but probably mostly because he was being paid to.

I know to look into your eyes, Winona.

'Cut.' Havelski pulled his baseball cap low over his eyes and sat down. 'So, this is going to be a long, long afternoon. Take a break everyone and we'll try again.'

Rhona rushed off to get Havelski another treble shot of caffeine or gin or whatever he wanted. The people with clipboards and large watches gathered around Eddie looking concerned. Naomi joined their huddle.

'They're not going to get to you for a while,' she told us when she came over a few minutes later.

'Can we go and eat?' asked Carlo.

Naomi reached into her bag and pulled out a couple of energy bars. 'Er ... look behind you.'

Dick was waving at us from the sidelines, because why waste time eating bacon rolls when you could be mastering the short sword?

~~WAITING~~

WORKING

- % of time spent on Sound Stage A: 23% (the best, even the bits when I was waiting and/or being told off by Eddie for standing in the wrong place)
- % of time spent training with Dick: 15% (felt like 95%)
- % of time spent in dressing room watching daytime TV: 65% (if I ever found myself with a really dysfunctional family life I would now have the skills to distract myself with property makeovers). Apparently this percentage would drop steeply in term time when I would swap my dressing room for a similar room, designated The Classroom.
- % of time spent in buggies making not entirely necessary trips around Fairmount: 3%
- % of time spent with Archie: 0% because of work and because of mothers (a lethal combination)
- % of time texting Archie: not enough on account of all the stupid rules about phones
- % of time thinking about Archie: undisclosed because I am a strong and independent working actress

From: Stella at the Haden Agency
Date: 27 August 14:12
To: Elektra James; Julia James
Cc: Charlotte at the Haden Agency
Subject: *Straker* (working title)

Dear Both,

Panda have just been in touch. Hungary's definitely out as a location but they are now looking at filming just a couple of the scenes on location in *Mali*! So exciting! Could you check with Elektra's doctor about the current guidance on malaria in that region?

Kind regards,

Stella

CHAPTER 15

'In a way you do create a monster when you go out with someone well known.'

Emily Blunt

'Mum, there's really no point searching the internet for malaria symptoms. I'm not going to have contracted it just because they've suggested that we might go to Mali. I don't think it works that way.' I went back to marking up the latest version of the script with a yellow highlighter. Each new version came in a different colour, we'd already run through blue, pink and yellow. This one was green so at least I was making the pages look pretty.

'I'm not searching for symptoms,' she said. 'I'm researching risks.'

Researching risks was one of my mother's

all-time favourite things to do. I looked over her shoulder. 'So what are they?'

'Death,' she said, briskly closing the lid of her laptop. 'I'm not happy about this.' Obviously I wasn't happy about the risk of death either.

'I can take tablets,' I said. 'Forget about Mali. I'll make you a cup of tea if you stop talking about death.' She opened the laptop again. 'Now you're researching risks of malaria tablets, aren't you?'

'*Anti*-malaria tablets, yes.' She wasn't even apologetic.

'Tea? Will you make me one while you're at it?' asked Dad, coming in as I was filling the kettle. 'And who needs anti-malaria tablets? Are we going somewhere nice?'

'Elektra is going to Mali,' said Mum. 'At some undisclosed date. Supposedly.'

'That's brilliant,' said Dad calmly. 'See the world while someone else is paying.'

'It probably won't happen. They changed their minds about Hungary they'll probably change their minds about Mali.' But I really hoped they wouldn't.

'I'm not happy,' Mum said again. 'I mean why *Mali*?' she asked in a tone that was frankly disrespectful to that country.

'I think it's for the caves,' I said.

'I thought the film was set in a forest.'

'There are caves *and* a forest,' I said. 'Well, there are in this version.' I waved my copy of the script at her. 'Caves *and* forests *and* a lake.' I was a bit troubled by the scene in the lake, but I wasn't going to dwell on it because there had to be a decent chance that they'd revise that away.

'Quite a few ecosystems going on in this script,' said Dad. 'I thought nobody could get around because of all the disaster stuff.'

'They can't. I think it's just that the usual rules of geography haven't survived the environmental disaster.' If I sounded vague, it's because I was vague. The script rewrites weren't making the plot any easier to follow. 'And they're not just ordinary caves.' I skimmed through. 'Listen: "Jan and Straker, their mud-stiff clothes torn and stained with blood, gaze awestruck at the entrance to the cave. It is a narrow entrance the height of a cathedral carved by man ... or worse."'

'That doesn't make structural sense,' interrupted Dad. 'Who's advising these people?'

'Maybe it means that the carvings are made by man ... or *worse*.'

'Worse? What? Creative wolves?' Dad shook his head.

'I think you need to suspend disbelief a bit,' I suggested.

'And all rationality?'

'Won't it be dangerous filming in real caves?' asked Mum. 'And what about school?' Now she was sounding really panicked. 'It's bad enough that they're expecting Elektra to miss some term time,' (it really wasn't) 'without her having to drop everything and gallivant off to *Mali*!'

'I wouldn't be gallivanting, I'd be working. Anyway, maybe it will be at half term,' I offered, but she just did some angry *tssking*.

The doorbell rang. 'I'll get it. Moss is coming round to plan my birthday party.' I practically sprinted. It wasn't Moss, it was Eulalie, and that was still good. 'Come in, quick, my mum is melting down about Mali.'

Eulalie looked surprised and followed me back to the kitchen. 'Is it too early for a tiny glass of wine?' she asked, pulling out an obviously still-cold bottle from her enormous bag. It was quarter past midday so *probably* not. '*Bonjour, bonjour.*' She kissed my parents. 'So explain to me, Julia, this problem with Mali melting? Global warming?'

'No, it's *Mum* that's melting . . .' I started, but this was quite hard to explain. 'Never mind. Mali is fine, just fine. We might be going there to film.'

'Ah! This is *formidable*! You must go and see the Great Mosque of Djenné.'

Why did everyone think that filming on location was just one big opportunity to sightsee?

190

'And there is a tiny restaurant in Bamako that is cooking the best *fufu* in the world. Patrice's favourite meal.'

'Who is Patrice?' I asked. I had no idea where Bamako was and I had never tasted *fufu*.

'Just a man from long ago,' she replied. 'A very beautiful man. Unfortunately he is being dead.'

'Oh, I'm sorry.'

'It was his passion for bull running, his life was always going to be short.'

I filled her glass. 'Will you help me plan my birthday party, Eulalie? Moss is coming over, we're going to have a summit.'

'You didn't ask me to this summit,' said Mum.

'Nobody's really going to notice if I leave now, are they?' Dad was already edging out of the kitchen.

'*Bien sûr*,' said Eulalie, who was an expert on partying. 'We are starting with *le catering, non?*'

'*Non*. I don't think it's going to be that sort of party,' I said.

'It's not,' said Mum, though she poured herself some of Eulalie's wine, which made me optimistic. 'But let's *plan*. Let's make a list.'

Oh, God, she was *taking an interest*. Sure, if the party was actually going to happen in this (with the exception of my bedroom) very tidy house, Mum had to have a say, but how much of a say? Her enthusiasm was both unexpected and troubling.

'This is SO exciting,' she said with her pen poised. 'I haven't arranged a birthday party for you since the mishap with the Animal Man in Year Six. Are you going to invite just the girls in your year?'

What had I started? 'No, Mum, I'm not going to invite *just* the girls in my year and I'm certainly not going to invite *all* the girls in my year.'

'You don't want to hurt anyone's feelings,' she said, looking worried.

'It's not primary school. I think people will be *fine* about it. Anyway, I don't think I even know the names of everyone in my year.'

'That can't be true!'

'There are at least a hundred girls.'

'A hundred girls! I meant your form,' she said. 'You'll invite all of them?'

'Nope. I'll invite most of them, but not all.'

'Is this about you not getting on with that Flissy girl?'

I shrugged. 'I'm not going to invite her, but don't worry. She has no feelings.'

'Everybody has feelings.'

'Well, hers are very far from the surface. Anyway, she won't care. She wouldn't want to come to my party.'

'I swear, Elektra Ophelia James, that we could have been having this exact same conversation when you were seven. How many people are in your form?'

'Twenty-seven.'

'Well, that sounds like the right sort of number. And if you're not going to invite all your form,' she looked disapproving, 'you can invite a couple of others. You can invite *Archie* and Moss's Torr boy.'

'Archie might still be on location,' I said. Also Torr might not still be Moss's boy, but the status of that changed daily so I wasn't going to say anything. 'Twenty-seven isn't really enough people for a party. That's more of a gathering.'

'One hundred people is being the perfect number for a small party at home,' said Eulalie with conviction.

'If we had one hundred people in here there'd be limbs hanging out of every window,' said Mum.

If it was a good party there was a risk that there would be limbs hanging out of every window anyway, but I judged it best not to point that out. 'Sixty?' I asked hopefully. (Well, not that hopefully.) Mum shook her head. 'Fifty-five?' She shook her head again. 'Fifty? Come on, fifty is reasonable.'

'Fifty is being half a good party,' added Eulalie.

'You can have forty.'

'But—'

'Forty. Final decision.'

I gave Mum a hug because given the starting position this had turned out better than expected.

'Canapés,' announced Eulalie suddenly, as if she'd stumbled on some brilliant solution to one of the world's more serious problems.

'Sorry?' said Mum.

'The little yummy food things.'

'I know what they are. I just don't think they're going to be served at Elektra's sixteenth birthday party. Although,' Mum paused and gave it some thought, 'some crudités might be nice?'

Great. I was going to be throwing a very small party serving carrots and hummus. I was living the dream.

'What will you drink at this nearly-a-party?' asked Eulalie, waving her glass at me.

'Best not to mention drink,' I whispered in her ear as I filled her glass.

The doorbell rang again. 'Right, I am so ready to get this party organized,' said Moss before she was even inside the house. She was on a mission. Possibly to distract herself from whatever Torr stuff was – or more likely wasn't – going on, but probably just because organizing parties was new territory for us. 'I have a feeling this situation calls for a list,' she said.

'It does. Unfortunately my mum is already drawing one up.' We went into the kitchen and

Moss and Eulalie hugged for so long that I started to feel left out.

'What have you got so far?' Moss asked, joining us at the table.

'We have ...' I picked up the list, 'forty guests maximum.' Mum had written 'maximum' in capital letters and underlined it three times. 'Crudités, carrots? Celery? Popcorn ... Mum, why did you cross out popcorn?'

'It'll get everywhere,' she said.

'What do you think, Eulalie?' asked Moss, who was beginning to look as panicky as I was feeling.

'I think there should be a hundred people and interesting drinks and everyone should be dancing until dawn. *Bien sûr*. Also no carrots.' She was being less helpful than she thought she was.

'We need to go, Eulalie, if we're not going to be late,' said Mum, looking at her watch. They were going to see something arty together, working on the step-mother-daughter bonding thing. 'We'll finish this party planning later, Elektra. Eat properly, there's soup in the fridge and bread.'

Or maybe Moss and I could just eat biscuits and finish the party planning without interference. 'So, let's start again,' I said once they'd left. 'Coloured gel pens or felt tips? Or maybe metallics?'

'Elektra, restrain yourself. This list is purely functional.'

I went with the metallic pens. Obviously. Moss could eye-roll as much as she wanted; it wasn't going to get in the way of what was truly important to me.

'So, if your mum's agreed to forty, then fifty?'

'Why not?' Obviously that was a rhetorical question.

'If we want fifty to actually come,' said Moss, 'how many do you think we need to invite?'

'Erm, I'd say probably one in eight won't be able to come.' I had no idea.

'So then how many do we have to invite to get fifty turning up?'

I got the calculator. We both stared at it. This was veering dangerously close to maths.

'What do we do with it?' Moss whispered, as if we needed to dispose of a corpse rather than do some basic mathematics.

'We could try dividing fifty by eight?'

'Six point two five? That doesn't look right.'

'And then maybe times it by ten?'

'Sixty-two point five seems more like it. Let's just go with that.'

'Who's going to be the point five?'

'Archie, because he'll just spend his time following you around.' Moss was nothing if not a problem solver. 'Right,' she said. 'I'll come up with suggestions and you say "yay" or "nae". Jenny?'

'Of course.'

'You've got to say "yay", Elektra.'

'Why?'

'It sounds more official. This is a momentous occasion – it's our first proper party.' That was true. This list would probably be preserved in years to come, like the Red Sea Scrolls or the US Constitution. Thank God I'd had the foresight to use the metallic pens.

Ten minutes later we had this:

1. Me
2. Moss
3. Daisy
4. Hayat
5. Lyathe
6. Sofia
7. Keira-Joan
8. Tilly
9. Jenny

'I've just blanked.' Moss reached for a biscuit. 'I suddenly can't think of a single name.'

'We must have more than nine friends,' I reasoned.

'Actually, only seven friends so far,' Moss helpfully pointed out. 'It's nine including us and it's a bit sad if we have to be friends with ourselves. Let's go through our Facebook friends.'

I had to start a new list so that I could take advantage of Facebook's alphabetical name organization without any ugly crossing out. Moss judged me, but there are some things you have to prioritize over friendship. I ran through the A's (Abi, Abayomi, Alex), Caitlin, Daisy ... Hana, Lauren ... Rachael, Radiya, Zara. 'Even if Archie and Torr come, we can't have thirty girls and two guys.' I said.

'But if they were *our* two guys we would feel quite smug ... No, you're right, we *need* more guys,' Moss nodded sadly. I wasn't entirely comfortable with that statement but I knew what she meant. 'Carlo!' she declared, like it was a breakthrough.

'Not Carlo,' I said.

'Why not? He's fit, he's cool and it will make Archie jealous.'

I glared at her. 'Stop trying to make it sound like some sort of love triangle,' I said. 'It's just not like that.'

'But that kind of thing always happens on film sets,' she said, forgetting for a moment what Archie was doing this summer.

'Only because nobody ever gets a chance to see anyone they're not working with,' I said bitterly.

'But it's *perfect*. Archie in *lederhosen* in

Transylvania, Carlo on-set in Slough and you in the middle. It's the dream.'

'Firstly, Archie does not wear *lederhosen*. Ever. It's unthinkable.'

'And yet we are now both thinking about it,' said Moss.

'Secondly, you can't make some love triangle happen just because you think it would be quite entertaining.'

'But Carlo flirts with you.'

'He does, but as I've explained to you about five hundred times, he flirts with everybody. I've worked him out. It's just how he communicates. Also he's already got with about five different people on set. He's *busy*. Sorry, Moss, to mess with your fantasy, but I'm not feeling it and it's not going to happen.'

'You think he's hot, though.'

'That doesn't mean I want to get with him.'

'You have kissing scenes coming up . . .'

I sighed. 'I am aware.'

'You should still invite him.'

'Nope. Carlo goes out with the sound guys and is never separated from his fake ID. I am not going to invite him to a gathering at my house with crudités and background music. It's not happening.'

'What about other people from your acting class?'

'Issam and Ian, but that's it. Half of them are, like, thirteen and I'm not desperate enough to invite Christian or Brian. This is hopeless. And I'm still hungry, I need toast.' And with toast came inspiration. 'We're missing the obvious! We can ask some of the boys from St John's.'

'Brilliant plan,' said Moss sarcastically. 'Let's randomly ask some near-strangers from the neighbouring boys' school because that's what they're there for.' Put like that, it didn't sound that inspiring. 'Also Torr will hate it. He'll get all up himself about having to socialize with boys from his school in the year below.' He didn't mind socializing with girls from the year below, but I let that pass. 'Let's ask Daisy to bring some guys from her school?'

Sure, because if you're going to ask random near-strangers to your party it's better to get someone else to do the dirty work. 'OK, I'll ask her,' I said, making a little annotation beside Daisy's name in gender-normative blue.

'Ask her *now*,' said Moss desperately.

I sighed and got out my phone.

Planning my b'day party ALREADY. Unfortunately I know no guys. I have no life. HELP

You are DATING ARCHIE MORTIMER and are on set with HOT CARLO. I have no sympathy

I don't need sympathy. I need boys

200

I am screen-shotting this to hold you to ransom 😊

You wouldn't be laughing if you went to an all-girls school

Good point. I'll bring random guys. How many do you need?

'Loads,' suggested Moss, looking over my shoulder.

I ignored her. **Ten? And not TOO random. You've met my mother**

Moss looked under the table. 'Where's Digby? I want to give him my crusts.'

'He's in the corner in his basket,' I said, 'but he probably won't want them. I'm worried about him, Moss, he's still not right.'

Moss had been feeding Digby her crusts since she was a toddler. She went straight over to check on him. 'Hello, old boy,' she said, patting him. Digby gave a gentle snore but didn't move. 'He's lost weight,' she said.

'I know.' He was too skinny and I didn't like it. 'Mum says he'll be fine – well, the vet says that – I'm not sure if Mum believes him, I keep catching her checking him out. Digby, not the vet.'

'I suppose it's just old age,' said Moss. 'How old is he in dog years?'

That was maths again so we looked up a doggy-age calculator. Digby was eighty-five.

'Don't worry,' said Moss, seeing my face. 'My

dad's dog lived to be over a hundred in dog years, and Toto is already nearly thirty *in human years*.'

'Toto is a tortoise, Moss. I really don't think it's the same.'

Digby woke up and lazily crunched at one of the crusts Moss tempted him with. 'See?' she said. 'He'll be fine.'

My phone barked. **What's up in sunny London town?**

Not much. Just party planning with Moss. And it's raining

You can't be more bored than me. Everyone else is in a scene that I'm not in and I've spent literally six hours on BuzzFeed and my trailer's boiling and I can't sit outside because we're not allowed to get suntans because of continuity and the whole Plog general deathly pallor vibe. Also party?? Am I invited?

Tea party for Eulalie. Champagne and conversations about shoes. Not sure it's your thing

'Why did you say that?' Moss was looking over my shoulder.

You can't keep me away from Eulalie forever, Archie replied. **You're just scared that I'll fall in love with her.**

'Are you mad?' said Moss, when I didn't reply.

'*Obviously* I want Archie at my party. But it's *ages* away and I'm not counting any chickens or, you know, boyfriends ... I mean, anything could happen, we're barely getting a chance to hang out and Archie's on-set with *her*.' I tossed a copy of *Fresh Celeb* magazine over to Moss. '*Rising Teen Stars*, number six, Poppy Leadley. Check her out.'

Moss flicked through until she found the right page.

'No, not the big article about Instagram making you fat, it's the small side column ... the one with the *photograph*.'

Moss's eyes widened. 'She's nothing special.'

'Moss, she is stunning and wearing a small red bikini. You are allowed to admit that she is not hideous. And Archie says she's really good fun.' I was quite glad when Moss put Poppy Leadley away (burying the magazine under a heavy pile of architecture books like it contained a Horcrux).

'Shall we have a little Facebook stalk?'

'We can't. Her privacy settings are like the Pentagon. All you can see is a couple of profile pics that are her headshots.'

'You could friend request her?' suggested Moss hopefully.

'We both know I'm not going to do that.'

'Well, whatever she looks like, she's irrelevant,' said Moss loyally. She grabbed my phone. **Actually, planning my birthday party. Probs third weekend in October. When are you around?**

'Moss, that is not OK. You wouldn't like it if I texted Torr.'

'Stop panicking. He'll come.'

My phone barked straight away. **I'll make sure I'm around. I'm not missing it. I'll text tonight x**

'Aaaaw, look at your little shiny, happy face. No wonder Hot Carlo isn't getting a look-in,' said Moss.

'Don't mock me,' I said. 'And it still doesn't mean he'll be able to come. He's just an actor, he has to do what he's told.' But he wanted to come and that made me happy. 'Do you want more toast? Jam or honey?'

'Yes please, a slice of each. Stop trying to change the subject. It's still all really good with you two, isn't it?'

'Yes,' I said, and glowed a bit more. Then, because it was Moss and we pretty much always told each other the truth, I added 'mostly'. I hacked at the loaf. 'It's going really well apart from the fact we've only seen each other about three times since we started going out and the last time I saw him it was for, like, an hour because he had to rush off to catch a plane and kill bats. I don't know ... I talk to him a lot, when we've got time and we're allowed phones, well, mostly texting. Sometimes I worry that it's a bit like having a really fit, really perfect pen friend.' I dropped the wonky slices of bread into the toaster. 'It's not exactly how I imagined having a boyfriend would be.'

'Trust me, it sounds pretty good,' said Moss. 'I have the smallest, darkest suspicion that fit pen friends might be the dream relationship.'

I handed her a buttery slice. 'So, are you and Torr on or off at the moment?'

'We never do anything as useful as have an honest conversation, as you know, but he's been texting me a bit more again and I saw him yesterday.'

'That's good, isn't it?'

'Sort of. It's just, like, sometimes Torr's so on it and sometimes he's just not really there. I don't know . . .' She trailed off.

The temptation to advise Moss was strong but a) she hadn't asked me for advice and b) she was drawing a little heart in the puddle of butter on the table.

'It'll be *fine*,' I said. I'm not sure that I convinced either of us.

I was ninety-nine per cent asleep when my phone barked.

Are you awake?

Now I am. But I didn't mind because it was Archie.

Sorry. I'll text you tomorrow. G'night xx

Noooo, seriously I'm awake. But why are you still awake? What's going on?

Couldn't sleep. Big galloping through the forest scene tomorrow

I hoped he wouldn't break his neck. **You'll be FINE. Angelina will look after you**

Even Angelina might not be able to make me look good. They'll have to tie me on

Can't they use a stunt rider?

They are for the really scary bits – I'm just doing the EASY galloping through the forest apparently

Are you wearing a helmet? Occasionally I was my mother's daughter.

No. They weren't much favoured by nineteenth century vampire slayers

Ah. Fair. Well, don't let them make you do any bits you don't want to

I won't

Like seriously, do not play the hero

I won't

Also don't die

I will try not to and that was not the most reassuring text you have ever sent me

Sorry

If I'm still alive I'm probably back in London next week. Yay, my pen friend was coming to town. **But only on Tuesday and Wednesday**

Ah. **I'm pretty sure I have filming those days**

We're not doing too well at this meeting up stuff
Nope

There was a downside to our weirdly successful summer.

This was it.

TheBizz.com

Bringing you the all the Best Backstabbing in the Bizz . . .

29th August

They may be facing the end of the world and the destruction of the human race, but it looks like the *Straker* (working title) producers have some more pressing issues to worry about.

With yet another writer set to join the team, and the writing room already sounding like a scene from *Cheaper by the Dozen*, you've got to wonder what cracks (read major screw-ups) they're trying to paper over . . .

We are also sad to announce that working title Straker is apparently no longer working. We have it on good authority that it has been ditched, but the studios have yet to announce a replacement . . .

So here are some of our suggestions:

JAN you be any hotter?

RAW Meat

Don't you WARRI

Yes we JAN

Over RAW-t

Too hot to JAN-dle

And we're out.

Leave your suggestions below! ⇩⇩⇩

CHAPTER 16

'There's nothing worse than being on-set with an actor that you have to kiss, and then they, like, get all weird. You're like, "Calm down, dude."'
Chloë Moretz

I'd now got used to getting up before dawn. Like, considerably before dawn. That bit before dawn when drunk people have all gone to bed but the birds haven't woken up. That tiny, tiny window when the world is asleep. It was *lovely.* I was wide awake, I wasn't going to school and I wasn't waiting at the bus stop. Instead a large black car was quietly purring outside my front door.

'You really don't need to get up every day to see me off, Mum.' She was standing shivering on the pavement wrapped in her dressing gown. Digby was shivering beside her, looking like he'd quite like a dressing gown. They both looked *exhausted* and I felt guilty. I told Mum every day not to bother and every day she did. I think she was worried that the one day she didn't wave me off would be the day I'd be carried off by an exploding bit of scenery or something.

'I'm not going to let you disappear at this time of day with no one to wish you luck.' She'd stopped saying 'break a leg' since I'd told her that Sam had twisted his ankle in a fight scene and they'd had to rework the schedule to do standing still/lying down scenes while it healed.

'Mum, I'll be *fine*. Have a nice day and look after Diggers for me.' I gave her a big hug and got into the car. I felt a bit bad because the windows were tinted, so I could see her looking anxiously in, but she couldn't see me stretching out in *comfort*, so much comfort. This car was the most ridiculously comfortable car I'd ever been in. Actually, it was one of the most ridiculously comfortable *places* I'd ever been in.

'Everything all right back there, Elektra?' asked Kerim, the lovely driver.

'Very all right, thank you,' I replied, snuggling into my squishy leather seat. I pulled down the little compartment in front of me to discover two fat, flaky croissants, a thermos of dark hot chocolate and a tub of perfectly perky blueberries. The usual, embarrassing levels of spoiling.

I looked at my pages of script again for that day's filming. I'd spent most of last night looking at them, but no matter how many times I wished that the words would reform into a fight scene or even a climbing scene, it was still very much a love scene. I only had five lines, and even I had to accept that I knew them back to front and upside down. That was not the problem. I stuck the scripts back into my bag. Out of sight was an attempt at out of mind.

As usual, Naomi was there to meet me at the gates and within seconds I had the lanyard round my neck and was jumping into the back of one of the little buggies. Everything Naomi did, she did fast and she did efficiently. 'Do you want the good news or the bad news?' she asked as we drove down Godzilla Avenue.

'The good news, obviously.'

'Your call time has been put back to the afternoon.' Excellent, anything to defer the kissing scene.

'And the bad news?'

'I've agreed with your mum to get to work on your French revision.' Great. 'I vote for a chilled-out breakfast, then French revision, then set.' I wasn't sure I could face any more breakfast. 'There are pancakes on the menu this morning.'

In that case ... 'That would be lovely,' I said.

Naomi was literally perfect, even if she was going to make me do French revision.

'Right,' said Naomi. 'Let's get started.' She actually said this in French, but for obvious reasons I'm writing it down in English.

'Is it even worth it?' said Carlo, who had apparently failed his French GCSE and so was sharing this lesson. I would've felt smug, but I'd probably end up failing mine too.

'Of course it's worth it! Molière, *coq au vin*, Chanel, Clémence Poésy.' Naomi had a little dreamy moment. 'The Louvre, croissants—'

'I didn't mean that,' interrupted Carlo. 'I meant that we're due in Make-up in half an hour.' He crunched another Extra Strong Mint.

'Which means you've got thirty minutes to learn something,' said Naomi. 'Remind me, what scene are you about to do?'

'The one where Winona comes in when we are kissing,' said Carlo. Then he waggled his eyebrows at me and I didn't know whether to laugh or cry.

Naomi looked at me with sympathy. 'Ah, yes. Well, let's practise for it, and learn French at the same time.'

Carlo whooped. 'I am so up for that. First good idea for a French lesson I've ever heard.'

I laid my hot face on the cold table, closed my eyes and died a little.

'We will practise translating the *dialogue*, Carlo,' Naomi said, and I breathed. 'We will *not* practise the *action*,' I died again. 'Elektra, can you pass me your pages for today?'

I lifted my head and handed them over. I checked Snapchat under the table while she read them through. Archie had storied six hours ago, with the two-hour time difference meaning he'd posted at *four a.m.* I held my breath and clicked. There was some blurry movement, then a close-up of Archie's face and some flashes and, oh great, a couple of maidens of outstanding beauty. It wasn't that easy to work out what was happening without sound, but the caption read: *Impromptu bonfire party*. I switched my phone off.

'Well, some of these lines don't make a lot of sense in English,' said Naomi, looking up from the script, 'but we're going to try. Pens at the ready? Right, let's start with an easy one. "It just happened."'

'Er ... that's not that easy,' I said. 'Can we just say "It happened"?'

'Try both ways. Go on, write it down, have a go,' said Naomi.

'"It *just* happened" is actually quite an offensive line, now I come to think about it,' said Carlo.

'I mean, the kiss didn't "just happen" – Straker kissed Jan because she could no longer resist the overwhelming attraction between them.'

'I think Jan kisses Straker, actually,' I said.

'"They come together like attracting magnets" – that's what the stage direction says,' Carlo pointed out.

'Why don't you both have a go at translating "they come together like attracting magnets", too?' Naomi said. 'And before you ask, the French word for magnets is *aimants*. What is the meaning of the verb *aimer*? Carlo?'

'I literally have no idea.'

'I think you do. *Je t'aime, tu m'aimes . . .*'

'You OK, Elektra?' Naomi asked me later, as we walked over to the stage set. 'Are you nervous about the scene?'

'Honestly? A bit.'

'You've kissed someone before, right?'

'Yes,' I said, glad that I didn't need to lie. 'This is different though, isn't it?'

'I think it'll be easier,' she said. 'It's just work.'

'I'm not sure,' I said. Most people's 'work' didn't *require* them to kiss their colleagues while their other colleagues captured forty-eight frames a second. And I still hadn't recovered from the trauma of the last time I'd been kissed for 'work' by the overenthusiastic Damian in the final *Straker* callback.

'Think of it as mechanics. None of those *feelings* to worry about.' She said 'feelings' like other people would have said 'pneumonia' or 'atomic weapons'.

Naomi was right, though I was pretty sure that if I was to act the scene well, I would have to summon up some sort of feelings. At least on the surface. Also 'mechanics' was a creepy sort of word.

'I just wish it wasn't Carlo. I mean, I quite like him, but I'd rather kiss a complete stranger. Carlo will tease me.' And the whole stupidly hot thing didn't help either, but I didn't say that.

She slung her arm round my shoulder and gave me a hug. 'He probably will tease you, but you know what? It won't kill you. You could always tease him back. Also . . .' She paused. 'I don't want to be really annoying, but remember this is acting. *Straker* is going to kiss *Jan*, Elektra is not going to kiss Carlo.'

That *was* quite annoying. It was also exactly what Daisy and Moss had said. I hadn't asked Archie for his opinion.

'So,' said Havelski. 'Ready for today?'

'Yes,' said Carlo. 'Oh, yes.'

'Maybe remember to be *professional*,' said Havelski,

by which I think he meant no tongues. This was torture.

I didn't say anything. I don't think it was helping that in my head this scene was always going to be The Damian Scene.

JAN
(Jan looks up at Straker and this time his voice is firmer, more the voice of a man than a boy.) I promise you, Straker, I *will* keep you safe.

STRAKER
(Straker is crying now.) Nobody can keep anyone safe here, not any more. You shouldn't make promises like that.

Crying on cue is so much easier than kissing on cue.

JAN
(Jan puts his hand up to her face and brushes away a tear. They are standing very close.) I won't let you down, Straker.

Except that the way it was now written, Damian's lunge in rehearsal wouldn't have been improvisation.

STRAKER

(Takes Jan's hand and is very gentle.) I
know. *(They come together like attracting
magnets and kiss.)*

'Maybe if Carlo puts his hand on your face first?'
suggested Havelski.

'Maybe hold the eye contact?' added Ahmed.

'Also your shoulder, Elektra ... Not quite sure
why it's at that angle?' That was Havelski again.

'Yes, she's blocking Carlo's light,' butted in one of
the lighting guys.

Today would, of course, be the day when every
direction was given using our real names. Too
many people have an opinion on kissing. I'm pretty
sure we'd have had less direction if we'd been
stabbing a wolf or something. This had all gone
very smoothly when I'd practised with Archie. Now
I was regretting practising, it felt a bit messed up.

'OK ... *Good*,' Havelski said unconvincingly.
'Maybe one more? Maybe if you lean back a bit
more, Elektra, and Carlo, can you be more ... *over*
her.'

I wanted to go home.

I leaned back, Carlo hovered over me – so, so
close to me – and I looked up to see Sound Dan
looming over us too, holding the boom. His T-shirt
had ridden up and I was struggling not to focus on

the carpet that was his belly hair. He caught my eye and winked. I really liked Sound Dan but this was not helpful.

'Hey,' said Carlo quietly, 'I'm the one you're meant to be looking at.' He didn't wink; maybe it would have been easier if he'd winked.

'Let's try again,' said Havelski. 'Tap into some of that great chemistry.'

We tried, but there's a lot of difference between kissing and chemistry equations.

'You need to make it longer,' said Ahmed, when we'd cut again. 'We need you to be kissing when we cut in and kissing when we cut out, so, you know, much longer than you would kiss in real life?'

We wouldn't kiss in real life.

'OK.' Havelski clapped. It wasn't applause. 'Let's try a run with me counting? One, two ... three ... four, five and, OK, breathe. Take a break while we reset.'

I lay very still on the polystyrene rock while Carlo manoeuvred himself off me far too carefully. He was moving really awkwardly, like people do when they nearly bump into each other and both try to go the same way. There was no eye contact. None. And suddenly I really did need a break.

'Do you want a mint?' Carlo said a few minutes later, fumbling in his pocket. We were standing on the sidelines while they reset some lights. I felt like they should have given us those tinfoil blankets that they give trauma victims. 'I don't mean you *need* a mint ... You know what, E, I don't think either of us is enjoying this as much as I thought we would.' I was way past the point of getting offended.

We sat down side by side, leaning against the nearest tree (real trunk, fake leaves) and crunched through the mints. I was thinking about Archie and I had no idea who Carlo was thinking about, probably more than one person. I hoped that thinking about Archie would help me feel better, but it didn't. I was pretty sure that I was having a lot less fun than he'd had at his impromptu bonfire party or whatever kissing scenes he'd had to do.

'Let's just go for it, E,' Carlo said after a bit, 'because otherwise we're going to be here forever doing take after take after take, and it's going to get weird.'

It was already very weird so I just nodded, and then Continuity and Make-up bore down on me with brushes and wipes and powder and declared me 'good to go'. Optimistic.

'So?' said Havelski. 'We take it again from the start.'

And we did. Again and again, until everyone

was happy with the speed and the position and the sound we were making and the length and the placement of my hair and Carlo's hand and my right foot. Apparently my right foot was very problematic.

It didn't get any easier.

It didn't feel like mechanics.

It felt like someone was kissing me.

It felt like the wrong person was kissing me.

It felt confusing.

My phone barked and I jerked awake. The back of the car had almost become a second (more luxurious and much tidier) bedroom to me, and I was used to falling asleep on the way home. Today had been an especially tiring day. Carlo had gone out with Eddie and Andy and was probably doing some practising with random girls in case we had to reshoot the kiss. But I just wanted to get home.

Have you got your key? It was Mum.

Nope x I never had my key. I rarely needed my key.

I'm out so go to Eulalie's and wait till I text you.

Where are you?? I was a tiny bit put out that she seemed to have a life. I mean obviously that was great, but if she could have waited until a time when I was also having a life or had left home or even had just had an easier day that would be

220

better. **Are you annoyed with me?** I asked. They were oddly cold texts. I must have done something to make her cross. I scrolled the possible reasons in my head – yes, there were plenty of candidates. **Was it my bedroom? I'm SORRRREEE I'll tidy it up when I get home xxx**

No reply for ages. And then: **At the vet's. Digby's not great.**

CHAPTER 17

'I want less me. I want people to have less me.'
Jennifer Lawrence

'I don't think you should stay. It'll upset you.' A fat tear was hesitating on the end of Mum's nose.

'Maybe I should stay and you should go out?' She wasn't a 'sobbing in the kitchen' sort of person. I was worried about her.

'No. I want to stay and hold his paw.'

'I do, too,' I said. I sort of did, but I was scared. Digby came and leaned against my legs. I wanted to think it was love, though I'm pretty sure it was mostly for support. He was trembling. I patted him and could feel every single rib. He'd got skinny so fast. I knew why we were going to do it, but that wasn't making it feel OK. I got that itchy feeling in my nose that meant I was going to cry. Maybe it was hay fever. No, it wasn't hay fever. Mum silently handed me a tissue and a biscuit.

'At least he'll be in his own basket, at home.'

My phone barked and we all jumped.

Digby?? 🐾 Do you need me to come over?

I did quite want Moss to come over because she wouldn't have been as messed up by it all as the rest of us, but I looked at my mum and I knew it wasn't a good time. **Maybe later?**

Are you OK?

Two seconds later: **Of course you're not OK, sorry, call me when it's done**

When it's done.

Two seconds later: **SORRY everything's coming out wrong. Call me when you can**

I tried to give Digby my biscuit. Six months ago – even two months ago – he'd have wrestled me to the ground and fought me to the death for it. Now he just looked at me and basically shook his head. I hugged him – but gently, so I wouldn't break him.

Dad came into the kitchen with his phone in his hand. 'I just got a message, she'll be here in ten minutes.'

'She' was the travelling Doctor Death for pets. Her website didn't describe it that way – I'm paraphrasing.

'I'd better make a fresh pot of tea,' said Mum, but stayed where she was – crumpled in a heap at the table.

'I don't know if the vet will have time for tea. I think it's pretty quick.' Dad patted Mum's head, a bit like she was a dog.

I looked at Digby and gulped. He looked back at me and I swear his expression was more trusting than ever. I felt like a hangman.

When the vet arrived she seemed much too young and much too smiley and much too pretty. She crouched down and scratched Digby behind the ear, and he gave her one of his 'love at first sight' looks. He didn't wag his tail, though, and he didn't get up from his basket.

'Poor old boy,' she said in a strong Australian accent. 'You're not in a good way, are you?'

'It happened fast and even so, I think maybe we left it a bit long,' said Dad, because Digby couldn't answer.

'Everyone does, it's hard to let them go.'

Yes.

I was holding it together until she opened her bag and I saw all the syringes. That was too much. Dad put his arm round me and I tried to dry my eyes on his jersey, but the tears kept coming.

'Say goodbye to him now, Leggy,' Dad said. He

hadn't called me Leggy since I was about four. 'I don't want you to stay. We'll be with him.'

I kissed Digby on his nose. 'I'll miss you,' I said.

Ten minutes later I heard the front door bang shut and then a car engine. The vet had gone, which meant that Digby had gone too. I felt horrible. I should have stayed with him. A whole part of my childhood had just left the house and there wasn't anything I could do to make it not true.

'Do you want a cup of tea?' my mum yelled up the stairs. Her voice was all fake normal.

'No, it's OK,' I called down, equally fake normal.

Footsteps and then a knock at my door.

'Elektra?' Dad put his head round the door. 'Are you all right?' I wasn't all right and this was one of the few times he couldn't make it better. He looked at me. 'No, of course you're not. Move up.' He sat on my bed and didn't even comment on the fact that I hadn't made it and that I'd snuck in a neon cushion amongst my pillows. 'I'm not all right either. Who am I going to watch the football with now?'

'I'll watch football with you, Dad.'

'No, you won't,' he said, 'but that's fine.'

We sat there for a bit without talking, shoulder to shoulder.

'You know we didn't have a choice?'

'I know,' I said, and I did. 'What was ... it like?' I had to ask because otherwise I was just going to keep imagining.

'Quick. It wasn't horrid for him. He just went to sleep.'

'Really?'

'I promise.' He looked at me. 'Do you want to come downstairs?' he asked. 'Your mother's making tea and I'm ninety-nine per cent certain she'll start baking any second now.'

I shook my head. 'I just want to be on my own for a bit. Is that OK?'

'Of course it is. I'll call you when something comforting comes out of the oven?'

'Thanks ... I love you, Dad.'

'I love you, too.'

I wasn't going to text Archie because it wouldn't help.

But I really wanted to text him. Digby had loved Archie, it's what he would have wanted.

Hey?

Archie didn't reply. I spent a miserable half hour plaiting the fringes on my bedspread and leaking tears.

I wasn't going to text him again. Ten more minutes of solitary sobbing and I picked up the phone.

You about?

Double texting and no reply.

I needed my dog.

I got into bed with all my clothes on and screwed my eyes closed tight. All I could see was Digby. My phone barked and I scrambled for it.

Sorry. Mad time sword fighting. Ah, yes, because we were having parallel lives on different continents. **Poppy is annoyingly good**

I'm sure she was. I couldn't even bother caring. **Digby's gone**

Gone where?

No, really gone. Had him put down today

Are you OK?

I stared at the phone. I don't know why, but I'd expected something different. A bigger reaction, more dramatic, more *sorry*. **Sort of**, I texted (lied).

You're not OK. Two seconds later: **Of course you're not. That was a stupid thing to say. Sorry. Call me?**

My text conversations today were falling into a pattern. I didn't call him, I wasn't sure what I would say or if I'd even be able to speak.

The phone barked. He was phoning. I didn't pick up. Five minutes later it barked again and I wondered if it would be callous to change the ringtone. This time it was a text. **Elektra??**

I still didn't pick up. I just looked at the phone and it looked back at me. I was regretting the screensaver too – me and Digby in matching Christmas jumpers.

Long minutes passed. The phone barked again.

Really, really sorry. Diggers was an awesome dog

He was the best dog in the history of dogs, I replied.

He probably was

How's stuff in Transylvania? I have no idea why I asked. I didn't care. In my head 'Transylvania' sounded sarcastic. I hated Transylvania.

Does that mean you don't want to talk about Digby any more?

Yes.

Stormy

I didn't mean the weather. Although I was quite glad that the sun wasn't shining in that miserable, vampire-populated, tree-infested, soul-sucking, Archie-stealing place.

There's not much going on. I haven't had any scenes for 2 days. We've mostly been sitting eating Jaffa Cakes

Digby had sincerely loved Jaffa Cakes. And who was 'we'? I didn't have enough energy for this conversation. I put the phone in the drawer beside my bed. It barked again within seconds. I looked at the drawer. The phone barked insistently. I took it out, wrapped it in two pairs of woolly black tights and put it back. It barked again and again, just more muffled. I gave in and read my messages.

I'm REALLY sorry about D Then: **Miss you.** Then: **Miss you xx** Better. Then: **Come and see me**

Sure, I'll be there tomorrow. That was not a helpful suggestion. What did Archie think I was going to do? Just hop on a plane? The midnight flight from Luton to Cluj-Napoca would probably be the best one. Or maybe he expected me to nip down to St Pancras and get on a train to Paris then change stations and get the train to Munich and then catch the sleeper train to Budapest and then find a train to Bucharest that goes via Barsov and then I don't know? Get a taxi? Ha! Easiest, cheapest thing in the world to get to Dracula country.

Not that I've given it any thought.

I don't think that's going to happen, I texted, just in case my last message hadn't been sarcastic enough.

Because of your mum?

Right, because otherwise I'd just race across countries at his beck and call? And that would make everything OK? Sure. And actually no, I wouldn't abandon my mum right now because she was probably crying in the kitchen.

No, not my mum. I shouldn't have started this conversation. Digby had made me all vulnerable. My phone barked again.

We could split the fares?

Thanks but no. I switched my phone off, properly off this time, and pulled the duvet over my head and closed my eyes. The room was very, very quiet.

Moss rang the doorbell when we were having supper. It was an unfestive feast. For the last couple of weeks Mum had spent all her time boiling chicken for Digby and feeding us pizza, and now she'd been cooking for hours in some sort of displacement frenzy and the table was groaning with food. But nobody was eating anything so we all leaped to answer it. I got there first.

'I hope it's OK that I came round?' Moss held back, like she was a bit nervous, and then just sort of launched herself at me. It was nice, really nice. 'It's just, you weren't answering your phone and I knew my texts had been all wrong and I just wanted to see you.'

I'd wanted to see her too; I just hadn't realized it. 'My phone was off,' I said. 'Come in. There are enough sausages to feed an army.' And we both looked at each other, thinking how very much Digby would have enjoyed an army's worth of sausages.

'Did you speak to Archie?' asked Moss. We'd escaped from the gloom in the kitchen and were curled up together in my bed. Moss had refused to go home and I hadn't tried very hard to change her mind.

I shook my head in the dark.

'It might help?'

'I don't think so.' It wouldn't help because Archie wasn't around. I didn't want his words or even his voice. I wanted a real live person. But I had Moss on one side of me, smelling of chocolate, and Digby's blanket on the other side of me, smelling of Digby.

I felt as OK as I could feel. Which wasn't very OK.

TheBizz.com

Bringing you the all the Best
Backstabbing in the Bizz . . .

31st August

Rising English teen star Archie Mortimer (see what got him cast as a sexy vampire hunter in The Curse of Peter Plogojowitz _here_) has, as predicted, been taking full advantage of every on-set opportunity. Our mole tells us that he's been - killing it - on-and off-set with the ladies.

Tragically, we couldn't find anyone prepared to name names. But we're problem solvers here at The Bizz, and after an extensive campaign of Insta-stalking our bets are on Poppy Leadley, seventeen, who plays 'Ana' in the new TV series. She was pictured standing next to Archie in a post from just last week. Which she posted to her own Instagram.

Being undead has never looked so fun . . .

☆
CHAPTER 18

'I love what I do, but I'm also surprised I'm still sane. Or somewhat sane.'

Nick Jonas

'This is really good of you, Eulalie,' said Mum, opening the door and simultaneously pressing a cup of very strong black coffee into Eulalie's hand. 'It's the one day I can't go myself and I think it would be nice for Elektra to have someone with her today.'

Part of me (the mature-working-actress part) thought that I should protest, but a bigger part of me (the too-sad-to-pull-off-mature-anything part) wanted Eulalie there. It was five thirty in the morning and even though my dog had just died, I had to go to work. Eulalie would be nice to me but, more importantly, she wouldn't ask me every five minutes how I was feeling like Mum would.

'Of course I will be going,' announced Eulalie, gulping down the coffee in one and presenting her cup for a refill. I'd never seen her so early in the morning before. She, unlike anyone else standing in our very tidy kitchen, was made-up and sparkly and ready to go. 'What do I have to be doing?' she asked. 'Other than being nice to Elektra. Can I be giving my opinion on everything?'

'No, no, *non*. Whatever you do, you can't be giving your opinion on *anything*,' I said with a panic in my voice. Eulalie and 'Quiet on-set' would be an interesting mix.

'I've been on film sets before and *everybody* was wanting my opinion, but maybe that was because I was having *un petit moment* with the star.'

'Who?' I asked, momentarily diverted.

'*Pff*, I can't be sure exactly. It was the very early eighties, so it was maybe Mr X. He was having *a lot* of *petit moments*. Or maybe it was Mr Y, he wore the most beautiful suits. Maybe it was both of them.' The names I'm not repeating were instantly recognizable. Also I'm not sure that they were both alive in the eighties, though I let it pass. 'Even on this sad day I am thinking it will be *très* interesting.'

'You need to eat, Elektra,' said Mum, gulping her own coffee.

'It's fine. I can have something in the car.'

She shrugged like it didn't matter. Her eyes were all puffy; I think she'd cried more than I had.

My phone barked and everyone flinched. It was Archie. **You're probably still asleep but I just wanted to say that I'm really sorry that I'm not around x**

I'm awake. I'm glad you texted x

Going to set?

Yep

That's tough for you today. I've got a free day. Thinking about you. Good luck xx

'Archie?' asked Mum. I nodded. 'I thought so, it's nice to see you smile.'

I didn't manage to stay smiling. We all stood in the hall in silence for long, painful minutes waiting for my driver. Not even Eulalie could think of anything to lift the mood.

'Mum?'

'What?'

'You keep looking over at Digby's basket. It's not very healthy.' Also it was freaking me out. I half expected to see his little spectral face poking out over the edge. I swallowed. 'Maybe we should throw it out?'

We looked at each other and shook our heads. Too soon.

'OK,' I said. 'I'm just going to move it into the big cupboard in the hall.'

'I'll do it,' Mum said. 'I'll clean it out and hide it away and in a week or two I'll give it away.'

'Will you be all right today?' I asked, feeling more sorry for her than for myself.

'It's just a filling. I'll be *fine*,' she said. We both knew I hadn't been talking about her dental appointment.

'Say thanks to Moss for me.' I hadn't had the heart to wake her.

Mum nodded. 'I'll drive her home.'

Eulalie got her phone out of her magnificent handbag. 'I shall be twittering the news.'

'Oh, please don't tweet about Diggers.'

'Of course I'm not twittering about Digby! That would be disrespectful, *non*?'

Oui. I looked over her shoulder as she typed.

Off to Fairmount with DG. 'You are "DG",' she explained to me proudly. 'Darling Granddaughter.'

'I don't think anyone's going to know what you're talking about.' Which was not a bad thing.

'But of course all my followers are knowing who DG is, and why she is going to Fairmount. I am cheeping of you often.'

Oh, God.

'At first there was a little confusion because they thought I was spelling *dog* wrong—' She broke off and looked guilty.

'It's OK,' I said, giving her a hug, 'you can say the D.O.G. word.'

'Sometimes I put a little picture of you to make my food chain look prettier.'

'Feed.'

'Sorry?'

'Your Twitter *feed,* not food … never mind. How many followers do you have?'

'Not many.'

Good.

'40,354 … Oh, no, 40,355 …' She stared at her screen for a bit. 'You are having ninety-seven favourites already.'

'So where are you wanting me to be?' asked Eulalie, bouncing up to me for the fourth time since we arrived on-set.

'You just stay in that chair,' I said, pointing.

'But I am not being *helpful* in that chair.'

'Really you are being very helpful in that chair,' I said. What I meant was that her getting out of the chair would be very unhelpful. Eddie, who'd been trying really hard to be lovely to me since I'd told him about Digby, was on the verge of a nervous breakdown. Sound Dan had already medicated him by playing several verses of *Take a Chance*, but the effect had been somewhat marred by Eulalie's enthusiastic attempts to join in. 'Please … Mr Havelski's coming over.'

'It's a great pleasure finally to meet you, Madame.'

Finally? *Finally?*

'Sergei!' she said, and kissed him on both cheeks – twice.

Sergei? 'Er ... you two know each other?' I asked.

'Almost,' said Eulalie. 'We are being friends on the social media.'

They were standing *very* close together. 'Social media?' Please don't let it be Tinder. Please. The thought of Eulalie swiping right on my director was the stuff of nightmares. Realistic nightmares.

'We are Twitter friends,' explained Havelski. Well, he obviously thought it was an explanation – it wasn't clearing much up for me.

'We are following each other,' said Eulalie, and they both beamed. They were exactly the same height. They might also have been the same age, but with Eulalie it was hard to tell. 'I am finding out all about your director ...'

'... and I am finding out all about your grandmother.'

They were finishing each other's sentences. I panicked. What embarrassing things had I told Eulalie? And especially what had I told Eulalie *about Havelski?* And what had Eulalie told *everybody* about DG? This was dreadful. I badly needed to get hold of her phone but Eddie had confiscated it after an earlier (unfortunate) Snapchat episode.

'So, let's find you a more comfortable chair. My chair, maybe?' He snapped his fingers and had someone carry over the folding chair with DIRECTOR printed across the back. I'd never seen him sit in it, I think it was just a prop to add to the whole vibe of fear and awe. 'And later—' he twirled Eulalie into the chair – 'later, you and I can get to know each other IRL.'

'*Ooooh, in real life,*' mouthed Carlo. He was very much enjoying my discomfort.

'So,' said Havelski, turning to me. 'Eddie told me about Digalot. Are you all right?'

'Digby,' I said, although Digalot would have suited him too. 'Yes, I'm fine.' I wasn't fine, but I was here to work.

'Well,' he said, giving me an unexpected hug, 'if suddenly you are not fine then just shout and we will stop everything.'

He'd stop everything for a dog?

'*So!*' It was one of Havelski's let's-crack-on 'so's and without him saying anything else, the right people started milling round doing whatever bits of technical magic they needed to do.

I watched with the script in my hand.

JAN
No, Raw, don't hurt her! (*Winona cowers.*)

RAW

The woman has food. (*Jan stands between Raw and Winona. Raw brandishes a spear.*)
Get out of the way, young fool.

JAN

(*Jan stands his ground, confident that Raw will not hurt him.*)
She's Straker's mother. Leave her alone.

On the page, this was a perfect moment. Action, emotion, family. On the set, there was all the blocking and standing in and light tinkering, and then all the usual takes from different angles and resets and interruptions when the sound quality wasn't pure enough or something else got in the way.

RAW

(*He laughs bitterly*) Family means nothing here. Nothing. Get out of the way.

WINONA

Family means everything here. Family is the only reason I get up in the morning. The only reason I forage, the only reason I eat these (*she gestures to a bowl of squirming grubs*), the only reason I bother

to try to clean myself or the places where
I shelter. Family is the only reason I
keep any respect. Family is the only thing
that keeps me human. (*Breaks, looks at
Raw*) And you, are you still human or are
you an animal?
(*Raw looks past Jan, makes eye contact
with Winona. There is a spark of attraction
between them.*)

'CUT!' roared Havelski. He stood with his arms folded across his chest, stretching up to his full, not very impressive height. He was in grumpy dictator mode. Eulalie was loving it. 'Are we all working from the same script? Because the directions that are in my script say: "There is a spark of attraction between them". Yes? Good. So is there any chance that you two could look at each other with something other than dislike?' He wasn't bothering with any of the sugar-coating that Carlo and I usually got. Eulalie had grabbed *my* script and was ostentatiously fanning herself. She was enjoying this way too much.

'That wasn't *dislike*. If I'd wanted to look at *Winona* with dislike, you'd know about it,' said Sam, glaring at Amber with even more animosity than in the last take.

'There's a thin line between dislike and

attraction,' said Carlo, forgetting where he was, and speaking so loudly that Eddie, Havelski, Ahmed, three sound guys, a huddle of random lighting and electrics guys and two girls from Continuity all turned and glared at him.

'Well, thank you for the life advice, Carlo,' said Amber. 'What are you? *Sixteen? Seventeen?*'

I could see where she was coming from.

'That's not what's happening here,' said Sam, and he and Amber shared a long look.

'I don't care,' said Havelski. 'I really Do. Not. Care. Let's go again.' He motioned for the relevant people to spring into action.

'Hang on, we need more grubs,' said a very brave and junior person. Amber shrieked. To be fair, if I'd been standing where Amber was standing I'd probably have shrieked too. The bowl had overturned and there were little white maggots wriggling everywhere. It was revolting. I edged backwards in case any of them escaped at high speed in my direction.

'*Cherie!*' said Eulalie from behind me. 'This is so *passionnant!*'

'Get some more grubs. NOW!' Havelski stamped aggressively on the wriggly line of intrepid bugs that had made a break for the big time and were investigating his shoe. It was too late to say that no animals had been harmed in the making of this movie. It wasn't really my idea of a *passionnant* moment.

It took some time before everyone was ready to go again. Amber had to have a little private meditation behind some scaffolding. Some things can't be hurried.

'Quiet on-set ...'

WINONA
Family means everything here. Family is
the only reason I get up in the morning.

If Amber were my mother, I don't think I would get up in the morning.

The only reason I forage, the only reason
I eat these—

Her deep emotional moment was disturbed by a barrage of yapping. Kale tore across the 'grass' towards Amber's boulder like The Dread was after him, not just a horribly frazzled-looking assistant-pom-pom-wrangler.

'Cut!' roared Havelski. 'And will someone get that damn dog off my set!'

'*Baby*,' cooed Amber to Kale with more warmth than I suspect she'd ever shown towards a human. 'Come to Mummy.'

It was a big boulder and a small dog, but Amber's assistant was plainly more afraid of Amber than she was of Havleksi. Sound Dan hoicked her up and she handed the dog to Amber.

Amber cuddled Kale to her famous and much-photographed bosom. Kale looked understandably smug. He was such a snake.

'Were you feeling jealous?' Amber cooed. (To him, not me – even in my newly dog-less state I did not envy her Kale.) 'There is *nothing* to be jealous of. This nasty man—' she paused, looked at Havelksi and Sam in turn and settled on Sam – 'isn't going to be your new daddy.'

'No, mate,' Sam spluttered. 'Nothing to worry about there. But if I was, you'd be the first casualty.' He looked at the grinning dog with loathing. 'It's almost worth a quickie marriage.'

Eulalie laughed loudly.

'Will somebody take that ... *thing* away?' Havelski was quite red in the face now. No one stepped forward. 'Do I have to do everything around here?' No one replied. Havelski moved towards Kale – in fact, he pretty much launched himself at Amber's cleavage, which must have been a troubling trip down memory lane.

More yapping, more swearing, a snort of suppressed laughter from someone who would probably have to fire himself from the production immediately. I wanted to look away, but I couldn't.

'Ow! He ... It bit me!' Havelksi swore. 'It ...' he swore again, 'bit me!'

'Are you being all right?' asked Eulalie, who had escaped from her chair, again hotly pursued by Eddie.

Havelski turned back to the assembled masses like a returning war hero. 'I am being all right.' He held up his finger which was bleeding. 'But that *animal*—' he left a dramatic pause – 'is banned from my set.'

'That animal' was currently licking up a couple of escaped maggots with the sort of joy I reserve for Oreos.

'You'll need a tetanus shot for that,' said a nurse who had magically appeared.

'See how your ... *creature* has poisoned me?' Havelski said to Amber. I really hoped a camera was still running.

'You provoked him. He's *stressed*.'

'WE'RE ALL STRESSED!' It was a very loud statement of fact. 'And mostly because you two are now massacring what is already a rat's nest of a script.' He turned to Rhona. 'Get me the writers. NOW!' Then he turned to me and Carlo. 'The chances of getting to your scene today is less than zero. I'd say learn your lines for tomorrow, but frankly what's the point? They'll have changed them again by the morning.' Then there was a rant in Hungarian that I'm pretty sure none of us would have wanted to understand. Eulalie quelled him with the tiniest of dark looks and he remembered he was meant to be being nice to me and said in a much gentler voice, 'You go home early, Elektra. Rest up and tomorrow will be easier.' He looked back at Eulalie, who was probably enjoying the whole drama more than anyone else. 'So, Madame, another day, perhaps? A time when I am not ridden with maggots and wounds and an execrable script?'

'*Bien sûr*,' said Eulalie, with the confidence of a woman for whom broken dates were always rearranged.

He smiled at her and turned back to the chaos that was his set. 'OK, everyone, I give up. That's it for today.'

Havelski had stopped everything for a dog, but it was definitely the wrong dog.

Dear Parents,

I hope that your daughters are enjoying the last days of summer holidays and have had just the right balance of relaxation and work. I'm sure that they are ready to take on what promises to be an exciting and challenging year! A parent-teacher meeting is scheduled shortly, but in the meantime just a handful of notices:

1. We are confident that your daughters are well prepared to take the GCSE exams in their stride. Whilst they will need to work hard, we will be aiming for as stress-free an experience as possible and we would respectfully ask parents to help us keep anxiety levels low.
2. The Head of Year this year is Mrs Green who will be assuming all the usual pastoral responsibilities alongside her language teaching.
3. UNIFORM – last year witnessed an unfortunate upsurge in a frankly anarchical approach to the uniform policy. Many of you will be aware that a petition was delivered to the school requesting changes to that policy. After careful and fair deliberation, this petition was rejected. This year, detentions will be freely 'awarded' for breaches of the uniform code. Please support us on this – we are sure you agree that it is important for the girls to be well turned out and we are proud of our distinctive uniform.
4. May we please remind all that PE is not an *optional* subject.

Too many girls have been failing to turn up to lessons or producing wafer-thin excuses. If your daughter is suffering from some rare condition that involves weekly menstruation, please do not hesitate to schedule an appointment with the school nurse to discuss.

We wish the girls a happy and successful year.

Best wishes,

Jonathan Tibble (Deputy Head)

Berkeley Academy: Believing and Achieving since 1964

★
CHAPTER 19

'If you're already attracted to someone and they play your love interest, it becomes very easy to fall in love.'

Kit Harrington

EXTERIOR: DARK MOONLIT NIGHT. EARLY EVENING (CLOUDY)
The Girl and Hot Guy sit close at an outside table. The mood is romantic. Everybody looks uncomfortable. The Girl is being squashed by a seriously large woman at the next table who is talking at her silent, chain-smoking, depressed-looking companion.

THE GIRL

It sounds brilliant! I'm so happy you're
having so much fun!
(*The Girl sounds a little too bright. She
means it, but is conflicted. She waves her
hand in front of her face, the smoke from
her neighbour's cigarette is making her
queasy.*)
The scene where you finally declared
that you had risked life and limb for
Ana's true love must have been fun to
film . . . being on horseback . . . in the
moonlight . . . with the violins.

HOT GUY

Thanks.
(*Hot Guy looks at the Girl like he knows
she's pretending.*)
There weren't any violins.

THE GIRL

There will be. Yep, it sounds like such
a fun production. Can't wait to watch it.
And it must be such fun that you guys
all get on so well together. You and the
maidens of outstanding beauty. Fun.

HOT GUY
Pretty much everyone's nice. Yeah, I'm not
going to lie, it's a good crowd.

THE GIRL
Are you all, like, one big happy family?

HOT GUY
God, no! It's way more fun than that.

THE GIRL
Yay! (*Awkward pause*)
So pleased for you. Honestly. (*Another
awkward pause*)

HOT GUY
But you're having fun on *Straker*, right?
(*In a casual but heroic gesture, he takes
off his jumper and slings it over the
shivering girl's shoulders. He's that kind
of guy.*)

THE GIRL
It's not called *Straker* any more.

HOT GUY
What's the new title?

THE GIRL
RAW.

HOT GUY
Good title.
(*Hot Guy quickly realizes that was not the most sensitive response.*)
Sorry. I mean not as good as *Straker*.

THE GIRL
I don't care about the title.

HOT GUY
Sorry, sorry . . . of course you don't.
You're only thinking about Digby right now.

THE GIRL
(*Hesitates. Obviously struggling with the effort to be honest and trying to understand her feelings. Shrugs.*)
Let's not talk about Digby any more. We're nearly out of time and all I've done is sob and go on about it. Let's talk about what you're doing.

HOT GUY
You can go on about Digby all you want.
I'm here for you anytime.

THE GIRL
But not *actually* here . . .

HOT GUY
You're annoyed with me. (*It isn't a question.*)

THE GIRL
No . . . It's just . . . I am genuinely pleased that it's going well. And I'm really happy for you that it's a good cast and everyone is hanging out and . . . having bonfires and stuff. I just wish . . . I just wish that you weren't in Transylvania.

(*There's a long silence, broken only by the sirens of a passing ambulance. The large woman collects her bags and her silent companion and they leave. The Girl spreads out a little in the space; that means she has moved away a little from the Hot Guy. He doesn't seem to have noticed. He's staring at the contents of his coffee cup as if they might provide him with the answer to all of life's problems. The girl fears that she's one of his problems. She is also troubled by the fact that Hot Guy now drinks coffee.*)

253

THE GIRL

(*Speaking in a small voice, regretting actually being honest for once.*)
Now you think I'm all weird and clingy and stalker-ish.

HOT GUY

You know I'd far rather I was filming over here. I don't want to spend months stuck in Transylvania.
(*The Girl notices he hasn't actually contradicted her on the clingy stalker comment.*)

THE GIRL

Yes, you do ... bears, Angelina Jolie, the maidens, bats ... impromptu bon— (*she stops herself*) ... sword fighting. We don't have any of that in Slough. Actually, we do have sword fighting ... impromptu sword fighting, and now I come to think about it we might have bears, but our bears will be green screen bears and ... (*The Girl trails off because she realizes she is making no sense.*)
We definitely don't have any real haunted forests in Slough.
(*An eavesdropping waitress very slowly wipes the table. She is definitely trying*

254

to catch *Hot Guy's* eye. But then, who
wouldn't? The Girl glares at her.)
Or vampires.
(The Girl traces patterns in the sugar
that she's spilled on to the clean table. A
little bat. A star.)
Come on, be honest, you can't wait to get
back.

HOT GUY
(Leans over and draws a little heart in the
sugar, because he is really quite sensitive.)
Okaaaay, I am sort of enjoying myself.

THE GIRL
I know, and I'm honestly so happy about
that. I truly am.

HOT GUY
But I do miss you. More Skype?

THE GIRL
Sure.
(The Girl's voice is unsure. The single
word conveys that she knows she looks
weird on Skype; it makes her head look
like a pumpkin — a pumpkin that doesn't
know where to focus. Maybe it's not Skype,

maybe it's just how she looks, but she's
resistant to that explanation.)

HOT GUY
More texts?

THE GIRL
Maybe you could just reply a bit more?
(She instantly regrets saying that.)

HOT GUY
That was just last week, the schedule was
mad. Look, it's less than three months
until I'm back.

THE GIRL
Three more months.
*(It comes out as a wail and she
immediately regrets it. Not cool. Long,
long pause. So long that Hot Guy looks at
his watch. She notices.)*

HOT GUY
*(Puts his hand over The Girl's — a little
bit as a romantic gesture and a little bit
to stop her playing with the sugar. It has
become a little manic.)*
I'm sorry about the texts. Well, not about

```
the texts, about the not-texting ... We're
still good. It's cool.
```

THE GIRL
(She avoids eye contact.)
```
It's all cool.
```

'Elektra?' said Moss in a worried voice. 'What is *this*?' She waved a scrap of paper at me.

'Er ... it's a script,' I said.

'It's a *script*,' Moss said slowly, 'of your *life* ... ' She was clearly struggling to understand. 'What are you doing?'

'It was just a ... creative writing project ... for going back to school ... '

'Yeah, sure it was,' said Moss. 'A project that involved you writing a script casting yourself in the third person as "THE GIRL"? Also, we agreed not to mention the whole going back to school thing.' She looked at me sternly. 'Come on, explain yourself.'

'Nobody was ever meant to see it.'

'That I can believe,' she said, shaking her head.

'It's a very bad script,' I said. 'Shall I show you some yoga?' I did some ostentatious alternate nostril breathing – Amber was beginning to rub off on me.

'No, it's not a very good script,' said Moss, completely ignoring my selfless offer to help her be more at one with her body and the universe. 'But

I think we both know that that's not the issue.'

'Is it a bit weird?'

'It's *extremely* weird,' she confirmed. 'The third person thing freaks me out, and let's not even go into the blatant objectification of your boyfriend. But more importantly ... was that actually what happened?'

'Sort of. It wasn't good. It got awkward and I wasn't very nice to him and I got insecure—'

'*Plainly*,' Moss interrupted unhelpfully. 'Why didn't you tell me?'

'It got better. Much, much better.' That wasn't why I hadn't told her.

'You didn't write about any of the good bits.' Moss looked like she didn't believe me.

'There were fewer words in the good bits,' I explained.

Moss laughed, but not for very long. 'You're mad, Elektra. You messed up one of your only meet-ups?'

'I was a wreck because of Digby. Also the fact that it was one of our only meet-ups was part of the problem,' I said defensively.

'You didn't need to be so mean. Archie's lovely. He's practically perfect.'

'Stop saying he's practically perfect. Everyone says he's practically perfect. No doubt that includes at least half the cast of *The Curse of Peter Plogojowitz*.'

'That's tragic. Anyway, why should you be the only person that gets to have fun on-set this summer?'

I shrugged. 'I'm not having the sort of fun that gets remarked on in gossip columns. I'm not "killing it on- and off-set with the ladies".'

'I'd be surprised if you were,' said Moss. 'And I really doubt if Archie is ... you know, doing anything *off-set*. He's not like that.'

'I know.' I really hoped I *did* know.

'What's he posting?'

'Nothing. His Facebook is dead, but then so is mine – there are so many rules about what you can and can't post from set. It's not really about that, it's that he's *not around*. I literally never see him and I *miss* him. Neither of us is any good on the phone – in fact, we're painfully bad – and texting is stressful, not least when the person you're texting with is "too busy" to get back to you. None of it's as much *fun* as I thought it would be. And this was meant to be my Spectacular Summer of Love,' I said bleakly.

'Be very grateful, Elektra James, that I am the only person that heard you say that.'

'I was going to roll in flower-scattered meadows and write poetry and learn Italian and—'

'Sounds rubbish. Why is there no chocolate in here?' She'd turfed the contents of the drawers out on to the carpet. There were two fudge-bar wrappers and a quite good origami bird made out of Kit Kat foil, but Moss was right – there was no actual chocolate.

'I'm stressed,' I said. 'What do you expect? I'll go and forage in the kitchen.'

'I'll go,' she said. 'You just lie there and do some of your weird breathing.'

'If you can't find any biscuits in the tin, look behind Mary Berry,' I said, closing my eyes.

'At least Torr hasn't left the country,' I said, sitting up from corpse pose when Moss came back armed with half a packet of digestives that she'd found behind *Eat Like a Caveman, Look Like a Gazelle*. (I needed to have another little chat with my mum.)

'He might as well have,' she said gloomily.

'Has he disappeared again?' I asked sympathetically.

'Not exactly – I saw him in Starbucks yesterday.'

'That's great,' I said.

'I saw him through the window.'

'Was he with someone else?'

'No, he was on his own which was worse, as he'd literally just texted me to say he was in his bedroom finishing coursework.'

Ah.

As one, we folded into child's pose.

School Resolutions

1.

Write notes. In all my lessons. Pretty ones with highlighting
and topical doodles and handwriting that looks like typing. Every other year I've
attempted this I've got halfway through the first lesson, drawn a weird arrow and
decided I'd start again the following year. Not this time.
This is my year.

2.

Buy and not lose perfect stationery. Preferably with witty and
ironic slogans on.

3.

Be above petty in-fighting and unnecessary arguments. As a woman with a
career it's important that I maintain dignity.

4.

But also keep up to date with all petty-in-fighting-and-unnecessary-
argument developments. I'm going to pretend that this is what people mean
when they tell you to keep up to date on 'current affairs'.

Archie Resolutions
<u>Personal Development Resolutions for</u>
<u>the Improved Running of my Romantic Affairs:</u>

1.

Stop refreshing Bizz.com for updates. It's creepy.

2.

Remember that enduring minor and vague gossip-mongering is a small price to pay for being the official girlfriend of a vampire-slaughtering TV heartthrob.

3.

Find a way to remind Archie that resisting an endless stream of maidens of staggering and even merely outstanding beauty is a small price to pay for being the official boyfriend of a world-saving action heroine who has endured two and a half months of Dick's personal training and can now run normally. Sort of.

4.

Just generally stop being a psycho jealous girlfriend. I will be so laidback that people will start asking me if I surf and/or teach yoga. I will probably spontaneously develop beachy waves in my hair.

5.

Be cool. I, Elektra Ophelia James, am a strong independent woman.
sassy clicking

6.

Be self-aware. Know that sassy clicking is not something I will ever be able to pull off.

CHAPTER 20

*'It can be really surreal going from walking
through a manmade jungle with fake blood all over
you to a chemistry exam. But hey ho.'*
                                        Ella Purnell

'If you don't get downstairs within the next thirty
seconds I am going to feed your breakfast to—' and
then Mum remembered – 'I'm going to eat your
breakfast myself.' Her voice shook the stairs and
rattled my bedroom door.

I wanted to stay in bed and perfect my lists. I
very much did not want the day to begin.

'Come on, Elektra! You. Are. Not. Going to be late
for school on the first day of a new year.'

My uniform was laid out neatly because during
the midnight epiphany that had produced the
lists, I'd resolved to become a super-organized and
basically perfect person, so I'd got out of bed and

sorted *everything*. I looked at it and sighed. It was just so *purple*. My phone barked.

SCHOOL 😩 😩 😩 😩 😩 😩 😩

I'm pretty sure Moss was looking at her uniform too. **I KNOW!**

I wish I'd done my holiday coursework now

I had less empathy than usual because of Naomi and Mum's combined efforts, but it wouldn't help Moss to know that.

I KNOW, I lied.

If I'm in the same form group as Flissy I will literally kill myself . . . or her

I KNOW

If I'm not in the same form group as you I will have no one to talk to 😩 😩 😩 😩 😩 😩 😩 😩

SAME ♥

We will meet daily in detention

Hahaha

I wasn't being funny

The harsh reality of our academic life was all flooding back.

'Elektra! Downstairs, right now!' yelled Mum.

Meet at bus stop at 8

At least no choice in clothes meant no decisions . . . Although tights or no tights? No tights because it was still sunny and hotter than it had been in the whole of the holidays? But maybe tights because my legs were white and hairy? I looked more closely. *Very* hairy.

Right, tights. Good decision.

'Elektra! Ten, nine, eight, seven . . .'

The tights barely made it past my thighs. No tights, then. I looked like Chewbacca, a Chewbacca with extremely poor taste.

'I made you scrambled eggs,' said Mum when I got to the kitchen. 'But you're too late. They were going cold so I ate them.'

Good. The thought of eggs was turning my stomach. 'I can't face anything,' I said. 'I'll get something at break.'

'Don't be silly.' She was already whisking up more. 'Students who eat breakfast have higher test scores than students who skip breakfast.'

'Sure.'

'It's true. Hunger affects performance.'

'It might affect my performance if I was going to run a marathon, but I doubt it's going to make any difference to how well I function in double maths this morning.' And then I wished I hadn't mentioned maths because I felt even sicker.

'You've got time to eat an egg,' Mum said stubbornly. 'An egg is protein and protein is necessary for the release of energy. To be precise, proteins provide the amino acids necessary for the functioning of neurotransmitters.'

'What?'

'Without enough good protein, your neurotransmitters will be insufficiently efficient to get you through the exam timetable that is Year Eleven.'

Well, that was depressing. 'Have you been looking up brain food on How To Have A Clever Child websites again?'

'No,' she said. 'You left your biology textbook on the kitchen table yesterday – Food and Nutrients module.'

'My first biology class is on Thursday,' I said. 'And I'll be on-set.' I sat down quickly and started to eat before she started back on the whole missing-school-is-a-disaster rant. 'Have you seen my phone?'

'It's in front of you,' she said, peeling me an orange for after, presumably because my neurotransmitter function was so poor she didn't trust me to do it myself.

'Ah, I missed that school uniform,' said Dad, coming into the kitchen. 'So tasteful.' He shuddered. 'Do you want a lift to school? Help you to get over the shock of not having your limo pick you up this morning?'

'I said I'd meet Moss at the bus stop.'

'We can pick her up, if you want?'

My dad is in a strangely good mood and has offered to drive us to school. Will pick you up en route. BE READY.

I love your dad. Will get out of bed now

'Such a big year,' said Mum.

I willed her not to say it . . .

'GCSEs.'

She said it.

'Is there any tiny, teeny chance that you could wait until, say, six months before the exams to start winding me up about them?'

'It's just that it's *exciting*!' That was absolutely not the word I would have used. 'Now, is your bag all packed?'

I nodded.

'Have you remembered your coursework?'

'Yes, I am now super-organized.' And smug.

'Are you *sure* your coursework is in your bag? Check.'

I sighed ostentatiously and checked just to humour her. Ah. 'Um . . . have you seen it?'

'I saw it,' said Dad. 'It was under the sofa in the sitting room.'

'Thanks,' I said, getting up.

'That was last week,' he added.

'It's definitely not there now,' said Mum. 'I hoovered yesterday.'

'Where did you move it to?'

'I didn't. It wasn't there. Your homework is your responsibility.' And then she drifted into her everything-is-your-responsibility-now-you're-in-Year-Eleven lecture. Which was fine, except for the fact that I was still going to have to do whatever I was told. 'Anyway,' she concluded some painful minutes later, 'I believe you'll find your coursework on top of the bread bin.'

There was a perfectly logical explanation for why I'd put it there, but it had temporarily escaped me.

'So have you finished making your movie?' asked Mrs Gryll.

'Not quite,' I said.

'I think I would have liked to have been an actress,' she said wistfully.

'Really?'

Mrs Gryll was nice and easily distracted, which is a good thing in a geography teacher, but I would never have guessed she hankered after cinematic fame.

'Oh, yes. Never mind.' She pulled herself together. 'I get to perform in front of you lovely girls instead. Are you all ready for GCSE year?'

All us 'lovely girls' groaned. That exchange pretty much set the tone for the morning.

'Are you all ready for GCSE year?' Maths teacher.

'Well, I hope you had fun making your film.' Also maths.

'What do you mean, you're back on-set in a week?' Maths again, swiftly and sadly followed by:

'Don't think that means that you get to miss any homework.'

'What's Sam Gross like?' Mrs Lawal and Miss Browen and Mr Smith. Followed by: 'Well, no time to tell us now.'

'What's Amber Leigh like?' As above.

'Raring to go for GCSEs, Elektra?' PE teacher in corridor – I was both impressed and worried that he knew my name.

'Looking forward to seeing your action hero skills, ha! Hahaha!' The same PE teacher – what a wit.

'So when is your film coming out?' Ms Chan, Lost Property. I have no idea how I managed to lose my phone between geography and maths. It's a mystery.

*

Moss and I hovered with our prison-style trays and *despaired*. A bit because of what was on our trays (being on-set had spoiled me, I'd forgotten what normal canteen food was like) and a bit more because it was just all so first-day-back-ish. There were three girls crying in three separate corners, at least seven girls rolling up or down various bits of their uniform to display suntan lines, numerous girls copying each other's coursework and two girls proudly comparing love bites. Half the tables were so packed that the least popular girls were falling off the edge of the benches, and the other half were under-occupied, with girls sitting at strict diagonals so as to avoid any risk of eye contact. There was a sort of white noise of talk and cutlery and occasional yelps of either hilarity or misery.

'Which is the least bad option?' I asked.

'We can fit on the same table as Jenny if we only take up one place.'

'You can sit on me,' I offered. We headed over.

'Did you finish your film?' asked Jenny, the second I put my tray down.

'Nope.'

'Does that mean you get time off school?'

'Some. I'm backwards and forwards. But I have to do lessons on-set.'

'Still lucky,' said Jenny, which was fair. 'What's Sam Gross like?'

'What's Amber Leigh like?' asked Maia, who'd squished on to the other end.

I'd never had so much attention at lunch. To tell or not to tell? I mean, I knew stuff about the cast that I could probably *sell* (plastic surgery alone would take us through several lunches). But, no, I didn't even want to tell them anything about Amber. 'They were all really *nice*,' I said, and everyone glared at me. I'd let my audience down, not for the first time.

'What's Carlo Winn like?' asked Flissy, walking past without stopping.

'He's really *nice*,' I said.

'Is he *really*?' She turned back.

'Are you asking for a friend?'

She shrugged. 'Is he seeing anyone?'

'Mmmm I really shouldn't say ...' I said. I was enjoying this now.

'Come on, you can tell *me*,' she said, like she was the most trustworthy person in the world.

'I really can't,' I said. Conveniently, my phone barked. 'Oh, it's Carlo ...' I didn't pick up. 'But I really can't take this call here. Calls from the set are so *private*.' My phone barked again with a text. I looked at the screen, bit my lip and smiled. Flissy glared at me and walked away.

'You should so have taken the call and flirted with Carlo in front of her,' said Moss. 'It would have killed her.'

'I probably would have – if it hadn't been my mum asking what we were having for lunch and whether I'd handed in my coursework.'

'Are you still dating Archie Mortimer?' asked Maia.

'Yes,' I said, trying not to sound smug.

'Aren't you worried?'

'What about?'

'Well, he's filming that vampire series with all the hot girls in it, right?'

'Right.'

'Including *Poppy Leadley?*'

'Right.'

'I looked her up.'

I bet she did. 'I'm not worried.' I stared at my meatballs. They had a little greasy film on them.

'Wowww! That's so cute! It's great that you're so *secure* in your relationship. I'd be worried. I mean, I know Archie's like *practically perfect*, but he's a guy, right?'

First day back at school today. So grim. I'm home now, but think I'm in state of shock. I pressed send and then wished I'd gone with something a bit more upbeat. Archie had been putting up with a lot of miserable texts since Digby died.

Ah, bad luck

Bad luck? No kisses. **Can't wait to see you at the weekend!!** I went for the upbeat double exclamation mark. No reply, so I started my maths homework. Three minutes, twenty seconds of quadratic equations was long enough to drive me to double texting (to be fair to quadratic equations, it didn't take much). **How was your day?**

Busy. Tricky scene involving reviving a maiden drained of blood. Well, nearly drained of blood – she had enough left to sit up and kiss me. Lots of retakes

Sounds like a tough day

It was ... It IS – we've got three more hours of shooting. Got to go. Text later x

Sure. It was a good thing that I was so *secure* in my relationship.

WAITING & WORKING

- % of time spent at Fairmount: 30% (of which 40% was spent on Sound Stage A loving every minute and 60% was spent in the 'classroom' with Naomi, who has a dark side)
- % of time spent at school: 50% (of which 25% was spent panicking about mocks and 65% was spent being distracted by real life stuff and trying to stay away from gossip sites)
- % of time spent planning/looking forward to my party: 4%
- % of time spent dreading my party: 26%
- % of time spent in the same place as Archie: 0%
- % of time spent texting Archie: 2% (which was higher than the percentage of time Archie was spending texting me, on account of his extreme busyness)
- % of time spent thinking about Archie and tragically scrolling all the old pics on his social media: undisclosed
- % of time spent missing Digby: 100%

★
CHAPTER 21

'Whenever I try to pick up a hobby and take it to set, I look like an idiot there with a ukulele.'
                                                            Kit Harrington

'Good morning. Good morninnnngggg!' Carlo slid into the chair beside me. Filming had been pushed forward to some as yet unspecified time because of a lighting 'screw-up' and Naomi had left me to my second breakfast in the canteen while she 'sorted out scheduling', which I'm pretty sure was a euphemism for shouting at someone for messing up her tutor time.

'Why are you so happy?' I asked him. It was seven in the morning, I'd been up since five thirty and I was getting over the end of a cold. I wasn't feeling happy vibes.

'I'm just a happy person, E, you know that.'

'You're even more annoyingly happy than usual. What happened? Did Amber let you take Kale for walkies? Did Sam let you join his poker game? Did you get with another extra? Did we finally get a date for Mali?' The last one was a serious question; now that school had started again I was very much up for a change of scenery. Carlo shook his head. 'What then? I know there's something.'

'Mayyybbee. Maybe not.'

'Come on.' I punched his arm. 'You have to tell me. I need the distraction.'

'I'm not going to share *confidences* with someone who assaults me.'

'Why not?'

Carlo leaned towards me. 'Because it's about you,' he whispered.

This couldn't be good. I took an emergency bite of apple Danish.

'Don't you want to know what it is any more?'

'Um ...' I really did want to know, but I also really wished I didn't care.

'It's probably best you don't know.' Carlo stretched. 'They say what you don't know can't hurt you.'

'What's that supposed to mean?' What had I done? I could feel myself going red because whatever it was, it was bound to have been embarrassing.

'I shouldn't have said anything.' He half laughed, then looked at me and said more seriously, 'I *really* shouldn't have said anything.'

'You have to tell me now.' I tried not to sound panicky, but, well, I *was* panicking.

'No, no. I shouldn't have—'

'Carlo.'

'Do you actually want to know?' He wasn't laughing.

'Yes. I do.'

'Dracula Boy's cheating on you.'

What? Everything suddenly seemed really quiet. It felt like the entire canteen was staring at us. I swallowed. *Breathe, Elektra, breathe.*

It wasn't true.

Of course it wasn't true.

Classic Carlo. He'd say anything for drama. How could he even know if Archie was . . .? He couldn't. Of course he couldn't.

I managed a wobbly fake laugh to buy myself some time. Had I read Carlo completely wrong? Was he was actually into me? It was the only explanation. It had to be. And he'd have to be into me in more than a bored-get-with kind of way to go to the trouble of lying about Archie. In a way, this was sweet. Tragic, but sweet. I'd humour him. Let him down gently.

'E?' Carlo waved a hand in front of my eyes and

did his best attempt at a concerned face. 'Are you all right?'

'Yes.' I sat up straight. I was going to deal with this in a kind and mature way. 'Carlo.' I put a comforting hand on his arm. 'I get it. I really get it. But you—'

Carlo passed me his phone.

TheBizz.com

Bringing you the all the Best Backstabbing in the Bizz . . .

17th September

On-set the young cast of *The Curse of Peter Plogojowitz* may be engaged in an all-encompassing war between the forces of good and evil, but off-set it looks like they're all a lot closer.

The group took the whole trying-to-murder-each-other-shebang down to a much more playful level on a recent paint-balling trip in the Hoia Baciu forest. Although they left their conflicts on-set, it looks like one scripted relationship could be creeping into the real world . . .

A recent Instagram set our hearts racing when Poppy Leadley posted it to her account. It showed Poppy perching playfully, paintball gun in hand, on the strong, manly shoulders of Archie Mortimer (the vampire-hunting hunk who we may or may not have mentioned – just a few times – before). The seventeen-year-old beauty captioned it: *Me and my main man ... come at us, Vamps.*

As if that wasn't enough, our on-set informant basically confirmed all our hopes/fears that this love story was not going to be confined to our TV screens. She said: 'Archie and Poppy are both great actors. Very committed. They'll do anything to get into character, no matter how ... method. Their chemistry is intense.'

While we would obviously be heartbroken to see Archie taken off the market, we have to admit that he and Poppy would make one fit vampire-fighting couple.

Of course, rumours are only that ...

I read it. I re-read it.

I forced a laugh. Carlo looked unconvinced.

'The Bizz? Come on, Carlo, you can do better than that.' I tried to slide his phone nonchalantly across the table to him. It clattered off the edge and on to the polished wood floor. 'I mean, The Bizz? THE BIZZ?'

Carlo picked up his phone. He handed it to a girl from Costume who was on the next table. She read it with her hand over her mouth and passed it to one of the sound guys, who was leaning over from another table. He read it and grimaced and gave it to Milo, who very quickly passed it to Andy, who'd come in for a coffee and stayed for the drama.

'Everyone knows that The Bizz just make stuff

up? Right?' I laughed again, but it came out *slightly* manic. 'I mean, they said the other day that Amber and Sam were back together. AMBER AND SAM!'

There was dead silence. Carlo looked at costumes girl who looked at another costumes girl who looked at sound guy who looked at Milo who looked at Andy who looked at the floor. Nobody looked at me.

'*Amber and Sam* – can you imagine? It just shows you how reliable The Bizz is. NOT RELIABLE. The opposite of reliable. They don't even pretend to be reliable. "*Rumours are only that* ..." Amber and Sam are literally the *last* people that would EVER ...' I tailed off. I'd been speaking really loudly. Two people from Production were looking at me like zookeepers who'd lost the tranquillizer gun just as their most psychotic rhino had gone on a full-on rampage. I wanted to run away, just stop talking and go, but I had to finish now. 'But, I mean, Amber and Sam?' I whispered. 'It's not like Amber and Sam would ever get back together.'

'Actually ...' Andy cleared his throat. 'Amber and Sam ... this week, well, they sort of got back together.' Everyone nodded. Everyone knew.

Well, everyone except me.

'But ... but they hate each other!' I choked.

'There's a thin line between dislike and

280

attraction,' said Carlo, and this time nobody contradicted him.

I sat on my own at the canteen table and picked a paper plate to pieces.

Carlo had been called to set for a green screen scene that I wasn't in. Some kind of nasty run-in that Jan had with the wolf-type things. I hoped the 'wolves' came out on top. I didn't want to see Carlo again. Ever.

Everyone else who had been around for Carlo's Great Reveal seemed to have disappeared. Probably so that they could talk about me.

No doubt Sam and Amber were getting ready to do some scenes with the right sort of chemistry.

I'd already tried to phone Moss, Daisy and Jenny. None of them had picked up, presumably because they were busy. Obviously I hadn't tried to phone Archie because he was clearly even *busier*. Eulalie was on a one-day spending spree in Paris, buying outfits to impress Havelski with IRL. Dad was at work and even my mum wasn't taking my calls. She was missing Digby so much that she'd arranged a manic programme of displacement activity, plainly leaving her too busy to pick up her phone and speak to her only daughter.

I'd rather have had an impromptu training session with Dick than sit alone at the canteen table for another five minutes.

'Are you moping, Elektra James?' said Naomi, coming to sit beside me.

'I'm just thinking about school stuff.' Obviously I wasn't. 'I've got a French test that I haven't revised for. Irregular verbs.' Actually, that was true.

'Are you sure that's what's wrong?' She scooped up the little molehill of paper shreds and chucked them in the bin.

'So presumably you know what's wrong?' I took a gulp of tea and scalded my mouth.

'I think so.' Of course she did. Being on-set was literally worse than school for gossip. 'Come on, give Archie the benefit of the doubt. Innocent until proven guilty and all that.' She wasn't being as reassuring as she thought she was. 'You know what it's like on-set. If anyone had had a camera when you pushed Carlo in the "river" last week it would have looked really bad.'

'We were just mucking about.'

'Yes. And Archie and Poppy and the whole gang of them were no doubt just "mucking about" too.'

'Do you really think so?' I felt a bit better.

'Uh huh. Probably. Yes. Anyway, you're not going to have time to think about it, because we're going over to the classroom and I'm going to help you revise your French conjugations. That'll cheer you up.'

*

'OK,' Naomi said, opening a French textbook. 'Irregular verbs. You can slay these. *Decevoir* ... no, actually not that one. *Mentir?* No, maybe not.' She skimmed a bit. 'Right, let's go with *vouloir*. Off you go, set the timer on your phone, it'll make it more fun.'

It was the most 'fun' I was going to have all day, so I put my phone on the desk and pressed start on the stopwatch. '*Je veux, tu veux, il veut* ...' My phone barked with a call before I'd got to five seconds. I looked at the screen – Archie.

'Take it,' said Naomi, who was sitting close enough to read the screen.

'No.' The barking stopped.

'That's not fair,' she said. 'You don't even know why he was phoning.'

'I'm assuming because he's seen that post.'

My phone barked again, he was texting. **Just found out I can't get back this weekend. Fingers crossed for next one. Are you feeling better? x**

I silently showed Naomi.

'He obviously hasn't seen the post,' she said. 'Nobody sane reads The Bizz.' I read The Bizz. 'They've probably just changed his filming schedule because of weather or something. You know how it goes.'

'What should I say?' I asked a bit desperately.

'If it were me, I'd go with something breezy

and confident. You don't want to come over as needy.'

I gave it my best. **Don't worry! Yeah, MUCH better**

That was a massive lie; my cold had nearly gone but I was definitely not feeling better.

'Good,' said Naomi approvingly. 'Now ask him about the filming.'

They're making you film all weekend? I was getting into the swing of this. I threw in a bit of sympathy which may or may not have been sarcastic. **Wow, poor you. That's intense**

Not all weekend. Filming on Saturday – intense vampire death scene, stake through the heart and garlic. Love triumphs over evil. There may now be violins. Free on Sunday. A few of us are going to go wild swimming in a volcanic lake near here and chill a bit. If we've only got one day off we're going to make the best of it. It's going to be awesome

Yes, it probably was. Great.

✩ CHAPTER 22

'It's been half a decade of severe mental trauma ...
I love it.'

James McAvoy

STRAKER
If winning means losing people I love,
then I don't know if I want to win.

WINONA
Losing means dying, you little fool.

STRAKER
Maybe dying wouldn't be so terrible.

I was saying my lines while running *backwards*, pursued by Amber who was wearing a particularly fetching little burgundy silk off-the-shoulder number. (I had on my trusted and by now quite smelly sack.) I was also being pursued by one large camera on tracks, one small camera on a very strong cameraman's shoulder, a guy with a light monitor, Sound Dan and his boom and one of the electricians who was running after them carrying a loop of cables like a bridesmaid holding a train. But I didn't fall over and I didn't even flap my hands. Well, I couldn't have, because I was carrying a dead, bloody rabbit. Not a real one, thankfully, but it was still pretty rank.

WINONA
I want you to grow up. I want you to have a child. I want you to know a little of the happiness I knew before *this*.

'And *cut*,' said Ahmed. 'Amber, can you summon me up some tears from about "happiness" or do you want Make-up to stand by with the tear stick?'

'It's fine.' She was already sniffing. 'Just give me a minute to summon up Coco.'

'Reset . . . and *action*.'

WINONA

I want you to grow up. I want you to have
a child. I want you to know a little of
the happiness I knew before *this*.

Her acting today was the best I'd ever seen.

STRAKER

I never want to have a child. How could I
bring a baby into all of this?

My voice broke on 'baby'. No cute babygros, no
stuffed animals, no Pingu or Sylvanians. Only tiny
brown sack clothes, a diet of grubs and Jan as a
possible dad. I didn't find it hard to tear up at all. I
didn't even need to 'summon up' Digby. Tears were
coming easily today. For so many reasons.

'Cut,' yelled Ahmed. 'That was fantastic. Good
job, guys. Give us twenty and we'll be ready to
go again.'

We'd been at it for a while, but I didn't want a
break. It was hot, though there was a wind machine,
and everyone seemed to be in a good mood; Eddie
had been de-stressed with his daily burst of Abba,
and Kale was nowhere to be seen. Maybe Sam had
managed to 'lose' him somewhere (probably in a
sack in the stream). I was working and busy and not
thinking about anything else. I was literally *refusing*

to let myself think about anything else. Even so, I was quite glad to hand the rabbit back to props and wipe my hands.

Naomi came over. 'This is looking so good, Elektra! Forget the personal stuff and just focus on your work. Good girl.'

Amber joined us. 'I think we might even finish early today. This is going really well.'

I beamed. I'd just received praise from an actual Hollywood star. Amber was unusually smiley, which may or may not have had something to do with the recent re-coupling with Sam.

Bo from Make-up came over too and patted the real sweat from my face, then spent a few minutes putting some fake sweat on instead.

'How's my mud?' I asked.

'Holding up well,' Bo said approvingly.

'She has dark shadows,' said Amber accusingly.

'She's meant to have dark shadows.'

'Yes, but under the make-up dark shadows, there are real dark shadows.' Amber was sounding worryingly like a real mum. 'Elektra, did you not get any sleep last night?'

'I slept perfectly,' I lied.

'Are you sure you didn't lie awake all night worrying about your boyfriend?' Of course she knew. 'Yes I'm sure,' I lied again.

'I don't believe you,' Amber said. She was literally

morphing into my mum. 'Everyone was talking yesterday about his little location thing.'

Great. So that had put an almighty full stop to the I-will-only-think-about-my-work plan.

'Alleged,' I said, slightly desperately. 'His *alleged* location thing.'

'In my experience, there's no smoke without fire.' Yes, that would be Amber's experience. 'On the other hand, it doesn't usually long outlast the filming.' Oh dear. We all looked round to check that Sam wasn't in earshot. 'Rise above it, Elektra. Rise above it like a phoenix.'

Easy for Amber Leigh to say that. There was no shortage of replacement guys for her.

'You need to focus on your work and put your boyfriend, if he still deserves to be your boyfriend, right out of your head.' Until her little *intervention* that was *exactly* what I'd been trying to do. 'Get in touch with the strong and independent woman that is lurking beneath the surface.' I had a bad feeling that the only thing lurking beneath my surface today was a huge spot.

'I already told her that,' said Naomi, and Bo nodded.

'There's no point just *telling* her,' said Amber. 'We need to give her the tools to become the Alpha woman we know she can be.'

I knew what was coming. I'm pretty sure from

Naomi's and Bo's attempts to wriggle away that they knew what was coming too. Within seconds, Amber had us all in a little circle behind the 'cliff' holding hands and chanting affirmations.

'Say after me, "I am beautiful".'

'I am beautiful,' we intoned as one.

'I accept myself and all my flaws.' Amber stumbled over the word 'flaws'. The rest of us didn't.

'I am a graceful and sexy woman at one with my body.'

I tried my best.

'Neither men nor women can resist my femininity and highly-charged energy.'

I lost it. Naomi started laughing.

'*Take this seriously,*' snapped Amber. She took a deep breath, readjusting her posture and no doubt her chakras. 'We'll try some physical affirmations. A few poses that will help you release some of that frustrated emotional toxicity. It's so bad for the skin.' She peered at me. I'm pretty sure she could see beneath my surface now. 'You know, Elektra, I think you need to regroup, forget about the unsatisfactory boyfriend and move on. A whole new start ... maybe become a vegan. What do you think?' She turned to Naomi.

'I think Elektra should do what makes her happy and I don't think she should believe everything she reads,' said Naomi. 'I certainly don't think she needs to become a vegan. Have you spoken to Archie, Elektra?'

I hesitated. 'Y ... e ... s.'

'And?' They were agog.

This was tricky. 'We're chatting, well, we're texting. He's got a really full-on schedule. But it's all good.' My audience plainly wanted more. This was problematic because I hadn't spoken to Archie. I hadn't even texted Archie since the whole wild-swimming-chilling-with-maidens exchange. And he definitely hadn't texted me. 'He said The Bizz stuff was rubbish,' I said, because I like to think that's what he *would* have said if I'd been brave enough to ask him.

'Rubbish?' Amber looked at me pityingly. 'Sweetie, the camera never lies.'

'You of all people should know that that is not true,' said Naomi quite snarkily.

'He didn't deny being with the girl?'

'Well, no ...'

'He didn't deny liking her?'

'Well, no ...' I didn't mention that he hadn't denied anything, because I hadn't *asked* him anything. 'He likes her *as a friend*,' I improvised hopefully.

Amber looked at me as if I was very naïve.

Maybe I was very naïve.

'I think you should forget about him and move on,' said Bo, parroting Amber.

'Or become a feminist and forget all men,' suggested Amber in a whisper.

'Er ... that's not what feminism—' began Naomi, but before she could talk any sense, Amber was back in her comfort zone.

'No, nooooo, what about Carlo? He's good-looking and he's *here*.' Location was obviously a big factor for Amber. 'What do *you* think, Sam?' He'd snuck up on us and was listening in. He didn't look that much happier to see Amber than usual, but plainly I knew nothing about how relationships worked.

Sam swung his arm around my shoulders and gave me a quick hug. 'I'd say forget about your vampire hunter – at least till you're both back in civilian world.' This was becoming a pile-up of advice. I looked over to Naomi for a bit of support, but she was being pulled away by Eddie to discuss something that was obviously more urgent than my love life. 'Long distance stuff is always a mess,' went on Sam cheerily. 'Take it from me. At your age it's not worth worrying over. Have some fun instead. Give someone else a chance. OK?' This was serious peer pressure, except that none of them were my peers. 'But not Carlo,' he continued. 'I like Carlo, but I understand Carlo. He would be a bad choice.'

'Why would I be a bad choice?' asked Carlo, appearing from behind a styrofoam outcrop. 'And what would I be a bad choice for?'

'Oh, probably lots of things,' said Amber. 'But right now we're focusing on Elektra. We're breaking up with her boyfriend.' *We were?*

'Text or Facebook?' asked Carlo, like that was the only decision still to be made.

'Text, I think,' said Sam and everyone – except me – nodded. Before I knew it Amber was conjuring up some fake emergency excuse and *ordering* some junior production assistant to break the rules and fetch my phone.

Minutes later I was looking at my screen. 'I don't know what to say.'

'Just put the usual,' said Carlo breezily.

'I don't know what "the usual" is.'

'Something like, "Hey babe, this isn't working. See you around." Or, if you want to make a point, maybe, "I'm not feeling it. Have a good life."'

He wasn't being helpful. 'I should wait and phone Archie,' I said. 'I should give him a chance to tell me what's going on. If there's anything going on ...' I tailed off. Naomi had vanished and the others were all looking at me with deep sympathy – even Carlo. I started to draft a text.

Hey Archie. I don't think this is working any more but then I guess you've known that for a while. I think

293

it's better if we both just admit it now and I really hope we can be friends when you get back x

'Take off the "x". It's too friendly and he definitely doesn't deserve it,' said Amber darkly.

'No, no, definitely keep the "x",' said Carlo. 'It looks cooler, you don't want him to think you care.'

I did care, but all I said was: 'Should I send it now?'

'Yes,' everyone said at once.

I shut my eyes and hit send. The decision had been made, but I wasn't sure it had been made by me.

'You're going to feel so much better now,' said Amber. 'It's like lancing a boil.' Everyone looked at my chin.

My phone barked. I definitely wasn't feeling better. **What??** Then: **Is this Elektra??** Then: **Seriously?** Immediately followed by: **WHAT??**

And then, after a pause: **I'm so sorry**

'I'll bet he is,' said Amber, who was looking over my shoulder. 'Now it's public.'

I stared at the messages. He was saying sorry. He wasn't even trying to deny that something had been going on and I'd felt so paranoid for even suspecting him. This looked bad. No, this *was* bad. 'What should I reply?' My voice came out weirdly small.

'Nothing. Let him dig himself into a deep, *deep* hole.' I think Amber was relishing this. Sam gulped.

My phone started barking again.

It's been the weirdest week

Just so full on

I messed up

Just give me one more chance

I know it's no excuse but we've just been doing all these really intense scenes. So many scenes

Sorry sorry it's not an excuse

The phone barked with a call this time. I hesitated too long and he rang off. He texted seconds later.

I promise I'll be better. Give me another chance

Did Archie really think I was going to be chill with this? The Bizz had made me very well aware of just how *full on* he'd been and just what an *intense* time he'd been having. My cheeks were burning with anger and humiliation. What did he think I was going to say? *Oh, haha, you're so right, cheating doesn't count on location?*

No. Sorry I don't think so

'Put in a full stop after "Sorry" too,' said Amber gleefully. 'Make those words like little bullets in his tiny man-heart.' Sam flinched.

Elektra, please, I swear I had no idea you'd mind so much. I know I've been crap, but I swear on my life I genuinely didn't realize this was a big deal for you

Are you actually KIDDING me? You didn't realize this was a BIG DEAL? I was done with pretending to be cool. Archie was trying to make this *my* fault.

Sorry, sorry, that came out wrong but you're not seriously going to break up with me over this are you?? I get how stressed you've been over Digby and Straker, but please, please don't make this decision until you've calmed down

Until I've calmed down?? You arrogant ... Amber and Sam nodded approvingly, **entitled ...** I was too angry to even finish. We watched the typing dots appear and disappear as Archie tried to think of some suitably (un)convincing response.

The phone barked with another call. I didn't pick up. He texted again. **Elektra, can I call you? Just give me a chance to explain**

I looked at Amber.

'No! No way.'

'But maybe it's better ...'

'Better for whom?' she asked sternly. 'Better for him, yes. If you hear him out, you totally legitimize everything. Do not let him dictate how this goes, you have to take back control. You'll talk if and when *you* want to talk.'

It was like having a personalized self-help manual voiced by an A-list actress. **No**, I texted dutifully, then added, **If you want to talk we can talk when you get back to London**

There weren't even the typing dots this time. I took a deep breath. I didn't care. I was totally justified. I didn't need him to reply. But he did.

Right. Yeah, maybe.

Wow. Everything he'd done and all I got was a 'yeah, maybe' with a passive aggressive full stop. Everyone here had been right.

It just seemed so final.

WAITING & WORKING

- % of time spent at Fairmount: 17% (which was not nearly enough because I liked working and I didn't even mind the 59% spent in the 'classroom' with Naomi)
- % of time spent at school: 60% (which was too much and of which 23% was spent avoiding questions about my personal life and avoiding gossip sites)
- % of time spent planning my party: 0.1%
- % of time spent dreading my party: 36%
- % of time spent in the same place as Archie: 0%
- % of time spent texting Archie: 0%
- % of time spent resisting temptation to text Archie: undisclosed
- % of time spent thinking about Archie: undisclosed
- % of time spent missing Digby: 100%

From: Stella at the Haden Agency
Date: 28 September 15:04
To: Elektra James; Julia James
Cc: Charlotte at the Haden Agency
Subject: *Raw (Straker)*

Dear Elektra and Julia,

I wonder if you both have time to drop by for a chat after school one day this week? Any day will be fine, just drop us a line, but as soon as possible really.

Kind regards,

Stella x

P.S. I can't get used to that new title!

★
CHAPTER 23

'When you're young, you think everything is the
be-all and end-all and I'm learning to let it go, to
not think if I [mess] this character up I'll never get
another job again.'

Lily James

'We have a Colin the Caterpillar cake,' said
Stella. Her voice was suspiciously bright, and for
the first time in the history of humanity Colin
was contributing to the bad vibe. It felt like
overcompensation for something. Charlie brought
us mugs of tea and slabs of cake. 'So.' Stella paused
for just a fraction too long. 'I've had Panda on the
phone.'

'Not more delays,' moaned Mum. 'I mean, Elektra
has a life to live. She has *exams*.'

Life at its most lived, right there.

'What did they say?' I asked.

'They said there remain a few issues with the writers.'

'I know *that*.'

'And that Havelski has asked for more rewrites.'

'Asked?' I didn't have a lot of experience of Havelski 'asking'. And I was used to rewrites. I had scripts in every colour of the rainbow.

'A little bit of reshaping,' said Stella vaguely. 'Trying to make sure that they really get an ending that will resonate with audiences.'

The Grand Finale was going to becoming the even Grander and probably Longer Finale. 'So are they going to muck about with the schedule again?'

'Sort of,' said Stella. 'We're nearly out of cake! How did that happen?'

I really had no idea.

'Anyway ...' she said. 'The rewrites this time are ... quite extensive.'

'How *extensive?*' I asked. Mum was uncharacteristically silent.

'Very extensive,' said Stella.

'*All* my lines?'

'Nooooo,' said Stella, as though that were a ridiculous idea.

Excellent.

'Well, not all the lines you've already shot ...' She trailed off. 'It's just that ...' For someone who must be very used to giving out bad news, she was struggling. 'Going *forward* it's pretty much ... all of your lines.'

I mentally scrolled through the script. We'd shot a lot of the scenes I was in, but not all of them. 'So why don't they just send me the new lines? I don't understand.'

'Well, they've rewritten the scene where you're injured.'

'I'm injured in most of the scenes.'

'*Badly* injured. The one with Jan trying to save you?' Again, that was most scenes. 'You know, the one with the gash in your side with blood pouring out? Jan *distraught*? Raw racing up to the *rescue* just as everyone thinks that you're going to die?'

'Oh, *that* scene, yes.' I nodded. I did know that scene. It was a big dramatic moment – Jan and Raw, with only brute heroism and testosterone on their side, plucking me from the jaws of death. I was word-perfect on that scene. It was a big moment for Straker. I was going to nail it.

'Well ... in the rewrites, Raw doesn't race up to the rescue.'

There was a long pause.

'Raw doesn't rescue me? So someone else does?' Straker needed to survive; she had a pretty crucial role to play in the Grand Finale.

'Not really.' Stella looked awkward.

'They're ... *killing* me off?'

'Well, they're rewriting that particular *Straker* scene as a death scene.'

'*Raw* scene,' I corrected.

There was another long pause. 'It's not about you, Elektra,' said Stella, 'and it's not about Straker.'

'Well, it sort of is about Straker. I mean, last month she survived to the end of the film and now she's dead. I'd say she'd be interested in that.'

'Don't be sarcastic, Elektra,' muttered my mum from the sidelines.

'It's more about Raw and Winona, actually,' said Stella. 'The aim of the rewrite, as far as I understand it, is not to lessen the Straker and Jan roles, it's to deepen the Winona and Raw roles, putting their fiery relationship at the heart of the story.'

'So you're saying I'm collateral damage?'

'In a way. Look, don't forget that you'll still have a good credit in a big movie and you're not even sixteen. And, in many ways this is a positive, because now you'll be free to start going up for other roles. There's some great stuff around, isn't there?' Stella looked at Charlie, who made lots of excited, affirmative noises.

My mum shuddered. Too soon.

'And Mr Havelski has been so pleased with

everything you've done. I'm sure you'll all work together again some day. It's done your *career* nothing but good.'

'And did you see that lovely shout-out for you and Jan in Sam Gross's interview with the *Weekend Record?*' said Charlie. 'One for the scrapbook.'

I shook my head. I didn't care. I didn't want a scrapbook. I wanted to be too busy working to have time to make a scrapbook. Actually, all I wanted was not to be killed off in cold blood. Was that really too much to ask?

'So how do you feel about it all, Elektra?' Stella had broken the news of terminal diagnosis now and, hands full of painkillers, she was putting on her very best bedside manner.

I said nothing for a bit, because it's important to have a moment of respect for the dead. '*Fine*,' I said. I pointedly helped myself to the last slice of Colin, the slice with the face and two feet.

'Now you need to tell me how you *really* feel,' my mum said, as soon as we got back in the car.

'Fine,' I said shortly, kicking an old lead of Digby's under the seat so I didn't have to see it and searching for my phone. This car was nothing like my *Straker* limo.

'Answer me properly,' she said, narrowly avoiding running over an innocent pedestrian.

'I know how *you* feel about it,' I said. 'It's perfect, right? One more day off school and – *whoop, whoop* – back to preparing for mocks.'

'I'm not going to pretend that I can't see the advantages,' said Mum, taking the wrong turning, 'but I don't want you to be worried or upset about it.'

I shrugged.

'You had such an exciting summer filming and there weren't many scenes left anyway.' There were actually quite a few scenes left. Also now I wouldn't get to go to Mali. There was literally no escape. Mum was still talking. 'And Stella was very emphatic about how pleased everyone was with your acting!'

'Stella's lovely,' I said. Where *was* my phone?

'Do a U-turn, if possible,' said the car. Sound life advice.

'You really mustn't be disheartened, it could be worse,' Mum went on brightly.

'Please, Mum, no.'

'No, what?' asked Mum.

'I am fine, but please don't give me the whole count-your-blessings lecture.'

'I wasn't going to—' she protested.

'Yes, you were.'

'I just think it will be great for you to have some *ordinary* time.' Wow, great, months of ordinary time stretching ahead of me. 'And you'll have time to go to the movies instead of making them . . .'

'I don't want to go to the movies,' I said petulantly.

Mum sighed. 'Is this all about *Straker*? Or are you missing Archie? Are you still not talking to him?'

'I'm not, and no,' I said. I was tempted to add, 'We agreed that you wouldn't ask me about Archie any more,' but the less I said the better.

'I just don't really understand why you're not speaking to him,' she said.

That would be because she didn't read The Bizz. 'I told you, it wasn't working with us both on-set in different places.'

'But now you're not going to be on-set for much longer.'

'Is that meant to cheer me up?'

'I just thought maybe . . . Oh, I don't know what I thought. It wasn't the right thing to say. I'm sorry.'

'It's not your fault,' I said. I texted Daisy. Daisy would understand.

I've been killed off 🔪 ⚰️

'And it's not all bad,' Mum started up again. I ignored her.

Daisy wasn't picking up and I was running out of death emojis. I wanted to text Archie. Archie would be nice to me about it. Archie *would have been* nice to me. Whatever, I wasn't going to text him.

My phone barked, but it wasn't Daisy. **You are missing coolest day ever** Great. Good timing, Carlo. **There are extras everywhere. Eddie is having a nervous breakdown. I'm up on one of the scaffolding platforms watching Dick train them all to do some sort of synchronized tribal dance. It's wild**. Whoop whoop. I was glad someone was having a good day. **Ha! There are, like, twenty little silver elves**

Actual elves?

No, Elektra. Not actual elves. School kids. Really little ones. What are you up to?

Not much He'd find out about the rewrites soon enough. I wasn't going to tell him. He wasn't the one dying. I switched off the phone.

'I only wanted to say that at least this happened before the lake scene,' said Mum, bravely trying again.

I nearly smiled. 'How did you know I was dreading that?'

'You can't dive, you're scared of deep water, you don't like the cold and you can't open your eyes underwater – you'd have been mad if you hadn't been dreading it.' She stretched her hand out, only taking her eyes off the road for a minute or two. A car honked. I took her hand.

We made it home alive, but only just.

*

I was curled up on the sofa wallowing in a costume drama binge when my phone barked. I paused *Pride and Prejudice*. (In the absence of Digby, Darcy was the most reliable go-to male in my darkest moments.) It was Daisy.

'I just got your texts,' she said.

'It's brutal,' I said. 'And embarrassing.'

'*I know*,' said Daisy. 'It happened to me on *Sound Bite*. I knew it was coming because they were running out of money, but it was still not OK.'

'And the more they say it had nothing to do with anything I did, the more I worry that it did.'

'I doubt it. You'd have known if they weren't happy. It will just be production stuff.' Neither of us knew what 'production stuff' was, but it was a comforting explanation. 'And it could have been worse, they could have cut your role completely.' True. 'At least you'd filmed most of it already.' True. 'And you got to spend the summer at Fairmount, not on holiday with your parents.' True again. 'And you got lots of free personal training sessions.' That was a true but also not an entirely positive thing. 'Just think, they might have finished the whole thing and it might have never made it to distribution, or it might have been a disastrous flop.'

'Both those things could still happen,' I pointed out, ignoring the fact that my mum was yelling at me to do something.

'Eeek, that's true. Sorry, not helpful. I know what will cheer you up.'

'Nothing will cheer me up.'

'This will. Major *Fortuneswell* gossip. I probably shouldn't tell you . . .'

'*Tell me.*'

'OK, but don't tell anyone else until you've read it somewhere or Lucy will get into trouble. Georgie Dunn hasn't turned up to set for a week.'

'Partying?'

'Epic partying.'

'Can you PLEASE bring me my phone?!' Mum yelled down at me again. 'It's somewhere in the sitting room.' Reluctantly I put down my own phone and searched for hers (role reversal). I found it behind the arm of the sofa.

Thanks, Mrs James!

I read it again. Three words. Not that startling – except for the sender's number. I jabbed at the screen to see the conversation thread. Since when had my mother passworded her phone? I pelted up the stairs.

'Why are you exchanging texts with Archie?'

Mum put down the pile of sheets she was holding and stretched out her hand for the phone. 'Could I have the phone, please, Elektra. It is absolutely not OK for you to be reading my texts.'

'*What?*'

'I don't read your texts, so I'm sure you'll understand

that I don't want you to read mine. Hand it over.'

I held on to it. 'Except you *do* read my stuff,' I said.

'Not your texts,' she said, which was a weaselly denial.

'Mum, it's from *Archie*.' There was a strong possibility I was going to cry, but only because I was angry.

'Yes,' she said simply, like that was an adequate answer.

'Did you get in touch with him to tell him I was upset about *Straker*?' This was *so* humiliating. 'I mean *Raw*,' I corrected myself for the hundredth time.

'I haven't told him about that,' she said.

'Then what did you tell him? Please, please don't tell me that you got in touch with Archie to tell him I was upset about *him*?' Could today get any worse?

'I didn't get in touch with him, actually,' she said, not even having the decency to look guilty.

Today had just got worse. 'My *ex-boyfriend* got in touch with my *mother* because he was worried I'd fall to pieces without him.' Offensive as well as humiliating.

'Don't be such a drama queen, Elektra. Take these sheets, please, and put them in the washing machine, will you?' It wasn't meant as a question.

'Why are you being so mean to me?'

'I'm really not,' she said calmly.

'I need to know what you said ... I also need to know what *he* said.'

'Well, that's not going to happen and I'm not going to fight with you about it. Also, if you want to know what Archie said, then maybe you should talk to Archie.'

'You are being completely unreasonable!' I said, painfully aware that I sounded a bit like her.

'The sheets are not going to walk downstairs on their own,' she said, shoving them at me. It was hopeless.

'Dad,' I said, going into the kitchen and dumping the sheets on the floor. 'Mum's just done something unbelievable. Even for her.'

'You must tell me about it sometime,' he said. 'But those sheets aren't going to put themselves in the washing machine.'

'She's gone too far,' I said.

'Careful, Elektra,' he said quietly. 'I'm not going to stand here and listen to you having a go at your mother. I appreciate you've had a tricky day—'

'But, Dad—'

'No.' He put up a hand to silence me. 'I'm not listening. Stop being a drama queen and listen to me.' Why would nobody just let me be a drama queen? 'Your mum told me about the rewrites. I can understand that the fact your part in *Straker* or whatever it's called now, has ended up smaller than you wanted is annoying.' He saw my face and added, '*Really* annoying. But you need to have a bit of perspective. You got a big part in a film and you've had an experience that lots of girls your age would kill for. And if you're going to keep doing this, I expect you to be professional about it. End of.'

The utter lack of sympathy would have been brutal except that, deep down, I agreed with him and, more importantly, *Straker/Raw* wasn't what was upsetting me right then. 'But, Dad—'

He cut me off. 'But nothing.'

'But it's not—'

'Whatever it is will wait until the sheets are in the washing machine,' he said calmly.

I glared at him. He pretended not to notice. I picked up the sheets and started to bundle them into the machine. I was tempted to go and find a red sock and add it in, but on balance that was probably a poor idea.

My phone barked at midnight. It wasn't going to be Archie. I checked. No, it wasn't Archie.

If it had been Archie I might have answered.

Sam Gross in the Raw ...

You've been a heartthrob for a couple of decades now ...

You make me sound so old! But, yes, I suppose I've been in this game a long time. Any more of Havelski's films and I'll need new knees though (ha, ha) ... Anyway, I reckon I'm playing second fiddle in the heartthrob stakes this time to Carlo Winn. He's playing the young lead Jan and he's going to be on a lot of teenagers' walls by this time next year. Both the kids are strong actors. It's a big chance for Carlo and the other young star Elektra James ... but they shouldn't neglect their school work (ha, ha) ...

So you're playing action hero Raw and your romantic interest is being played by Amber Leigh?

Yes. That's not really your question, is it?

What is it like to be working closely together again?

We have some good scenes together. Yes. It's an extreme type of relationship. Yes. I'm not telling you anything else (laughs).

And does your rebel side come out on set, Sam?

God, no! Havelski runs a tight ship. Most rebellious thing we ever do is change the dance tracks from Abba to One Direction.

So *Raw* has a 'contemporary' sound track?

What? No. That's an in joke (ha, ha...)

Is *Raw* going to be a massive success?

It's going to blow you all away.

Stop Press: Diary News:
Georgie Dunn was seen being helped out of Wre Nightclub in London's fashionable Mayfair for th second time in one week. This time she was on t arm of notorious player and party boy, Max Ma wol. It's fair to say that she was very much the wo for wear and that her pre-season Gucci mini dr hadn't survived the night any better than she h Her management has refused to comment on whe she has returned to her old partying ways...

⭐ CHAPTER 24

'As soon as you start to really fall in love with a character we just kill them, so goodness knows who's next.'

Emilia Clarke

'Morning, Elektra, croissants are in the usual place and I won't judge you if you watch cartoons all the way to Fairmount ... again.' I was going to miss Kerim. There weren't many people who could manage to say the right thing at five thirty in the morning.

'Morning, Elektra,' said Dave at the gate. 'Don't forget to drop your pass back when you leave tonight.' I was even going to miss Dave. I wondered if I could 'forget' to give back the pass. I wanted to keep it as a souvenir.

'Morning, Elektra,' said Naomi, putting down her

clipboard and giving me a hug. I gulped a bit, I was *really* going to miss Naomi. 'We're going to have the best day today,' she said, and we walked arm in arm over to Costume.

'Morning, Elektra,' said Dick, popping his head round my dressing-room door. 'Have we got time to fit in another training session before you go?' I'd *thought* I was going to miss Dick. '... Only joking!' he said, and gave me a hug that nearly broke my ribs. 'And just so you know, you've turned into a surprisingly credible action hero.' He squeezed my non-existent bicep. I *was* going to miss Dick. 'See you later. I'll come over to set before you're finished. I've got to see that run one last time.'

I didn't want to be finished. I walked all round my dressing room, saying goodbye to my little summer home. I said goodbye to the miniature sofa and the fruit bowl that was disappointingly full of hard green pears. I walked over to the mirror and stroked its cold lightbulb frame.

'Have you got any lipstick?' I asked Naomi. 'Cheap lipstick.'

She rummaged in her bag and handed one over. I swivelled it, bright neon pink, perfect.

'Could I ... Could I *waste* it?'

'You absolutely can.' She smiled at me. She knew what I was planning.

Love you all
BIG time -
Don't forget me!

(the-not-so-
world-saving)
Straker x
♡E

I was going to miss this dressing room, no matter how many bored hours I'd spent in it. I was especially going to miss this mirror. Whoever was in here next had better appreciate it. My reflection was all blurry. I put that down one hundred per cent to the lipstick-covered glass. Naomi handed me a tissue.

My phone barked.

Are you having a beautiful white gown for le dying?

Non. I was going to have to disappoint Eulalie. **I am having the brown sack comme toujours for le dying**

You must channel your inner beautiful-white-gown-wearing dying heroine, non?

Eulalie had taken to giving me direction since she'd embarked on her flirtation with Havelski. **I'll try!** And I really would.

There was a tap on the door and Carlo came straight in. 'Hey, E. Are you OK? You're not *crying*, are you?' I was maybe going to miss Jan more than I was going to miss Carlo. 'I brought you this.' He handed me a plum and I laughed. It was definitely the smallest plum he'd been able to find, though I appreciated the gesture.

'Thanks, Carlo.' I hugged him too. I was hugging EVERYONE, but I'd also pretty much forgiven him.

'I'm going to miss you,' he said.

'You'll find plenty of distractions,' I said.

'I will, but it won't be the same.' He hugged me again. Amber would have been having heart palpitations by this point. Naomi just looked on like a proud parent because we weren't fighting.

Sam and Amber came in together without knocking. Soon there would so many people in this tiny room that my mum would call it a party.

'We won't be around this afternoon, so we wanted to say goodbye,' said Sam, presenting me with a rose. *Sam Gross gave me a rose.* Not only did that rhyme, but it was an epic moment (even if I recognized it as one of the kind that Amber had delivered to her dressing room on a daily basis).

'I wanted to give you a present, too,' said Amber. 'Well, the true gift I hope I've given you is belief in the power of nostril-breathing, but I wanted to give you this as well.' She handed me a glossy black-and-white photograph of herself. To be fair, it was personalized. *'To little Straker, my screen daughter who died too soon, with love from Amber and Kale x 🐾.'* That was quite dark, but I'd miss them both. Sam and Amber that is. I wouldn't miss Kale.

'So what's the schedule?' I asked Naomi when everyone else had gone.

She consulted her clipboard. 'You're going to be hours in Make-up and Costume because this is a very *bloody* scene. I'll bring you breakfast while they're sorting you out. Eddie says to tell you—'

'Not to be late and not to leave my phone anywhere except where I'm meant to leave it,' I finished for her.

'No. Well, that, obviously, but he also says don't steal any souvenirs from the set because he'll choose you a really good bit when they take it down.'

I laughed. I'd miss Eddie. 'Ask him to save me one of the cave carvings.' I wasn't sure how my dad would react to me bringing home a twelve-foot painted fake wood carving of something warlike, but I'd cross that bridge when I came to it.

'I will,' she said, as if that was a perfectly reasonable request. 'I'm guessing you don't want me to ask if you can keep any of your costumes?'

Er, no. I wouldn't miss my costumes.

*

We'd blocked the scene already, my stand-in had stood in for me for the last time, Make-up and Continuity had checked me a dozen times and this was it. I knew this was it because of all the people who hugged me on my way over to Ahmed and Havelski. I felt a bit gulpy.

'Remember to breathe, my lovely Straker,' said Naomi, materializing at my side in her near-magic way. 'I have emergency Haribo for after.'

I looked at my script for the final time.

Sc. 32. EXTERIOR. FOREST: NIGHT

Jan and Straker are lying, exhausted, against the trunk of a mighty oak. They are both wounded. Blood stains their clothes. There is a gash in Straker's side. Blood is pumping out. Jan has his hand pressed to the wound, but Straker is weakening.

'So,' said Havelski. 'Elektra? Let's make this the best scene in the whole movie.'

I would do my very best. If I couldn't command attention while I was actually expiring in Jan's arms, I didn't deserve another part.

'You're weak. You've lost a lot of blood, you're still losing blood.'

'Are you going to be OK with the spurting?' asked Ahmed a bit anxiously. My squeamishness had caused enough retakes already.

I nodded. I'd finally got used to film blood. I was ready.

'Good girl.' Havelski was all 'proud father' today. I was definitely going to miss him. 'You know you are dying before Jan knows. You accept your fate before he does. He will never accept it. Never.' He turned to Carlo. 'You are scared, scared that you going to lose Straker. So?' Carlo nodded seriously, already becoming Jan. 'You are going to fight it, rage against it, feel frustration, fear. But this time you are going to lose.' He looked at us both. 'Remember, there's no wrong way to do this. I just want you to *feel* it and then it will work for the camera. I promise you.'

'Hey, marker,' Ahmed shouted and we got into place. 'Action.'

JAN
Hold on, Straker, hold on.

Carlo had tears in his eyes. I looked up at him.

You're going to be all right, just hold on.

His voice caught.

I'll find you some help.

STRAKER

No ... don't leave me, please. I'm afraid
that if you leave me ... Just hold my
hand, please ...

JAN

I'm not going to leave you, Straker.
I'm never going to leave you. Help us
somebody, help us.

But nobody was coming. These were my last lines. Straker's last lines. Ever.

'And cut.'

Not quite Straker's last lines because we reset and re-did lots more times, with endless make-up touch-ups and washing off blood and applying fresh blood, and light changes and angles and a quick and wholly inappropriate burst of *Our Last Summer* where even Havelski danced.

I was going to miss everyone.

I'd have done more takes all night, but suddenly everyone was clapping and I was crying and Straker was dead.

★
CHAPTER 25

'I'd love to punch [a photographer]. I really would. I'd be so happy. I dream about it at night.'

Cara Delevingne

I moved version 17 of the *Straker/Raw* script (this one was orange) out of my eye line – I couldn't bring myself to throw it away – and picked up my French homework.

Write 500 words describing a typical day. Include reference to food eaten, subjects studied and family and friends.

Wow, inspiring. I'd rather practise love scenes (strictly words-only) with Carlo under Naomi's beady eye. What was the French for pudding? Did they even have pudding in France? At least my mum had made me pudding before she'd abandoned me to go to some random evening class. I got up and looked for my phone.

Hey Naomi, any chance you could do my French homework?

That's not going to happen. Your mum would kill me

What's going on on-set?

I have no idea. I was hired to tutor you! I started on a different set today teaching a twelve-year-old who thinks he is too important to pick up his own clothes. I miss you

I miss you too

And stop trying to find out what's going on on-set. When it's over it's over. There was a pause during which I tried and failed to get my head round 'when it's over it's over' and then she texted, **But we'll both go back for the wrap party, right?**

Yes!

Good, now go and finish your homework x It was like she was in the room.

But five minutes later she texted again. **I'm not at all sure if I should be telling you this but have you seen Bizz today?**

No. I've gone cold turkey on Bizz. Also you told me that nobody sane reads it

I also told you that your life wouldn't be complete if you didn't master the imperfect subjunctive. Maybe take a look?

I took a look. *Of course* I took a look. I took another look.

And then I reached for my phone.

'How did you get here so fast?' Ten minutes later and it was like Moss had Apparated into my kitchen.

'I will always travel fast and far for you –.well, for gossip.' She slung down her bag and opened the fridge door. 'Also my mum drove me. I told her we had urgent partner work to do for chemistry.'

'And she believed you?'

'She wanted me out of the way. Haruka was having a massive meltdown.' That made perfect sense; I'd been witness to plenty of Moss's little sister's meltdowns. 'This way, Mum could strap her in the back of the car for a bit and pretend that it wasn't just unlawful restraint. Will your mum mind if we finish this?' She waved the leftover pudding at me. 'I haven't eaten yet.'

'Help yourself,' I said confidently, because feeding up Moss was one of Mum's favourite things to do.

'So?' Moss asked through a big mouthful. 'This major gossip, it's about *Archie*, right?'

'What makes you think that?'

'Go and look in the mirror. Actually, don't, it will just mean I have to wait longer for the details. It's obvious.' She scraped the dish for the last sticky bits of pudding.

I laughed. 'OK, yes, it's about Archie.'

'He called you?' I shook my head. 'He texted you?'

'I wish. But ...' I paused for dramatic effect, 'according to The Bizz there have been developments.'

'I thought you were never going to read that scummy scandal screen of shame again.'

'I've decided it's actually an oracle of wisdom.' I got it up on my laptop and angled the screen towards her.

TheBizz.com

Bringing you the all the Best Backstabbing in the Bizz . . .

8th October

Poppy Leadley has just posted a link to _this_ fundraising campaign on her Facebook page, accompanied by an obviously heartfelt caption in which she opened up about her own experience of homophobic bullying at school and proudly told the world she was gay. YOU GO GIRL!

So if Poppy Leadley gets with girls, that means that she's probably not having a thing with Archie Mortimer who will, if you follow our in-depth reasoning, now be free ... to get with girls. Today, my friends, is a good day for womankind. Today the sisterhood won.

And then, because it was The Bizz and it couldn't help itself, there was a half-page of possible hot girl pairings for Poppy and a whole page for Archie.

'Forget the sisterhood,' said Moss, flipping down the screen and high-fiving me, 'this is a very good day for *you*.'

'*Extremely* good,' I said, presenting her with a packet of custard creams in celebration (and also because half a chocolate pudding wasn't nearly enough supper for Moss).

'So what happens now?'

Well now, I just wanted to enjoy the moment, run round my kitchen and then obviously get with Archie. OK, I especially wanted to get with Archie but given the minor Transylvania impediment that would have to wait a tiny bit longer.

'All you have to do is *un*-break up with him, right?'

I stopped abruptly mid-victory-lap. I'd somehow managed to forget for the last hour that I'd broken up with Archie. Moss was right: I had to un-break up with him. '*How?*'

'Man up, Elektra, just text him.'

'But I don't know what to say. I can't just be all, "Hey, great to read you're not getting with Poppy Leadley, can you get with me again please."'

'Maybe don't put it *exactly* like that.'

'You draft it.' I chucked her my phone.

Moss scrolled for a bit. 'Er ... Elektra? I don't get it. What are all these apologies for?' She started reading them out.

WHAT??

I'm so sorry

I messed up

Just give me one more chance.

I promise I'll be better

'*Stop*.' I could remember them now, all too well.

'But what was Archie sorry for?' she pressed.

'Not Poppy Leadley,' I said nervously, because I knew what her next question was going to be.

'Then who?' she asked.

This was going downhill quite fast. I tried to remember which maidens had been standing next to him in the photos.

'Or what?' suggested Moss.

'What' probably wouldn't be as bad as 'who', would it?

Would it? I had a bad feeling. I grabbed back my phone and scrolled up till I found my this-isn't working-text, back a bit more and there they were, my unanswered messages, my tragic double, triple, texts.

I read his texts again. **So full on ... / intense .../ so many scenes ...**

'What? What?' Moss was stressing out on my behalf. 'What did he do?'

'Not what I accused him of,' I said in a very small voice.

'I swear you didn't *actually* accuse him of anything, did you?'

I shook my head sadly. '*Text neglect*, Moss,' I wailed. 'He thought I was breaking up with him because of *text neglect*.' At that moment I nearly wanted *The Bizz* to be wrong, because the way this was looking, I'd screwed everything up for nothing.

'A bad case of text neglect?'

'Not bad enough for me to have totally lost it with him, and definitely not bad enough to have broken up with him. No wonder he texted my mum.'

'Stop panicking. We'll compose the perfect message explaining away the *tiny* misunderstanding and it will all be perfect again.'

'What? The *tiny* misunderstanding that resulted in me – and now I come to think about it, a couple of A-list stars – calling him arrogant and entitled, refusing to speak to him and irrevocably ending our relationship?'

'It'll be *fine*. Just say sorry and ... rekindle.'

'Moss, you don't understand. There's literally no possibility of rekindling *anything*. We haven't spoken at all since that conversation. He legitimately thinks I'm unhinged.'

'I'm sure if you just call him ...'

'Sure, because I can't wait to explain how I trusted

a gossip website over him. That'll go down brilliantly. Especially if I add in some colourful descriptions of my descent into jealousy and paranoia.'

Moss awkwardly patted my shoulder. I think she was bit scared. 'I wouldn't call it *paranoia*.' She too was a terrible liar. 'Maybe you could present it in a positive way? A ... sort of demonstration of how much you value your relationship?'

'What? The one I brutally ended?'

'OK, maybe how much you *valued* your beautiful relationship?'

'No, Moss, not the point. I really wasn't objecting to your use of tenses. I can't do it.'

Moss silently handed me a custard cream. I took it. It may have been a bittersweet admission of surrender, but it was still a custard cream.

'How long before he gets back to London?'

'I don't know, still weeks I think.'

'Are you going to try and talk to him then? You'll see him at your acting classes, won't you?'

I shrugged. 'He probably won't go any more now he's hit the vampire big time.' To be fair, I hadn't had time to go to ACT all term. Maybe I'd start again when he was back in the country, just on the off-chance of bumping into him.

'You know where he lives.'

'Great. So my only hope is to loiter near his house and pray for a miracle? That's creepy.'

'Well, you need a plan.'

It would have to be better than that. Maybe I'd just sit in my bedroom and obsess over why and how I had so monumentally messed up. I took some deep nasal breaths and briefly missed Amber. But not for her life advice.

'He might send you a birthday message.' Moss was scrabbling round for crumbs of comfort now.

'He probably will. One of those passive aggressive Facebook ones that just say "Hbd" or, if I'm lucky, "Happy Birthday". Or he'll just post a "hilarious" collage of all my stupid, stupid texts.' I deconstructed another custard cream quite savagely.

'Well, before your actual birthday we've got your birthday party ... that will cheer you up.' Moss looked up from checking her own texts and spoke in a voice of doom.

'Moss, I think you know that my party is not going to "cheer me up", but why are you sounding so depressed about it?' Bit late for that after literally months of *bullying* me to volunteer for what was looking more and more like social suicide.

'Guess,' she said.

'Torr?' She nodded sadly. 'He's not coming to my party?' She nodded again. 'Why not?' I didn't care for me, but I did care for her.

'He's not "free". Some "cool" girl in his year is

having a "surprise party" that he just can't miss.' She kept making little air quotes for every other word, in other circumstances I'd have laughed at her. 'The classic last-minute-surprise-party excuse.'

I'd never heard of that one. 'Did he not ask you to go with him?'

'She won't give him a plus one. According to this long and rambling text he's just sent me, he tried *really* hard to get me invited – right, sure. Anyway, I wouldn't have ditched your party to go with Torr. I don't even care that he's not coming.'

She obviously did care, so I just made vague supportive noises. From the most promising of starts this was turning out to be quite a traumatic evening. 'We'll have fun anyway,' I said. We both just looked at each other. 'OK, maybe not actual fun. Shall we cancel?'

'Too late,' she said. 'People will just come anyway. We're committed.'

And then there was an awkward pause where we both pondered Torr's particular commitment issues.

'We need to stop being negative and decide what to wear,' I said, in a desperate effort to channel my inner Eulalie. 'Effort or no effort?'

'Effort that looks like no effort, obviously,' she said, making an equally desperate effort to pull herself together. We weren't convincing, but at least we were trying. Not for nothing had we both endured a term of assemblies on the theme of resilience.

'Will you come over early and we can get ready together?'

'You mean panic together?'

That was exactly what I'd meant.

'As my alternative plan had been to go out with Torr and that is no longer happening, I will be at your house many, many hours in advance.'

WAITING[2]

- % of time spent convincing my mum that she does not need to email the parents of every person attending my party: 6% (This is very important, not least because I am not entirely sure who is coming to my party.)
- % of time spent panicking that I do not know who is coming to my party: 53%
- % of time spent convincing my mum that my Facebook event will not go public and end up on the Daily Mail website: 45%
- % of time spent creating completely irrelevant Party Pinterest boards: 62% (Your day will come, DIY glitter mason jar ice-cream bar, your day will come.)
- % of time spent texting Archie: 0% (starting to text and wimping out doesn't count)
- % of time spent missing Archie: 0%
- % of time spent lying about missing Archie: 100%
- % of time spent missing Digby: 100% (I've been doing some miserable multi-tasking)

---

[2]For my party . . .

CHAPTER 26

'I'm terrified of parties.'
Mia Wasikowska

Moss straightened one of the bottles of Coke for the hundredth time. She stepped back. 'Do you think it looks too organized now?'

'Yep, it's a bit creepy. It looks almost like we've been sitting here for an hour staring at it.' That is exactly what we'd been doing.

'It doesn't really look like a drinks table any more.'

'What does it look like?' I asked. Having a party was scary enough without a shape-shifting table thrown into the already weird and frankly disappointing mixture of invitees.

'Like a piece of really bad modern art?'

'Maybe we could mess it up a bit. So we look all casual and spontaneous.'

'Elektra, these people do know us.' We looked at the table. 'But we should maybe try.' Moss moved one of the bottles out of line and switched some plastic cups into different stacks, and stood back to admire her handiwork. 'Now I'm scared that it looks like we arranged it scarily precisely, and then moved a bottle and some cups to make ourselves look casual and spontaneous. That's like something a psychopath would do.'

'I think the best thing is probably just to leave the table alone now.'

'You're right.' Moss flopped on the sofa beside me. 'We should never have got ready so early.'

My mum came in. She'd got really dressed up in solidarity.

'You girls have a lovely evening,' she said, carefully rearranging the drinks table. 'I chopped up some crudités just in case – they're in the tupperware next to the hummus on the third level of the fridge. Right,' she said in the tone of someone about to go over the top during the Battle of the Somme, 'I'm going to Bridget's house.'

Moss and I had helpfully offered to book a range of dinner reservations on the opposite side of town, but Mum had decided that a cup of tea, a conversation with an annoyingly judgmental Cath-Kidston-style mum and, if she leaned right out of their top-floor window, a view of our garden was the better option. My father, on the other hand, had done a total Torr. He'd promised for weeks that he would be there to prevent anyone actually dying, but at the last minute he'd decided that a 'very, very important' and miraculously sudden client dinner was far higher on his list of priorities.

'If you need anything,' said Mum, 'or anything goes *wrong*, just text. I'll be on my phone the entire night.' That I did not doubt. 'Have fun!' The door banged behind her.

'What if literally no one comes?' I asked. Torr wasn't coming. Archie wasn't coming.

'Eulalie will definitely come if we text her.'

'Moss, I love you, but it wouldn't be much of a birthday party with me, you and my grandma. It would just be you two brutally excluding me.'

'I'm sure *some* people will come,' Moss said. She didn't sound very sure.

'I feel like maybe it's worse if a few people come because then they know no one else turned up.' I'd thought through every possible dire outcome. I'd probably done a more thorough risk assessment than they did for the whole of *Straker*: higher risk of social death and lower risk of actual death, also fewer flying elves.

'They'll all know, anyway,' added Moss helpfully. 'Because there won't be any snap stories this evening or pics on Facebook tomorrow.'

'I mean, unless we could ... fake some?' Moss looked at me like I'd gone mad, but she was in no position to judge. 'We could switch all the lights off, turn on some really loud music, maybe a YouTube video with some flashing lights and general shouting or something?'

'So to prove how cool we are, you are suggesting we should take photos and videos of each other alone in a dark, empty room with only some crudités and hummus for company?' This was not a good time for Moss to be at her most chillingly logical.

'You could dance crazily to distract people, or we could just do close-ups of our faces? We could get Eulalie to take the photos to prove there were at least three people? We could even get my parents ...'

The doorbell rang.

'Bagsie you go!'

'God, Elektra, how old are you?' Moss rolled her eyes but didn't go to the door. We looked at each other. It was all a bit opening-scene-of-a-horror-film.

'Let's go together,' I whispered.

It was the start of our first proper teen party and Moss and I, not a boyfriend in sight, were creeping into my hall, hand in hand.

The doorbell rang again. We both jumped.

'Hey.' The guy on the doorstep gave us an awkward wave.

'Erm, hi?' I was pretty sure I had never seen him in my life. I really don't meet many guys so I doubt I'd forget one.

'Sorry, who actually are you?' Moss wasn't renowned for her tact.

'I'm Sam ...' There was an awkward pause. 'Jamie's plus one?'

'Who's Jamie?'

'Daisy's plus one.'

Under the circumstances, that would do. We showed him into the living room like really awkward estate agents. He looked around. 'Is nobody here yet?' Sam clearly had amazing powers of deduction.

'Erm. No,' I said apologetically.

'I thought it started at eight?' Was he really going to make us spell out the fact that no one else had yet turned up to our party?

'It did.'

'Oh.'

Moss pretended to straighten the sofa cushions and I just stood uselessly in the doorway. I hoped it didn't look like I was trying to trap Sam, but I couldn't move now, the moment for moving was over. I also really needed to turn the lights down, but I felt that would be creepy at this point.

'I mean, it's only twenty minutes past eight and everyone knows eight means eight thirty.' I tried to sound as if I was just calmly explaining a point of party etiquette. 'Do you want a drink?'

'Oh, er, no. I think I'll wait for everyone else.' He looked out of the window pointedly, even though it was too dark to see anything. A *Little Party Never Killed Nobody* came on. I was beginning to regret our playlist decisions. Right now the *little*-ness of this party was coming very close to killing me.

The doorbell rang and we all breathed a major sigh of relief.

'Ahhh, Jenny, Maia, *thank God* you're here,' Moss practically screamed from the hall.

8.45 p.m.: Some people have actually turned up. Small talk is getting slightly less awkward. Tentative dancing beginning.

9.00 p.m.: Quite a lot of people have actually turned up. People are properly dancing now.

9.20 p.m.: There are really quite a few people in my house. Someone has brutally discarded our Taylor Swift and Ariana filled playlist in favour of something that sounds a bit like the *Straker* soundtrack.

9.35 p.m.: There are a lot of people in my sitting room but I can't find anyone I know.

9.45 p.m.: Alert. Alert. Commander Moss is Missing in Action.

9.47 p.m.: Text received from the mother: **Is everything OK????? Sounds quite loud?????**

9.48 p.m.: Follow-up text: **Is that chanting??? Sounds a bit like a satanic ritual??????**'

9.52 p.m.: Text received from the father: **Elektrsa, Can you pleasde confirm to your mother that therec is no satanic ritual being perforned in our kicten she is waorried.** Well, he was clearly having fun at the 'very very important client dinner'.

9.54 p.m.: Follow-up text: **If therec is a satanic ritual being perfomrd plese tell them not to use the kicthem – the white surfaces stain easily**

10.10 p.m.: I'm pretty sure I just saw Flissy . . .?

10.15 p.m.: Commander Moss is alive, well and getting with some guy I haven't seen before. Dark hair, stocky build, possibly wearing a rugby shirt. He is the anti-Torr.

10.17 p.m.: Quite stroppy text received from the mother: **Elektra. I'm not happy. If this noise doesn't quieten down in the next fifteen minutes I'm coming over.**

10.25 p.m.: There's a boy in the kitchen wearing a bucket hat. I think I'm going to cry.

'There's someone at the door for you,' said someone else I didn't know.

'Why are they not just coming in?'

'They want you to come to the door.'

Oh my God, I was literally going to get arrested. Or worse, it was my mother, too traumatized to cross her own threshold. Obviously I went because I was a respecter of authority. Unlike the person in the bucket hat.

I took a deep breath and opened the door.

'Hey, Elektra,' said Archie.

I stared. Was he even real? Had my poor little obsessed imagination just conjured up a lovely Archie-shaped mirage because I wanted him to be there so badly?

'Elektra?'

He sounded real. I'd missed his voice.

I didn't throw myself at him straight away. I had too much dignity for that. I gave it maybe another ten ... OK, eight ... OK, two seconds. 'I'm SOOOOOOO SORRRREEEEE!' I wailed.

'Woah, you're going to crush me.' Archie backed away fast, as if I really was going to do him some damage.

Well that was humiliating. 'I apologize for my enthusiasm,' I said, trying to make my voice sound cool and trying to forget that this was all my fault. There was a lot of space between us now. So much space he might as well have been a mirage.

'You'll hurt him,' he said.

Three months on a BBC drama and he was talking about himself in the third person? Too far. I got that he was upset with me, but why come if he was just going to give me the freezer treatment? I didn't know how to make this better. Part of me (the guilty, scared part) wanted to run back inside, but the other part (the part that kept staring at his cheekbones, and all the rest) wasn't going anywhere. Anyway, I couldn't get back in the house because Maia was now getting with Sam in the doorway. 'I'm having a party,' I said in a small voice.

'I know.'

'Did my mum tell you?' I managed not to add 'when you texted her' because that was too weird.

'It's more the hundred-odd people and the loud music that are giving it away.' He smiled. I'd missed his smile.

'Oh, God, Archie, I'm so sorry.' I started to word-vom. 'I didn't mean any of it. I totally messed up, I just thought—'

'Elektra.' He cut me off gently. 'It doesn't matter.'

'But it *does*.' Of course it mattered. 'I'm really, really sorry.' If I just kept talking super fast then I might come up with something that made sense. Or not. 'It was just a sort of misunder—'

'Shhh, stop talking. I want to show you something.' He started to undo the top buttons on his jacket. I was starting to feel kind of uncomfortable.

'Give me your hand,' he said. 'Can I just say

before we go any further that your mum is totally cool with this.'

OK, now I was feeling *really* uncomfortable.

He slipped my hand inside his jacket and both of us gave a little yelp of surprise.

Not me and Archie, me and the tiny bundle of puppy.

'He's called Plogojowitz,' said Archie. 'But I'll understand if you want to change that.'

It was a long name for the little dotty bundle that was curled against Archie's chest, but it suited him. 'Hello, Plog,' I said. He wriggled and stuck out one oversized paw. His coat didn't fit him properly yet.

'He was the runt.'

'He's perfect.'

'I know he's not Digby. He's not meant to be a replacement. Obviously.' Obviously. 'And I think maybe his dots are in the wrong places.'

'OK,' I said. 'He's not perfect.'

Archie looked worried. Plog looked worried.

'He's practically perfect,' I said. 'I like that.'

TheBizz.com

15th October

Roll up roll up fans of the Samber saga! We're in for a Season 2 and it's set to be pure DRAMAAAA ... OK, *so* last time didn't end so well: think public meltdowns, dog therapists and a literal Bonfire of the Vanities (when all of Sam's handmade Italian shirts hit the flames).

Despite all that, OK *because* of it, we here at *The Bizz* are MORE than up for a round two ...

We thought we'd play a little game – Samber Bingo. (Back off, we're trade-marking that.)

Sam tweets something passive aggressive about dogs	Pregnancy scare!	Samber spotted visiting couples' therapist	Amber cast in a movie with a different Ex
Amber posts something passive aggressive about goats	Samber declare intention to adopt cute but under-privileged child	Samber spotted visting a family therapist with Kale in tow	Sam repeatedly assures the media that he is FINE with said ex being co-star
Amber burns something	Sam punches a nurse (sorry we couldn't help ourselves it just never gets old)	Samber have a bust up at a restaurant	Sam wears an 'I <3 Amber...' T-shirt.
Someone cries on the red carpet	–next level– PDA on the *Raw* red carpet	Samber show People around their prematurely shared home	Amber swears off all men

So grab some popcorn, invite your most sadistic friends over and let's get watching ...

STOP THE ABUSE THAT IS OUR CURRENT SCHOOL UNIFORM

Dear Mrs Haroun and Governors of Berkeley Academy. We, the undersigned, are hereby petitioning for a change to the uniform policy of our school.

a) The colour of the uniform (variously described as purple, plum, aubergine or Berkeley Beetroot) is so 'unusual' that it draws attention to the wearers and thereby increases the safety risks we run especially when travelling to and from school. It is SO 'distinctive' that no lower cost items can be substituted for the official uniform which is unacceptable in the current austere economic climate. We petition for a change to black or grey or, at worst, navy.

b) We petition for the uniform to include the option to wear trousers. The suffragettes did not die for our right to wear a skirt (winter) or a pinafore (summer).

c) (Only if a) above is not accepted) we petition for a relaxation in the uniform rules so that full uniform need not be worn on any other than formal school occasions and especially that blazers need not be worn outside the school.

d) We further petition the school to relax its rules on hair, make up, accessories, tattoos and piercings. These rules are rooted in the traditions of the previous century and they interfere with our right to freedom of expression.

We the undersigned draw your attention to the United Nations Convention on the Rights of the Child and in particular articles 13 (freedom of expression), 19 (freedom from abuse and maltreatment) and 37 (freedom from torture and cruel and unusual treatment).

Let's CHANGE this school from the bottom up; sign TODAY to have your voice heard.

SIGNATURES:
Elektra
Moss

ACKNOWLEDGEMENTS

It's a wrap on *Take Two* and we want to thank everyone that has made our production run way more smoothly than *Straker/Raw*. If books had movie credits here's what ours would look like.

THANK YOU to:

Producer/Director Jane Griffiths

Unlike Havelski you've never subjected us to grumpy dictator mode. You are brilliant and always right (except possibly about 'basic' . . .). Keep pushing us.

Assistant Directors/Script Supervisors: Jenny Glencross (editing), Emma Young (copyediting), Mattie Whitehead (proofreading).

You somehow magically 'get' how our characters speak – you make it easy.

Production Designer: Jenny Richards

No squeaking boulders here – you know how much we love our covers and all the artwork (Hon: and thanks for 'making' me send you lots of pics of possible Archies – it was a hardship . . .).

Storyboard: thanks to the very talented Jack Noel for bringing our *Straker* storyboard to life.

Publicity: Jade Westwood

Jade, you're a STAR and thanks too to Hannah and Liz for all that you do.

Distribution: Elisa Offord and Laura Hough

Thank you for getting us out there on general release!

And to everyone else at Simon & Schuster, we are in the best hands and we hugely appreciate everything you do for us.

Grip: Hannah Sheppard

Our lovely agent who we're going to credit as 'Grip' because she does her very best to make sure that we don't lose ours. And to all at DHH, agents and clients (especially Team Hannah) thanks for the support, let's have a gin break soon.

Consultant: James Barriscale

Fine actor, writer and one of the nicest people we know. You bear absolutely no responsibility for the shameless way we have played fast and loose with what happens on a film set.

Supporting Cast:

We've been blown away by the support we've had from the children's & YA book blogging & reviewing community – there are too many to mention here but you know who you are. The energy and passion that you bring to what you do is amazing and we love you for it.

And huge thank you to family and friends (including new book world friends) who have had to put up with a lot this year. We've been selfishly unavailable for weeks on end because of deadlines and ~~near~~ delusional obsession with our characters. But you've been there, stoically listening to us worrying about whether we're doing this whole being-a-writer thing right and buying copies of our book for yourselves/children/dogs and feeding us cake and coffees and sound advice. We love you.

(Hon: and thank you to those of you who have sacrificed your dignity to become characters in the book – you know who you are ...)

Audience: Our readers

Last but not least, we thank you all. We've met some of you at school visits and we love it when you message us or write to us. We so hope you keep enjoying the series! xx

WAITING FOR CALLBACK

3

COMING SPRING 2018!

Permissions

Quotation Chloe Sevigny Chapter 1 [pg. 1] from *The Guardian* 14 May 2016 (Xan Brooks); quotation Lisa Kudrow Chapter 2 [pg. 14] from *The Guardian* 22 February 2015 (Rory Carroll); quotation Chris Hemsworth Chapter 8 [pg. 89] from *The Guardian* 19 October 2013 (Alex Godfrey); quotation Natalie Portman Chapter 11 [pg. 129] from *The Guardian* 19 August 2016 (Nigel Smith); quotation Nicholas Hoult Chapter 14 [pg. 174] from *The Guardian* 26 January 2013 (Shahesta Shaitly); quotation Cara Delavigne Chapter 25 [pg. 323] from The Guardian 15 June 2014 (Alexis Petridis).

All reprinted by kind permission of Guardian News and Media Ltd.

Quotations Mia Wasikowska Chapter 5 [pg. 50] and Chapter 26 [pg. 335] from *The Times Magazine* 27 August 2011 (Helena de Bertodano); quotation Jesse Eisenberg Chapter 6 [pg. 63] from *The Times* 15 April 2016 (Roderick Stanley); quotation Daniel Radcliffe Chapter 7 [pg. 72] from *The Times Magazine* 23 November 2015 (Janice Turner); quotations Kit Harrington Chapter 9 [pg. 98],

Chapter 19 [pg. 249] and Chapter 21 [pg. 275] from *The Sunday Times* 29 May 2016 (Josh Glancy); quotations Lily James Chapter 10 [pg. 112] and Chapter 23 [pg. 300] from *The Sunday Times* 20 December 2015 (Chrissy Illey); quotation James Norton Chapter 13 [pg. 164] from *The Sunday Times* 3 January 2016 (Louis Wise); Chloë Moretz Chapter 16 [pg. 209] from *The Sunday Times* 10 August 2014 (Chris Ayres); Nick Jonas Chapter 18 [pg. 233] from *The Sunday Times Style* 29 May 2016 (Giles Hattersley); quotation James McAvoy Chapter 22 [pg. 285] from *The Sunday Times* 29 November 2015 (Jonathan Dean). **All reprinted by kind permission of News UK and Ireland Ltd.**

Quotation Kate Beckinsale Chapter 3 [pg. 25] from The Telegraph 27 May 2016 (John Hiscock); quotation Eddie Redmayne Chapter 12 [pg. 151] from *The Telegraph* 19 February 2016 (Georgia Dehn); quotation Emily Blunt Chapter 15 [pg. 187] from *The Telegraph* 25 March 2016 (Celia Walden); quotation Jennifer Lawrence Chapter 17 [pg. 222] from *The Telegraph* 19 May 2016 (John Hiscock); quotation Emilia Clarke Chapter 24 [pg. 315] from *The Telegraph* 30th June 2015 (John Hiscock). **All reprinted by kind permission of the Telegraph Media Group and pursuant to Licence dated 6 July 2016**

Quotation from Asa Butterfield Chapter 4 [pg. 36] and quotation from Ella Purnell Chapter 20 [pg. 261] from an interview they very kindly gave to our website.

Thank you to all.

FIND US ONLINE

website: waitingforcallback.com